PENGUIN BOOKS

A PRIVATE VIEW

Anita Brookner was born in London in 1928 and, apart from three postgraduate years in Paris, has lived there all her life. She trained as an art historian and taught at the Courtauld Institute of Art, where she was a Reader, until 1988. She now reads and writes for her own amusement.

Also published in Penguin are the novels *Lewis Percy*, *A Start in Life*, *Brief Lives*, *Hotel du Lac*, *A Closed Eye*, *Providence*, *Family and Friends*, *Look At Me*, *Fraud* and *A Family Romance*.

ANITA BROOKNER

A PRIVATE VIEW

PENGUIN BOOKS

PENGUIN BOOKS

Published by the Penguin Group
Penguin Books Ltd, 27 Wrights Lane, London W8 5TZ, England
Penguin Books USA Inc., 375 Hudson Street, New York, New York 10014, USA
Penguin Books Australia Ltd, Ringwood, Victoria, Australia
Penguin Books Canada Ltd, 10 Alcorn Avenue, Toronto, Ontario, Canada M4V 3B2
Penguin Books (NZ) Ltd, 182–190 Wairau Road, Auckland 10, New Zealand

Penguin Books Ltd, Registered Offices: Harmondsworth, Middlesex, England

First published by Jonathan Cape 1994
Published in Penguin Books 1995
7 9 10 8 6

Printed in England by Clays Ltd, St Ives plc

I

George Bland, in the sun, reflected that now was the moment to take stock. Nice, a town which he had not visited since his first holiday abroad, some forty years earlier, spread its noise and its light and its air about him, making him feel cautious; he was not up to this, he reckoned, having become unused to leisure. He had been here for four days and had found nothing to do, although there was much to occupy his thoughts, most of them, indeed all of them, proving unwelcome. Nice had been an unwise choice, though in truth hardly a choice at all; it had been more of a flight from those same thoughts, which faithfully continued to attend him here. He had sought a restorative, conventional enough, after the death of an old friend, Michael Putnam, who had inconveniently succumbed to cancer just when they were enabled, by process of evolution, or by that of virtue rewarded, more prosaically by the fact of their simultaneous retirement, to take their ease, to explore the world together, as had been their intention. They had waited for too long, and the result was this hiatus, and the reflection that time and patience may bring poor rewards, that time itself, if not confronted at the appropriate juncture, can play sly tricks, and, more significantly, that those who do not act are not infrequently acted upon.

His friend Putnam, whom he sorely missed, had left him a quite respectable sum of money, which, added to his own capital, made of him a fairly wealthy man. The irony of this did not escape him, for he had started out poor, and poverty was imprinted on his mind and no doubt in his heart. If he were spending freely now it was in an effort to get rid of some of his money and in so doing to allay the pain of Putnam's death. Yet the incongruity displeased him. Seated in an expensive restaurant − as it might be Le Chantecler − all he could remember was his last sight of Putnam, skeletal hand clutching the latest of a series of Get Well cards from former colleagues, great eyes turning to the window in shock and doubt, then turning back to his friend with a look that was timid, wistful, almost eager, for he had trusted in life right up to the end. That the look had to be met, sustained; this was not easy. In time it had proved almost unbearable, but the effort was made, day after day, until, at the end of a mere three weeks, the eyes had closed for ever.

Bland was shaken by his death, had sought comfort in late out-of-season sunshine, which now struck him as garish. No one, he thought, could understand their friendship, as they themselves had understood it. Both unmarried, they somehow did not impress the outside world as lovers, yet their closeness was remarked upon, puzzled over. In fact, what they had in common was their origin in shabby beginnings and their slow upward rise to middle-class affluence. This was their gleeful rueful secret. Lunching together on a Sunday at the club, or at one of the better London hotels, they might test each other with a brand name with which to conjure the past. Both appreciated sweet food and strong tea. Both, before making a purchase, had the same instinctive reaction: Is this allowed?

Sharing the past, any past, but particularly their own, made it more comfortable. Now that he was alone Bland found the present irksome, shot through with a sadness he had not previously suspected. And this was not merely the sadness of Putnam's death, for that was more properly grief, but a sadness for the life they had lived through together, keeping up each other's spirits, applauding in each other the middle-class virtues which, to their surprise, had come to them quite naturally, so that from an initial bedrock of misgiving and suspicion had flowered charity and judicious benevolence and a hard-won fair-mindedness. He had loved Putnam; now that Putnam was dead, he, George Bland, felt half dead himself.

With Putnam gone the rest of his life must be assumed single-handed, until it was his turn to lie in a hospital bed and to embrace friendship as if it were love, for so it would seem in those last heightened moments. With Putnam gone the past was his alone, and the present too. For the time being the present was the more problematic, although he knew that time, in passing, would annihilate his comfortable harmless days and restore to him early sights and sounds, and with them the emotions that had always accompanied them. Above all, in his new unsupported state, he felt a curious sense of shame, that he had saved his own life to so little purpose. He was comfortably off, and he was superfluous. He had no family, no wife, no lover; he had lived so carefully that he occasionally caught sight of himself as an object of ridicule. He and Putnam, working contentedly in the same organisation until the retirement which Putnam had not lived to see, and which he, Bland, must now shoulder unaccompanied, had been cautiously happy. This grotesque interlude in Nice, for example (when he and Putnam should by rights be on their way to the Far East, as they had planned), offended him in some obscure way, nagged at him as some social mistake might have done. He hoped that he might meet no one he knew and be forced to explain himself, and to explain a presence which he would be hard put to justify.

But Putnam's illness had made him shaky, as if for the first time he had realised that he was a man of sixty-five, not old, but elderly, upright, still slim, but with thinning grey hair, a more prominent nose. All at once, in the golden sunshine, with the breeze still warm in this late season, he felt alone, as he had not done since he was an adolescent. It seemed to him that he knew no one, that the office, the comfortable background to his life for so many years, had evaporated, or passed into other hands, leaving him adrift, to spend too much time sitting in cafés, or staring at the sea. He was newly aware of the pathos of their lives, his and Putnam's, each leaving the other his life's savings, since they had excluded the possibility of there being other beneficiaries. And all those sad thoughts, now unshared, threatening to overwhelm him, as they once had. He had fought against them, successfully as it seemed, in the years of his maturity, but Putnam's decline, mercifully short, had made him vulnerable again, and he was subject now not only to aching muscles if he walked too far, but to a backward-looking cast of mind which made his present comfort seem nugatory, as if it were built on sand, as perhaps it always had been.

Sometimes, in the absence of Putnam, he had to activate an inner voice, or voices, which he imagined to be those of tutelary deities, a surrogate family, bold decisive aunts, loyal unquestioning cousins, quite unlike the relations, or rather relation, he had known, his aunt Lilian, with whom his mother had quarrelled enjoyably for as long as he could remember, as long in fact as they were still alive. These voices urged him to indulgence, even to excess. 'Why not?' they said. 'You can afford it.' Yet there was nothing he wanted, so that the function of the voices was dubious, and indeed unhealthy, for their encouragement seemed to belong to a phase of his life which was now

4

safely behind him: the poor boy from Reading, unwittingly involved in the machinations of disorderly parents, for whom he had felt alternate bouts of love and hatred, a conflict which persisted in him and which he had never managed to resolve. To his bewilderment and shame his parents had descended the ladder of bourgeois respectability to the undistinguished level at which they felt most comfortable, so that his father, once a sports journalist, was now habitually to be found on the racecourse on his own account, and his mother, once a nursing sister, spent most of her days smoking, reading undemanding novels from the library, or enjoying a passage of arms with her husband or her sister Lilian.

He had learned to look after himself from an early age. When his father dropped dead at Kempton Park, and Lilian arrived with a cheque, saying, in a tone which denoted triumph, 'I suppose George will be getting a job now?' he had known that his life was doomed. He had left Reading University after only one year, had entered the cardboard box factory as a junior clerk, and had cared for his mother until her death. It was at this point that the voices had first manifested themselves, urging him to run for his life, to sell the house, to request a transfer to the London office (which, in those days of easy employment, had been granted), and to all intents and purposes to disappear from sight, only to reappear some years later as a successful and trusted employee in the enterprise which had begun as a cardboard box factory and was now a prosperous conglomerate, the cardboard boxes having diversified into all forms of packaging, with a subsidiary which specialised in office materials. As these became more sophisticated, both staff and turnover increased, until the firm, known simply as Rogerson's, after the family that still owned it, was quoted as one of the more conspicuously successful achievements of the new commercially minded Britain.

The day that Putnam had walked in, a spry spare little accountant from Birmingham, the thought had occurred to Bland that they might be friends. He had asked Putnam whether he had found somewhere to live (he had) and whether he would like a quick meal on the way home. Putnam had accepted with alacrity, and over dinner in an Italian restaurant they had discovered numerous points in common. Thereafter life was harmonious. It had seemed that at last he would feel free, no longer obliged to dissemble or to apologise, and this freedom was to him so intoxicating that he had looked for nothing further, content with his work, his growing comforts, and the friendship of Putnam. In due course it was Putnam's approval that replaced the voices in his own head, voices which he now regarded as the poor companions of a starveling past, when he was still a prisoner, waiting for his sentence to end, as it had done.

Putnam had been attractive to women and had subjugated the likeliest of the organisation's female employees, but he was discreet about his adventures, and managed never to give offence, even when he was effecting a changeover from one woman to another. Refreshingly, he conducted his affairs without indulging in confidences, as would have been easy to do, and so no woman had ever come between the two of them. Putnam had had his affairs, and Bland had had his girlfriend Louise, or had done so until she married a doctor and went to live in the New Forest. He had known her since they were both adolescents in Reading; he had loved, and in fact still cherished, her peaceful fastidiousness, qualities almost unknown to him at the time, together with her white blouses and her frequently washed hair. They had pursued their love affair in borrowed flats and later in hotel rooms, finally in his own small flat, Louise's eternal good nature rising perpetually above the often sordid arrangements. But at the point at which their long-delayed maturity could be assumed and taken for granted, and their love affair already had reached and passed the twenty-year mark, she had told him that she was getting married, still in that placid tone in which she was wont to address him. For a time he had felt alarmed rather than upset; he had relied on Louise to keep him company and eventually to become his wife, although he had told her repeatedly that he was not ready for marriage. Indeed he was never ready, was still not ready even now. She had got tired of waiting, she had told him uncomplainingly. Her husband was much older than herself and something of a crank, but within a year Louise had had a son, and was thus able to tolerate her husband's relatively early death with much of her usual equanimity.

Bland had visited her, in Lymington, on hearing of this event; he had in fact read of it in *The Times* and had telephoned her straight away. In the course of his visit, which he had intended to be sympathetic, he had found himself distracted by Louise's son, then a boy of six, and repelled by the child's ugliness. Philip was untidy, restless, overpoweringly friendly. His teeth seemed broken, although they were in fact merely irregular; he spoke in a barely comprehensible monotone and laid about him with hot grimy hands. Louise was devoted to the boy; Bland knew that he had lost her, and resolved not to pay another visit. But their lives were too interwoven for one of them to lose the other. And now, many years later, when they were almost old, he telephoned her, or she telephoned him, every Sunday evening. He was still half bored, half comforted by her calm plaintive tone, and paid as much attention to it as he might to a bird outside his window. She gave him news of her son, now a successful marketer of computer games. He did little more than listen. They knew each other so well that conversation was hardly necessary. Once each had ascertained that the other was still alive there seemed to be nothing more to say.

The telephone call went with a certain Sunday evening melancholy, the light fading, only a rare car passing, windows reluctantly springing into bloom as the weekend was, by unspoken consensus, agreed to be over, and the working week about to encroach on what little liberty was left. But he had loved the working week, loved his large immaculate desk, looked forward to the Monday lunch with Putnam at the club, happy to espouse whatever outrageous proposition Putnam had thought up over the weekend. Holidays were planned, but not very seriously; more seriously was the retirement project envisaged, that long journey to the Far East, by the slowest route they could devise, and all the time in the world to talk it over.

It had never come about. Putnam, the sweat standing out on his forehead, had concluded their last Monday lunch with, 'I seem to have a pain,' this said with an air of ghastly hilarity. Bland had taken him in a taxi to the hospital, and when he returned to visit him that evening knew, from the altered cast of Putnam's features, that he was going to die. 'Looking after you all right, are they?' was all that he managed to say on that and subsequent occasions, but he bought him fine cotton pyjamas, arranged for a barber to go in and shave him daily, for Putnam had been immaculate for as long as he had known him. Later there had been bottles of Floris cologne to hide the smells of which Putnam seemed mercifully unaware, and that was the saddest time of all. 'All right, old chap,' he had said, laying a soothing hand on Putnam's forehead. There was nothing more to say. The fact that Putnam refused to believe in his imminent death broke the thread of effortless communication that had sustained their friendship and their life together. Bland felt this keenly: it was the single factor that more than any other brought home to him the fact that he was on his own.

And then Putnam's heartbreaking will, leaving him the money he no longer wanted or needed! He had, as his

8

Aunt Lilian would have said, done all right for himself. He had risen through the ranks to become Head of Personnel; he was thought to be good with people, an impression, since confirmed, dating from a tiny incident in his early days with the firm, when he had dealt with Mrs Bertram, Kenneth Rogerson's personal secretary, who had had something resembling a breakdown and whom he had escorted home proficiently to her large gloomy flat off the Marylebone Road. He had glimpsed an unmade bed through a half open door, and heard an unfed cat mewing angrily in an icy kitchen. He had taken the groceries day after day when his work was over, and, more delicately, had put in train the machinery for her retirement (a respectful word in the right quarter). He had even, in a small way, been responsible for her pension (another respectful word). The memory filled him with shame, as did most of his supposedly good deeds. Oddly enough he had not minded at the time. Kenneth Rogerson had noted his efficacy, and perhaps something more: his dutifulness. It had not seemed out of the way to Bland to perform the same tasks for Kenneth Rogerson himself, after the latter's stroke. He had visited him weekly, at his flat in St James's, again with groceries, and with the Sunday papers. Rogerson had been irascible by that stage, but after the man's death Bland had found himself richer by a respectable portfolio of shares. This too filled him with shame. He remembered in this connection not his own kindness but an initial humiliation, the disastrous occasion when Rogerson, thinking to do him a favour, had arranged for him to have a room in a flat belonging to his niece and nephew, a brother and sister for whom he professed to have no time and little liking.

'Punch and Alfreda Rogerson, my brother's children. We don't get on,' he had said, apparently without regret.

Bland had still been naïve enough to ask eager questions.

'Punch? What an unusual name,' he had said.

'His name is Peregrine. Naturally he dislikes it. In many ways he has always been problematic. However, that need not trouble you. I'll telephone him. Perhaps you'll do the same.' A piece of paper was handed over.

Bland, newly arrived in London, had accepted the offer eagerly, and that same evening had gone round to the flat in Radnor Place with his suitcase, bought in Reading just prior to leaving Reading for ever. The door had been opened by a very tall, very thin man, with a look of radiant goodwill playing around a weak mouth.

'Punch Rogerson,' he had said. 'My sister will be in later. Come in, come in! Your room's over here. You'll have to excuse me; we've got a meeting here this evening. Care to join us?'

'A meeting?' Bland had queried, his suitcase on the floor beside him.

'Prayer meeting; my sister Alfreda will fill you in on the details. I'm thinking of joining an Order, you see. You are a believer, I take it?'

But before he could answer the front door had opened again, and Alfreda Rogerson, as tall and thin as her brother, came in, followed by three women and two men, all of them talking in rather loud voices. These voices had continued to make themselves heard until long after dark, interspersed with bursts of high-pitched laughter. At some point Punch Rogerson, drunk with his own merriment, and also, it seemed, with whisky, had knocked on the door of Bland's room and invited him to join them. He had been rapidly introduced: 'Jamie, Caroline, Anna, Nigel, Cressida.' He had nodded, embarrassed. He felt tired and hungry, but found himself with a large glass of whisky in his hand. It was his first contact with the rich. He noticed how well they all looked, as if doctors and dentists had vied with each other to keep Cressida and

Nigel, and indeed Anna and Jamie, in perfect condition since childhood.

'We usually end with silent meditation,' said Alfreda crossly, 'but as it's your first evening . . . By the way, if you think of joining us, as I hope you will, we can put you in touch with Father Ambrose. Our people will take care of everything.'

'Everything?' he had asked, bewildered.

'That is if you decide to stay,' she said.

He had left the following morning, having spent most of the night composing a letter telling them of other plans, which he left on a console table in the hall. It was six-thirty; he had walked, with his suitcase, until he had found a workman's café, near Paddington Station, where he had breakfast. At nine o'clock he was at a local estate agent's. At nine-thirty he was at the bank arranging a loan. By the end of the week he was in his own tiny flat in a large red-brick building over Baker Street station. When Rogerson senior enquired how he was getting on he had told him that he had found a place of his own: no further details.

'Very wise,' Rogerson had said. 'You have a mortgage, I suppose? Well, if you are in any need . . .'

He had not finished the sentence, and Bland had never reminded him of his extremely vague offer. It had taken him years to pay off the loan, years of doing without, of living modestly but uncomplainingly. He sometimes thought that these years of careful budgeting, careful to the point of sacrifice, had cost him Louise. He had never at any point blamed her for leaving him. By that stage he was too conscious of his real advantages for that. His most precious gain was liberty, a fact of which he was well aware. And in any case Louise's departure was not rancorous: she was, and had ever since continued to be, thoughtful and loving. He was grateful for this too. It was, all things considered, a creditable relationship. And ever since then he had only to pick up the telephone to hear Louise's voice, still full of concern for him. She was, he knew, very slightly boring; perhaps that was why he had not married her. But kindness in a woman had always struck him as a precious quality, and she had always been kind. What he felt for her now he would have described as esteem, although they had nothing more to say to each other. They were linked by their long history, two aged siblings who retained a common language, which they tried, with only partial success, to apply to their now separate concerns. If she disappeared, or rather when she disappeared, there would be no one left who knew him as well as he knew himself.

Seated at a café table, in the syrupy warmth of out-of-season Nice, he reviewed his life and found it to be alarmingly empty. It had been built on flight, he saw, flight from an uncomfortable childhood, an unfairly victimised adolescence, an atmosphere of tension and contention, his father drinking too much, his mother ever handy with reproaches. If he had sought liberty, his own liberty, as a method of vindication for those clouded years, then surely he had gone about the only way of achieving it, although his life, by the standards of most normal people, must appear dim, limited. Who, in these volatile days, stayed in the same organisation for forty years? Who could boast only one long-term – in fact embarrassingly long-term – love affair? Who, at his stage of life, managed without a car, a second home, a flutter on the money markets, or a little property speculation, as did most of the people he read about in his newspaper, and indeed some of the men he had known in the firm, men at the same level of seniority as himself, or even a little lower? Who remained unmarried, or, as they said nowadays, without a partner? Who enjoyed a friendship of rare quality with another man which managed to be entirely sexless? Who was as dull as he was? And was this not the consensus of those who knew him?

At this point it became a matter of urgency to activate those inner voices, those imaginary companions to whom he was bound to listen when other, authentic voices failed him. These voices reminded him that he was healthy (so far), wealthy (incredibly so in the light of his earlier humility in this respect), and independent. This last fact was undeniable. He was the possessor of a comfortable flat a few minutes' walk from the park, where he could stroll without any limit on his time or leisure. Should he be ill he could avail himself of paid help, in the shape of Mrs Cardozo, his weekly cleaning lady, who, though noisy and unsatisfactory in almost every respect, was supposed to be devoted to him, or Hipwood, the downstairs porter, who sat behind a desk in the lobby of his apartment block, and who was amiable enough, although perhaps not entirely reliable. That was the rub: he was sixty-five, and illness, sooner or later would descend on him. The thought was frightening, but he told himself that he probably had a few more years in hand before he succumbed to pain or disability. He was hardy, he was free from immediate care, and he could afford to do as he pleased.

But nothing pleased him. His life of effort, of self-denial, of regular if tardy rewards, seemed to him almost shameful: that thought again. Shame was an emotion left over from childhood, but it had kept him company throughout many a year, always easily stimulated, quick to spring to the fore. Now he felt shame for this undeserved leisure, this pointless interlude in the sun. He had fled London as quickly as he could after settling Putnam's affairs; it had seemed to him then that nature might heal him, might remind him that growth and flowering were as possible as decline and decay. But he had encountered no nature worth speaking of in Nice, only mineral expanses, which, in their relative aridity, reminded him that he was without occupation. Perhaps that was the problem. He had had no time as yet to experience retirement, for his days had been filled with visits of a business nature, and with the sad task of disposing of Putnam's effects. When almost all had been completed, and only the flat remained to be sold, he had simply lingered in his own flat long enough to pack a lightweight bag and take a cab to the airport. The sun, he had thought: the sun is the cure for sad thoughts. But although the sun was unvarying throughout the day, the onset of night was sharp and disconcerting, reminding him that sooner or later he must return home. Then what to do all day? He had no calls on his time, and very few extravagances to indulge. He could walk in the park, of course, go to concerts. There was always the London Library, although not being a scholar he always felt a little shy there. He would read; he had always read voluptuously, and yet he still sensed his mother's withering eye on him as he buried his head in a book in order to drown out the sound of his parents' almost routine bickering.

One thing was certain: he would not go mad. He had never been in the least unstable, was in fact almost comically sensible. Any fantasy in his outlook had been supplied by Putnam. With that gone he was on an unenviably even keel. He knew that the days would be long, and probably empty; he knew that in due course Louise's telephone call would be the one fixed point in his life, but he also knew that he could and would endure his altered state, for was he not, when all was said and done, an extremely fortunate man?

Except that contemplation of his good fortune filled him with distaste. All the forbearance, all the obedience, all the acceptance that had cast their shadow over his formative years now disgusted him. Why and how had he come to this, to this idle afternoon at the café table,

14

out of everyone's sight, with past contentment suddenly turned to ash? If he stayed here it was partly to avoid going home; if he lingered on this café terrace it was to delay the moment of going back to his hotel room. Confinement seemed to him tantamount to concealment, and he wanted his moment of visibility, wanted to be the focus of someone's enquiry, wanted not to have to search for company. To all intents and purposes, to the waiter's eye at least, an ordinarily impassive Englishman, he was filled with all the sadness of loss, not merely for Putnam, but for his whole past life, for his refusal of adventure, excitement, commitment. And now it was too late, for no one found excitement at sixty-five; no one was even attractive at sixty-five. No more women: the thought struck him as a blow, though he had never been careless with women's feelings. There had been flirtations, the occasional sentimental friendship; above all there had been Louise, who had functioned as both wife and mother. There was still Louise, of course, but Louise belonged in essence to that past life which now seemed to him so distasteful. He sighed. At this, as if in answer to his sigh, the waiter came forward. Bland paid, added a tip. The waiter seemed a pleasant serious boy; Bland was anxious to learn something about him. But the waiter, obviously fearing an ulterior motive, refused to be engaged. '*Bon, merci,*' said Bland finally. '*A votre service,*' was the reply. They were the only words which had been addressed to him directly all day.

He wandered in the direction of the Place Masséna: the English papers would have arrived by now. The sea had taken on an opaque look, as if to cue the light to fade. He still had an hour before him in which to walk, but after that there would be a difficult interlude to fill before dinner. At home he would find it equally difficult, perhaps more so. And there would not be the solace of this beguiling golden light, this poignant late warmth. At home there would be greyness, darkness, the sultriness of central heating. Perhaps he would do better to stay here for a while, since he had no appointments. He caught a glimpse of himself sitting out the winter, an English tourist of an obsolete kind, no longer highly regarded because careful and solitary, not, when all was said and done, rewarding. He might buy a property here; he could, he reflected sadly, afford it. Without company his life would be penurious: it would be true exile, in comparison with which life at home would be relatively comforting. He thought of leaves falling in the park, the calm of libraries, the bustle of department stores. He felt a sudden ache of longing, or was it loneliness?

The light was now beginning to change, and it would soon be dark. He took a last look at the impassive sea, then, with a new urgency in his step, made his way back to his hotel and informed the man behind the desk that he would be leaving the following day. In his room he packed steadily, with a suspicion of haste. I was never meant to be here, he thought. I should be at work. I mean, I should be at home. He felt a moment of fear, as if he were no longer safe. Darkness, sudden as always, pressed against the window; cars roared along the corniche. He was aware of an alien life, nothing to do with him, utterly indifferent to whether he stayed or left. He wondered whether they could find him a seat on a plane that evening, but apparently this was impossible. Home, he thought, I must get home. This thought pursued him throughout a sleepless night. When he left, in the very early morning, it was with a feeling of infinite relief, as if he had outwitted a danger. Not until he was actually on the plane did he sense the vague stirrings of a species of nursery comfort, as if he believed the advertisements, a habit left over from a straitened childhood, as if British Airways would take care of him, and would have to, since in an emergency he could count on no one else.

Henceforth he would have to be his own prop and mainstay, a prospect which filled him with despair, as if he had been called to task by an enemy so intimate that he knew his security to be undermined, efficiently and inexorably, for ever.

2

Home is where the heart is. Alternatively, Home is so sad. Bland's attitude towards his flat was the somewhat shifting point at which these two attitudes conjoined. When he was away from it he thought of it longingly, as the place which would always provide him with a refuge from the world. When he was actually inside it, safe and warm and quiet, as he had always wished to be, it exasperated him, precisely on account of those same qualities for which he had felt such intense nostalgia. The quietness, which he cherished, tormented him. There seemed to be no way in which he could resolve this dichotomy of feeling.

The flat was situated on the second floor of a handsome modern block in a quiet street equidistant from the park and the Edgware Road; he could walk to either in less than five minutes, but rarely did so since most of his immediate needs were met by the shops in the small arcade which occupied the ground floor of the building. First impressions were if anything favourable. One entered a lobby, usually deserted, under the eye of the dubious Hipwood, who was on duty until six o'clock; the lift had not been known to break down; the lighting was adequate, although subdued. Once inside one was conscious that one had definitively left the outside world, where occasional cars passed with only a mild murmur.

It was in the flat itself that Bland always registered a faint sinking of the heart, something to do with the confirmation of his own unresolved state of mind. Yet the purchase of the flat, some four years previously, had been well aspected; Putnam had viewed it with him and had expressed approval, and indeed it had seemed a significant advance on the flat over Baker Street Station, not the one he had secured after his flight from Punch and Alfreda Rogerson in Radnor Place, but the larger gloomier apartment on the fourth floor of the same building which he had acquired with the enjoyment of greater affluence, and to which he had remained sentimentally attached for much of his working life, although truth to tell he hardly noticed it, and was indifferent to its largely undistinguished furnishings and the fact that there was a small crack in the bathroom window.

This present flat was different; it represented a conscious choice. It was to be his own creation, and to express his own personality, although he had no illusions on this score, and thought of himself, quite accurately, as an honest but faintly colourless man, not lacking in courage but disinclined to take risks. Its main advantage was that it was still near to Putnam's place in George Street; thus each was within reach of the other and could be called upon to attend in an emergency, if one were to arise. In due course the emergency had arisen but had done so in a public place, a fact which made it doubly painful to Bland, although at the time Putnam was so dominated by his condition that he was indifferent to his surroundings, as he was to be indifferent to the alien sights and sounds of the hospital ward, before he was moved to the small end room in which he had died.

Together they had surveyed the agreeable empty rooms, cheerily optimistic that they could enjoy the years of leisure that were due to them. But now those same rooms represented not leisure but emptiness, an emptiness which would have to be filled each day, until there was no time left to brood on what might have been in store for him, as it had been in store – and both of them quite unsuspecting – for Putnam.

The absence of Putnam was compounded now by the absence of labour. He had faced the prospect of retirement as honestly as he had faced most of the trials in his life, but the prospect had been mitigated by that vision of the Far East which he and Putnam had promised themselves, and which had never been and now never would be realised. The substitution of Nice for Indonesia seemed to Bland symbolic of his presently reduced condition. On his way up to his flat in the lift he had even felt a pang of regret for Nice, where at least he had been able to sit in the sun: here the day was dark and quiet, with a moody subterranean quality to it which he found dispiriting. The low wattage of the lights in the corridor, together with the mild stale warmth given out by the bronze-painted radiators, depressed his already jarred spirits even further, and once inside the flat he went straight to the window of his sitting-room and leaned out into the clammy but kindly air to look at the tree which somehow flourished on the edge of the pavement and was a glory of blossom in the spring. Now it could boast only a dozen or so tired leaves, all hanging down lifeless and waiting for the next wind to plaster them to the kerb which even now was darkening under a light sprinkling of rain.

As the damp air crept into the room and stirred the stagnant warmth Bland reminded himself to make plans for this coming winter. He had left a factitious pro-longation of the summer behind in Nice; here it was November, and London was at its most characteristic, its citizens already obedient to the folly of Christmas, longing to be diverted in a year which had been disastrous for all, not only for himself. With this thought came a·feeling compounded of despair and reassurance: if he was out of the race, at least he had fought the good fight. Blessings, it seemed, had once again to be counted, although the exercise brought him no joy. Dutifully he reminded himself that he was more than adequately housed; he was clothed and fed; he was fit, and healthy, and relatively wealthy, and although he might not positively appreciate any one of these attributes, tied as they were to the indisputable fact of his age, he was well aware how desperate his life would be if he had had to rely on a pension and lived in some distant undistinguished street in a remote part of town, far from the comforting amenities to which he was now accustomed.

He had seen such streets in the course of his long Sunday excursions into the suburbs, excursions on which he could not persuade Putnam to join him, for after their lunch together Putnam would settle down happily at home to watch an ancient film, while he, Bland, would·take a bus to Hammersmith or Camberwell, eager, anxious even, to see how ordinary people, the people with whom he was most in sympathy, were getting on. In reality there was no sign, either of such people's happiness or unhappiness, for the streets were deserted, and it was only on his way home, walking through the park, that he found a little animation, the Asian families out in groups, the tiny tired children, the self-conscious runners, sweat darkening the backs and fronts of their T-shirts, the imperious women throwing sticks for overexcited dogs. Was this where they all were, the undistinguished suburbanites with whose like he had grown up? He had retained a fondness for small communities, or rather for some enhanced idea, some fantasy, of such communities; he cautiously watched soap operas on television, but the characters were all too glossy, too healthy, too *young* to satisfy this odd almost painful atavism, this reluctant love for people whom he had almost certainly loathed as a boy, when forced to eat their meals and listen to their conversations and submit to their manners, customs and habits.

Putnam understood this, of course, although Putnam was free of this melancholy, which in truth was not really melancholy but rather a longing to be comforted, to be at home, in a home quite different from the home he had fashioned for himself, to be gathered in. Putnam understood this curious state but was not in sympathy with it. Putnam had lived quite contentedly in the present and had urged Bland to do the same, but it was precisely the present that now gave him cause for concern. On this dark quiet day he had a moment of panic, wondering what on earth he was to do with himself. He even thought of telephoning Louise, whose unvarying quietude he had always connected with a certain undefined feeling of homecoming, but it was Saturday, not Sunday, and he was unwilling to depart from established tradition. She would be there on the following evening, as she had never failed to be in all the years. For this reason alone he could almost persuade himself that he still loved her. The fact that he always trembled on the verge of such a conviction and never quite succumbed to it had something to do with Louise's own lack of imagination, but more perhaps with his own feeling that he did not want his life to end in this way, quietly and modestly and uncomplainingly, that if he did so he would be an old man within a year, whereas some part of him, an undeveloped part no doubt, was still waiting to be ignited, consumed.

If he were honest – and he was always honest – he feared old age, not merely for itself but for its humiliations. For how much longer could he contemplate the possibility of making love to a woman, without immediately wondering whether he could face the embarrassment of undressing in front of her? These things could be managed, he knew, but at the same time he knew that it would not be given to him gracefully to manage them. All in all there was nothing further to be said on this matter; he was elderly, if not yet old; he was as dignified as he knew how to be, and he must manage the rest of his life as best he could. And if he could not face the prospect of the end when it came he had the sleeping pills which his complaisant doctor had prescribed. They were good for two years, he had managed to ascertain, and in his mind he gave himself two years in which either to flourish or to be overcome by habit or by disappointment. The saving grace was his lucidity: he would know whichever of the two conditions presented itself, and what he would do to confront either one.

He had to come to terms with the fact that there was no consolation. He was an unbeliever: the comforts of religion had been reported to him, but they had sounded more like torments. The idea of being overtaken by unearthly bliss, by secret communion, was profoundly disturbing, like an intimation of madness. The example of the religiously minded, like the repellent Rogersons, had distanced him for ever. Nor did he feel moved to seek succour on his own account; he preferred a modest stoicism, which he saw as essentially secular. This meant a scrupulous attention to the tasks of every undistinguished day, and the good conscience that he occasionally felt at the end of such a day. Art was different, particular, separate; there was no possibility of tying it in to some vague impulse towards love. Art, and by this he meant painting and literature, music rather less, perhaps, stirred him with intimations of a world beyond his own small world. Great ideas, noble themes, opened up his mind and his heart. He went to libraries and museums as others might go to church. And he came away bemused, impressed by otherness, and grateful for the tremendous and no doubt painful energies that went into the fabrication of such artefacts, grateful too for his own tender responses. He could not share, but he could apprehend: that was enough for him. Some days he could only observe, but even these observations, such as a careful student might manage, caused him to experience respect, a respect mysteriously unavailable in other circumstances. He regarded himself as an unregenerate twentieth-century man, unlikely to be redeemed by last-minute revelations, or indeed by any revelations at all.

He took his unopened bag into the bedroom, checked that Mrs Cardozo had put fresh sheets on the bed, and went over to open another window. Already he was conscious of the lack of air, both in his inner and his outer worlds. He told himself that his brief excursion had done him no good at all, had merely unsettled him, whereas the task in front of him was to make the best of already easy circumstances, and be thankful that when he declined, as he undoubtedly would, there would be no witnesses to what would be his physical disgrace, that he could mop and mow without shaming any close relatives, for he had no relatives, having been the only son of a couple so feckless that he often wondered at his own mild equanimity. His long training in contained patience had been learned at his mother's knee, and at his father's too. For this he could not blame them, for the faculty had served him well, until now, that was. Again he felt tremors of some distant restlessness, which, as he knew so well how to do, he now disarmed by some sort of action, trivial though it might appear. To him it was a strategy which had long proved useful in moments of frustration; he would have recommended it to any young person, a son or a nephew, had such existed. As none did he was forced to benefit from his own advice. He would run a bath, he decided, make coffee, have a quiet half-hour with *The Times*, then stroll to Selfridges Food Hall to buy something interesting for lunch. He had taken off his

24

watch and was loosening his tie when to his astonishment the telephone rang.

His first reaction was one of alarm; it must be Louise, and she must be unwell, or in trouble of some sort. When he heard the delicate but decided voice he was unable to identify it; simultaneously he was aware of relief that it was not Louise and uneasiness that his bath was filling.

'Mr Bland?'

'Bland speaking.'

'Do forgive me for troubling you, Mr Bland. It's Mrs Lydiard. From upstairs, you know, the fourth floor.'

'Of course, Mrs Lydiard. May I just ask you to excuse me while I turn off my bath? I'll be with you in a minute.'

Mrs Lydiard, he reflected, laying down the receiver. Was she that rather handsome woman with the silver curls and the tall narrow body, always so well dressed, whom he sometimes crossed in the lobby or met at the lift? If so, then he approved of her, as he approved of all women who continued to fly the flag, decking themselves out bravely for a visit to the shops, never to be encountered in less than perfect order. He approved all the more of Mrs Lydiard inasmuch as she appeared to live alone, like himself, and did not seem to have been driven mad by it. He had never seen her in the company of a man, although there might of course be a bedridden husband upstairs. Somehow he doubted it. Mrs Lydiard, for all her careful glamour, had something resolute about her, as if there were no one to share in the mighty task she faced in keeping herself afloat. She was brave, of that there was no doubt. He had no idea of her age, having never given much thought to the matter. He supposed she might be the same age as himself, or a few years older. With women it was difficult to tell. These flats served as an unofficial retirement home for the elderly. She appeared embattled, largely because she gave an impression of having taken the matter of her own survival in hand. Lonely, he supposed, but dismissed the thought: the matter did not concern him, and in any event he was not disposed to lament the loneliness of others, having enough to cope with in the matter of his own.

'Mrs Lydiard?' he said once again into the mouthpiece. 'What can I do for you?'

'I am most dreadfully sorry to bother you, but I don't quite know what to do. There's a young person sitting on the stairs outside my flat. A young woman.'

'Have you asked her what she's doing there?'

'Of course I have. She says she's come to stay with the Dunlops. But the Dunlops don't live on this floor. They live on your floor, don't they? I thought it rather odd that she didn't know where their flat was.'

'Has one seen her before?'

'Well, I never have. But there's no reason why I should have if she's a friend of the Dunlops.'

He was as vaguely aware of the Dunlops as he was of Mrs Lydiard, easy to greet, just as easy to dismiss from the mind a few seconds later. She was called Sharon and he was called Tim: this much information had been imparted when they had asked him to keep their spare keys. 'We're both so mad we're liable to lock ourselves out for the night,' the girl had explained. She in fact had allocated to herself the privilege of being mad; the husband seemed by contrast rather orderly. He was aware of Sharon Dunlop only as a pair of feet thundering down the stairs every morning. She was a fairly successful free-lance journalist. Her husband followed her more sedately, but still rather noisily, a little later. He was a director of a small company somewhere south of the river. As neighbours they were acceptable. They sometimes asked him to water their plants when they were away and were duly appreciative when he did. He had been touched to receive a Christmas card from them the previous year, wishing him the compliments of the season in a large and looping

26

hand. Minutes later they had thundered down the stairs, on their way out to a party, or to parties, for he had been aware of a very late return, somewhere around four in the morning, just about the time when he woke briefly before succumbing to that irresistible warm sleep that presages the dawn.

'She said she was suffering from jet lag,' Mrs Lydiard's voice went on. 'Apparently she came here straight off the plane. America, she said. The West Coast. Quite a nice sort of girl. Nicely spoken. But I don't like to ask her in. Silly of me, I know.'

'If she says she's staying in the Dunlops' flat she must know them better than we do. What worries me is that the Dunlops might be away. I saw them just before I left, and they didn't mention that anyone was coming to stay.'

'I *think* it's all right. She seems quite above board. It's just that . . . Oh, I know you'll think me silly, but she is rather carelessly dressed, like they all dress these days, with those jogging shoes, you know . . .'

'Trainers.'

'That's right. And she seems to have no luggage. Just a nylon holdall.'

'I've just come back from France myself,' he said, as mildly as possible. Already he regretted leaving Nice so precipitately. These petty matters hardly concerned him. At the same time he saw his quiet day slipping away from him. And his bath was getting cold.

'I mean, and I hope I'm not being too silly, but don't you think it sounds a little unusual?'

'That would depend on how well she knows the Dunlops.'

'She says they're old friends. She says they said she could stay in the flat whenever she's in London.'

'Whether they're there or not?'

'So she says.'

27

'Well, I don't think we can interfere with their arrangements.'

'But if she's sitting on the stairs that must mean that the Dunlops *are* away, Mr Bland.'

'Yes. They do tend to go to America at about this time of year. She probably saw them while they were all there. The fact that we weren't told about any arrangement they might have come to is neither here nor there. I wonder they didn't give her a key, though.

'Yes, I thought that odd.'

'Of course they may not have another key to give her. I have their spare keys. They sometimes ask me to post on their mail when they're away, although they didn't this time. But of course I've been away myself.'

'Oh, I see.' In Mrs Lydiard's dwindling tones he could sense a growing lack of conviction. There was a brief silence.

'Where is she now?' he asked finally.

'Still sitting on the stairs. I don't quite like to ask her in, you see. I dare say I'm being silly, but living alone . . .'

'Why don't you bring her down here? If she says the Dunlops invited her I can give her the keys, and that'll be the end of it.'

'Do you think that's wise?'

'No, I don't. But we can't have her camping out on the stairs. And strictly speaking she's the Dunlops' problem, not ours.'

'Oh dear, I don't like it. And Hipwood won't like it, you know.'

Bland was well aware of this. If anything it made him more determined to take matters in hand.

'Why don't you both come down and have some coffee with me? We can introduce ourselves, find out a little more about her, and if possible persuade her to go somewhere else.'

'What a good idea! So very kind! Shall we say five minutes?'

'Five minutes will be fine.'

When the telephone was at last silent, he went into the bathroom, drained the bath, then, with no time even to change his shirt, he retied his tie, and slipped his watch back onto his left wrist. In the kitchen he filled the kettle, measured out the coffee, and put three cups and saucers onto a pretty japanned tray. He wished he had some biscuits: he was suddenly powerfully hungry. Almost immediately the doorbell rang.

Mrs Lydiard had arrayed herself for this informal visit in her usual finery. As was proper she had dressed as if for the street, in a navy skirt, a navy and white jacket, and a red wool shawl, the fringed end of which was flung bravely over her left shoulder. By contrast his other visitor was disarmingly pale, untidy even, but perhaps only by comparison with Mrs Lydiard's vividly made-up face and pearl ear studs. He had an impression of heaviness, of dullness, although her appearance was nondescript. She wore the usual uniform of jeans and a denim jacket, her feet encased in the grotesquely large shoes. He thought that divested of all this she might be more appealing, but it was impossible to say. Beneath her clumsy clothes she might be any shape at all. The face did not detain him; he was aware of a closed down-turned mouth, undistinguished, rather straggling brown hair. The skin, which was very white, was flawless: that much he noticed. The general impression, however, was indecisive; she might be any young person of her kind, without distinguishing characteristics. Her presence was tiresome. Something must be done about her, evidently, but he had already decided to do the minimum that was permissible in the circumstances.

'Come in, come in,' he said, a shade too heartily. 'I can offer you a cup of coffee, and then we'll decide what . . .

what to do. George Bland,' he added. 'And you've already met Mrs Lydiard.'

'Katy Gibb,' she stated, offering him a remarkably small white hand. 'What a charming flat.'

It seemed an odd thing to say on such short acquaintance, but then the whole situation was unusual. When they were seated with their coffee, he used the authority conferred on him by years as Head of Personnel to find out more about her. Yet for some reason he felt inhibited from asking his usual questions (Age? Income? Last address? Names of two referees?); she was not, after all, and perhaps regrettably, an employee.

'I'm surprised Sharon didn't telephone you,' said Miss Gibb. 'This was all fixed up when we met in New York.'

'You flew in from the West Coast, I think Mrs Lydiard said.'

'That's right. But we met in New York. I went there to see her before she flew on to wherever her sister lives.'

'Florida.'

'That's right.' She made a face. 'Ghastly plastic place. I was on a quick trip to New York, and we met up there. Wasn't it lucky? That's when we fixed up about my staying. She said she'd ring you, but you know Sharon.'

He was aware of an inconsistency in what she was saying, and also in her manner of saying it. The girl's voice contained a drawl that was almost patrician. This, however, was not constant; he had the impression that it could be mustered on certain occasions, when she was angry, for example, as she clearly was now. He registered this, but decided that her feelings were nothing to do with him. From time to time there was a certain American overlay to her pronunciation. He wondered what Professor Higgins would have made of her.

'Is there a problem?' This question was accompanied by arched brows.

Bland shook his head. He supposed all this to be above

board, although Mrs Lydiard's face was a study in both eagerness and alarm. But young people, he thought, they have these slapdash arrangements. Why should they expect us to approve? We don't, of course. But that is a matter of indifference to this girl. His hand retained the feeling of her small soft hand, so very different from Mrs Lydiard's wrinkled knobbed paw, different from his own, on which the veins stood out.

'How long would you be staying?' he asked.

'Oh, until they come back. Don't worry; I'll be careful. And Sharon knows all about it.' She gave a little laugh. 'Anyone would think you didn't trust me.'

His answer was to hand over the keys. 'Here you are then, Miss Gibb.'

'Katy.'

He made an effort. 'Katy, then. You know where I am if you need anything.' Although I hope you won't, he thought.

The girl yawned, and suddenly turned even paler.

'Oh, I'm sorry. It's just that I think I'll go to bed, if you don't mind. Only I'm liable to faint if I don't.'

'Of course,' they said.

At the door she turned and offered her hand again. 'You've both been very kind. Goodbye, Mrs Lydiard.'

'Moira.'

'Mr Bland.'

'George,' he said, sincerely annoyed. He did not intend them to be friends. 'I hope you'll find everything you need. You know where we are,' he added heartily. He was anxious to get rid of her before she passed out, as she threatened to do.

'I shan't forget your kindness,' she said, lingering.

He was surprised by the luminous, almost amorous look she gave him. But then the same look was bestowed on Mrs Lydiard, so he thought no more about it.

When the door finally closed behind her he felt a palpable sense of relief. Mrs Lydiard, on the other hand, seemed stimulated by her unusual morning and was inclined to linger. Bland coughed briefly to disguise the rumbling of his stomach.

'I wonder how she got past Hipwood,' he said.

'Hipwood must have been making his tea. I must apologise, Mr Bland. I can see that you think I have been too precipitate, but I couldn't just leave her sitting outside my flat, could I?'

Bland, who thought she had been precipitate only in the matter of introducing their Christian names, made a mild dismissing gesture with his right hand, thinking that the matter could now be concluded, that Mrs Lydiard could get on with whatever she had been in the middle of doing before this diversion, and that he could finally enjoy what remained to him of his day. Mrs Lydiard's response was to unwind her red shawl and to settle herself more comfortably in her chair. Lonely, he supposed; well, he could hardly grudge her a few moments' conversation.

'She reminded me of my daughter,' said Mrs Lydiard. From these words Bland immediately assumed that Mrs Lydiard's daughter was dead, and with a brief sigh prepared to lend a sympathetic ear.

'I didn't know you had a daughter,' he said.

'I hardly ever see her. She's in America, you see; that's what reminded me of her. Philadelphia at the moment, although her husband moves around a lot. I've never got on with him; that's what caused the breach. When I think whom she could have married I could weep. I have wept, Mr Bland, but that was at the beginning. Now I'm almost used to it, being alone, I mean. To be honest, I was never a very good mother, too restless on my own account, I suppose. Angela never forgave me for divorcing her father; you can hardly tell a small child that a marriage has run its course, can you? I always got on better with my son.'

'You have a son?' he asked, wondering whether to make more coffee, and deciding against it.

'In Yorkshire,' she said briskly. It seemed as if the prospect of her son, whether he were happy or unhappy, left her intact, whereas the daughter was clearly a thorn in her flesh. If the girl, Katy Gibb, reminded her of her daughter, he had an idea of how the daughter must have opposed the dead weight of her sulkiness to the mother's determined glamour, for Katy Gibb had seemed to him sulky, but at the same time intrusive, so that both he and Mrs Lydiard were marooned indoors on her account, whereas they should have been about their separate affairs, strangers to each other. This sudden intimacy was unwelcome, though Mrs Lydiard gave every appearance of welcoming it. He sighed again: her affairs were not his concern. He had appreciated her, if he had ever thought of her at all, for her excellent demeanour, for the pleasing picture she made as she set out on her morning pilgrimage to Marks and Spencer. He had thought she was making a fine job of supporting herself, both mentally and physically. Silently he had applauded her for making no claim on him, for so spectacularly not needing his help. Yet here she was, at nearly twelve o'clock on a Saturday morning, telling him her life story, whether or not he wanted to hear it.

Appearances were deceptive, he thought. To the outward eye this woman was self-sufficient, even exemplary, yet she too had a history, one which he was no doubt doomed to hear. People tended to tell him things, mistaking his polite expression for one of interest. The allusion to her daughter he thought conventional, possibly superficial. And where was the daughter in all this? He hoped that she did not figure too largely in Mrs Lydiard's account. Mothers and daughters were beyond his comprehension: even mothers and sons had proved difficult. He had harboured ambivalent feelings towards his own

33

mother; he suspected that he might, if they ever met, sympathise with the daughter rather than with Mrs Lydiard, who now looked refreshed and competent, having delivered herself of information which she clearly felt lay in better hands than her own. Bland had heard many confessions in his time, and had learned, if necessary, to guide them gently towards some conclusion, to search for some crumb of comfort, to point out the way in which some dignity could be retrieved, even in the most hopeless of circumstances. Mrs Lydiard, on the other hand, despite her admission that she had been a bad mother, did not seem disposed to dwell on the matter, and was even now smoothing out her gloves as if she had made him privy to some interesting new material and was now waiting for him to contribute something of a similar nature. He wondered if she were rather foolish, or perhaps simply as decorative as her own appearance. Yet she must endure lonely hours, as he was about to, and he owed her some sympathy, a sympathy he did not yet feel. He had preferred her in the abstract, when he hardly knew her, when she was simply an agreeable figure in the landscape.

'Any grandchildren?' he asked, somewhat desperately.

She made a face. 'My daughter has two; one black, one Korean. Adopted, of course. My son-in-law never had much sense of reality. You can see why we don't get on. Not that I want to burden you with my affairs. Well, I must leave you. So sorry to have ruined your morning. You'll let me know if Miss Gibb proves tiresome, won't you? Although I feel a little sorry for her. She looked so tired, didn't she? I remember that look: Angela had it when she was struggling with her homework. I'll leave you my telephone number, and of course I've got yours. That way we can keep in touch.'

But he did not want to keep in touch, he reflected, as he opened the door for her and at last shut it behind her. He wanted most definitely to be left alone, even if the prospect were unpleasing. He supposed that Mrs Lydiard was bored; he supposed that he himself was bored. But the bored do not necessarily attract others of their kind, and in any case he did not intend to sink into that half world in which any acquaintance is made to do duty for a friend. Despite a natural feeling for women he did not wish to know too many. Oh Putnam! And in any case he was after some stronger emotion in his life than that afforded by such Lilliputian concerns, stronger than resignation with what fate had offered him, stronger than the gossip of a Mrs Lydiard and her kind, stronger than irritation with the tiresome circumstances that such a day as today provided.

He glanced at his watch, saw that it was too late to go out and buy something for lunch, found and ate an apple, and sat for half an hour staring fixedly into space, his fingers occasionally drumming on the arms of his chair. He wanted life, more life; somehow the events of the morning, inconsequential though they had been, had brought this realisation to the front of his mind. He had never lost his heart, burned his boats, gone in search of something indefinable, out of reach. He had remained at home, cautiously, sensibly, even contentedly. He felt a pang of derision and despair that made his eyes blur with momentary tears. His fingers wiped them away; he felt incredulous. As always his reaction was one of gratitude that there were no witnesses. I must be tired, he thought. With an effort he got up from his chair and went into the bedroom. His unopened bag still stood on the bed. He removed it, still unopened, lay down, and within minutes was asleep.

3

He awoke with a start. A vibration in the dark room suggested either the telephone or the doorbell. He groped for his bedside clock and saw that it was four-thirty: he had slept through the entire afternoon. For a minute or two he lay on his back, wondering why he had awakened so suddenly, why in fact he had ever been asleep. The telephone was silent: he must have dreamt the noise. This period of unconsciousness alarmed him; he usually slept only at night, and then briefly, and with many interruptions. He was in the habit of leaving the radio on, enjoying the companionable voices in the peace of his own bedroom, enjoying the fact that he could simply listen and not be obliged to respond. In the course of his life many dinner parties had come his way, during which, as an eligible bachelor, and through the passage of time merely as a spare man, he had done his social duty to the best of his ability. For this reason, and no doubt for many others, unexamined, it was always a relief to return to his flat, to turn out the lights, and to listen passively to conversations which did not challenge or disturb him, and from which, swimming up from the depths of his light sleep, he could learn the occasionally interesting fact. An added bonus was that he was not required to remember such facts in the morning.

This sleep had been different, deep and strange. He had even had a couple of dreams, which, in his experience, was unusual. In one of them he had distinctly seen his mother's face, ironic and unfriendly, as it had appeared in her last illness, when she sat in a chair, hair and dress obscured by cigarette smoke and ash, eyes fixed on him as he attempted guiltily to read his book, a book pretentious by her standards, pretentious even by his at that date, but doing duty for a whole world which he was forbidden to enter. He had longed for her to die and had suffered ever since, had done penance for this longing, which was in fact a longing for freedom, and thus legitimate. He had been nineteen at the time, his heart swollen with grief and pity for this ruined woman, who, he thought, loved him as little as he loved her. He had done his best, perhaps better than a nineteen-year-old could be expected to do; he had been there at the end. Therefore the memory of her unsympathetic gaze had been deeply unwelcome, a reminder of times past. The other dream was more fragmentary, had been both trivial and vivid: a street somewhere, which he must once have known but now could not place, glimpsed in the silence of a suburban afternoon.

Of the two dreams, which, together with their attendant associations, had flashed past his inward eye in the space of less than a minute, it was the second which stayed with him as an after-image and seemed imprinted on his retina. Everything – the weather, the time of day – was present: it had seemed to him to be about four o'clock on a Sunday afternoon. Only the location of the street was imprecise, and in a sense irrelevant. He had walked down such streets in his youth, when he was anxious to restore peace to his soul after enduring the quarrelsome company, if it was company, of his parents for any length of time. A Sunday would have provided such an interval, since a large lunch was eaten in the middle of the day. He had been reduced to whiling away the blank afternoons until sheer weariness forced him home. But the second dream, though connecting with the first inasmuch as both took him back to adolescent hurts and soulfulness (was such a period of his life never to be over?), had seemed to contain later material, as if the suburban street were some sort of ideal far removed from his actual and extremely metropolitan setting, which by comparison – and all this in the split second of lucid dreaming – had seemed flimsy, meretricious, unconvincing, as if his slow steady rise to affluence had been an error, as if no happiness could ever come of it. With Louise he would have lived differently, he knew, possibly in just such a street, in a substantial but unpretentious house, in which the rituals of tea-time would have been honoured and all the neighbours known. Here he knew virtually no one: he sometimes wondered whether he could even tolerate this flat, which would have seemed to him unimaginably perfect in those early sore-spirited days. It is not home, he thought, staring into the darkness of the room: it does not comfort me, holds no warmth of memory. Not that memory, these days, was in any way propitious. If he had any spirit he would leave it until in the passage of time it lost some of its negative associations. He could go away again, not precipitately, but in a more deliberate fashion, could travel like a gentleman. And perhaps at the end of such journeying he would find, or make, another home, a real home. The image was becalmed but unnerving, as the dream had been. The emptiness, the silence! He registered the fact that although the effect had been peaceful it was a feeling of alarm that had woken him.

For this reason the doorbell, when it rang again, was almost welcome, although he wished he were in a better condition to answer it. Stumbling into his shoes, aware of his dishevelled state, he limped down the corridor, switching on the lights as he went. On the landing, and waiting patiently, stood Katy Gibb, looking considerably more amenable than when she had first appeared earlier that day. She had shed her jacket and trainers: indeed her feet were bare, and he had time to notice how beautiful they were, slim, white and unmarked. He remembered her hand in his, and the agreeable impression that had made. Her cheeks were now a healthy pink; her pale rather small eyes regarded him in a manner which conveyed both shyness and frankness. The only odd thing about her appearance, apart from her feet, was the fact that her hair was streaming wet.

'Hallo,' he said. 'Are you feeling better?' Though I am the one who feels ill, he thought.

'I came to thank you,' she replied, 'for being so kind to me this morning, and to ask if you could lend me some tea. There doesn't seem to be any in the flat.'

'The shops are probably still open,' he said.

'Oh, it's hardly worth going out now. And besides, my hair's wet.'

Conscious that he was not at his best, he was not anxious to ask her in, but as he turned towards the kitchen she quite naturally followed him.

'This is a nice flat,' she said. 'Do you live here alone?'

'Yes, I do,' he replied, rather shortly. 'Here's your tea.' He noticed that it was his last packet. He would have to do some serious shopping in the morning; it was, as she had said, too late to bother with now, and in any case he wanted to wash and change, feeling shabby after his long sleep.

'Thank you so much. And I was wondering, is there anywhere to eat round here? I'm not very domesticated, I'm afraid. Could you put me in the picture? I don't want to be a nuisance, or anything. Only all my friends seem to be away for the weekend.'

This could have been put more tactfully, he thought. But he was ashamed of his ruffled temper, which he feared may have been apparent to her, and conscious of the waif-like picture she made, with her bare feet and her wet hair.

'Why don't I give you dinner?' he said. 'We'll ask Mrs Lydiard to join us, and you can tell us all about yourself.'

'Lovely,' she said, all but clapping her hands. Don't overdo it, he thought, and smiled sourly at his own crabbed reaction. At the same time he felt a vague disquiet that he had descended the slope to misanthropy so quickly – he thought of it as misanthropy rather than misogyny, for he desired to see no one at all on this particular evening, neither man nor woman – and he felt balky and unattractive.

'What time shall I pick you up?' enquired Katy Gibb.

This too seemed tactless, but he put his irritation down to the fact that he had not yet managed to have his bath and had eaten nothing for what now seemed a very long time. And this morning I was in Nice, he realised with surprise.

'Shall we say seven-thirty?' he said. 'There's quite a good Italian restaurant round the corner. And we'll all meet up here first for a glass of sherry.'

He telephoned Mrs Lydiard, who expressed herself to be delighted at the prospect of this rather random invitation. Then he made himself a cup of tea with what was left in the caddy, wondered if he had time to slip downstairs to the shops, realised that he was cutting his arrangements pretty fine (his bag still unpacked) and resigned himself to coffee in the morning. He thought of hiding the coffee, in case Katy Gibb came back for it, then had the grace to laugh at himself and at last ran his bath.

As usual he contemplated himself sombrely. The body, he thought, was no longer good for much as an object of pleasure, or even as a subject of pleasure, yet it had served him well, and, more important, gave no warning of hidden illness, of imminent breakdown. There might be some anomaly waiting its time beneath the pale skin, behind the bony ribs, but for the moment it was leaving him in peace. If meagre, it was not altogether disgraceful; a little stooped, perhaps, but he could make an effort in that direction. He was powerless only with that which lay outside his normal competence, which might account for the fact that he had chosen so unexciting a partner as Louise. Yet even Louise had surprised him, and thus he had surprised himself. Nevertheless, he still felt somewhat ashamed of his constancy. It had never occurred to him to question hers.

Patting his body dry, and anointing it with Eau Sauvage, he turned his attention to his face, one eye widening warily over the old-fashioned razor as he registered a slight hairiness about the ears, rather too much domed forehead, a few broken veins round the outer rim of the nostrils. He made the same inventory every day, but it never ceased to amaze him, this evidence of decay of which he otherwise had no notion. Clothed, he was once again in command, an urbane, tall, rather thin man, with an undistinguished face and large hands, who had on the whole made a success of his life but who was now perhaps at something of a loose end. He must make plans for the future, he thought, as he arranged glasses on a tray; he must learn how to fill his days. If this afternoon were anything to go by he was in danger of slipping downhill, and not only of slipping but of ending up rather nearer to his early beginnings than to his later achievements.

When the doorbell rang, yet again – for it now seemed to him that it had been ringing all day – he hurried to answer it with some relief. Katy Gibb's third manifestation took him by surprise. He had registered the sullen hippy of that morning, and the pink-cheeked wet-haired schoolgirl of the afternoon. Now the creature who stood before him was a sulphurous sophisticate, clad in black silk trousers, a black silk jacket, and a black silk camisole. The body thus revealed, as opposed to concealed, was seen to be small and agreeably rounded, perhaps a little heavy on the hips. But the face . . . Her lips were now a brilliant red, her cheeks a dark reddish pink; the eyes were enlarged and darkened with cosmetic, the lashes freighted with mascara. Mata Hari, he thought, then realised that the name would mean nothing to her. He was amused in spite of himself, but at the same time touched that she had taken so much trouble. She smelt not of strange essences but of shampoo and face powder. He was aware of the white flesh beneath the camisole but was more beguiled by the bold and artificial colours of the face. The picture that she presented to him was compounded of both childishness and calculation; he thought the calculation outweighed the childishness, for given the effort and application that had gone into her appearance he did not see how it could be otherwise.

The effect was undeniably impressive. But more impressive even than all the colours, than the silent presentation of herself for his approval, and perhaps for his astonishment, was the evidence of amorous confidence, and of the self-knowledge and no doubt self-love that had inspired the whole performance – for that was what it was, a performance put on for his sole benefit. Everything that she wished to convey – her transition from girl to woman, the seductive power she had chosen to unveil – was present in the first sight of herself, as she stood on the landing outside his flat. He was amused, yes, but he was also intrigued, and if he was seduced it was by the picture she made and by the glimpse she afforded him of a world of pure femaleness that was almost a sacred mystery, like temple prostitution.

He had had little contact with such a world, and like most men was somewhat wary of it. Louise had passed from shy and virtually unadorned girl to modest if expensively groomed widow almost without transition; these days all he knew of her was her back view as she combed and patted her hair in his mirror. Or so it seemed to him now, faced as he was with this evidence of decoration, of polishing, of burnishing, of transformation of raw material into a work of art. It was as a work of art that he contemplated her, as if he were an unworldly scholar in a gallery studying a portrait of a courtesan by Veronese or Palma Giovane. There was the same hieratic passivity, as if she were waiting for his response to complete the sequence. In a way this mitigated somewhat against her appeal, for it was impossible not to regard her as one of a species, and only just incidentally as an individual. She was evidently on display, and knew herself to be so, for she made no movement, waiting for him to express some wonderment or appreciation. But he felt no desire for her, felt in fact little connection with this strange creature who had metamorphosed so unpredictably from the anonymous girl, whose appearance he could now hardly remember, of the morning.

His main emotion was one of gratification, of pleasure that he had been awarded an unusual and rather remarkable spectacle. It was a gratification quite devoid of intellectual substance. Somehow, despite the altogether enlightened effort that had gone into making her appearance what it was, he doubted if there were any evidence to suggest a mind of equal subtlety. He could not now remember anything she had said, which seemed sufficient indication that what she had said had not been memorable. A mind equal to her appearance would suggest a Queen of Sheba, a Cleopatra, and he doubted she would ever be in that category. Earlier he had registered something limited, almost obstinate. But he was ready to forgive her whatever character faults she might possess for her ability to confer on him an aesthetic surprise which he had surely not been led to expect from such a tedious morning. He thought of it as the Palma Giovane experience. He hoped that she would prove to be very silly. If not she would be formidable.

Perhaps tired of his silence, and of her own – the first indication that her judgment might not be perfect – she stepped forward, as if to brush past him. He was grateful that the whine of the lift heralded the arrival of Mrs Lydiard.

Mrs Lydiard too had made an effort, but unfortunately had also chosen to wear black, a black and white taffeta blouse under a black wool suit, which drained the colour from her pretty but slightly dissatisfied face. Mrs Lydiard, though decorative, though handsome for a woman of her age, and despite a very slight limp which he had not noticed before, having never before spent so much time in her company, was outclassed. She smelt strongly of scent, which he found disagreeable.

'Oh, it is good to see you again,' said Katy Gibb, giving her a kiss. Mrs Lydiard smiled and shook her too tight curls. 'And to see you too, my dear.'

'Sherry?' offered Bland.

Katy hesitated. 'You'll think me silly, but have you got any champagne?'

He had. A dozen bottles of Moët et Chandon, given to him as a retirement present and almost forgotten.

'Only whenever I start again in a new place I like to drink champagne.'

'Then we will drink champagne,' he said. 'But tell me, is this place new to you? I gathered that you had been living in America, but I assumed that you were as English as I am. As Mrs Lydiard is,' he added, remembering his manners.

'I may stay here,' she replied. 'I may decide to start my own business.'

This, he realised, was not quite what he had asked her.

'Oh, really, how interesting,' said Mrs Lydiard. 'I am

so in favour of women working. I always worked, you know, and I loved it . . .'

'A woman nowadays can choose her own lifestyle,' said Miss Gibb solemnly.

He had been right, he thought; her utterances were not up to the level of her appearance. If anything, this pleased him: he was now able to sit back and relax. He looked forward to an evening which need have no aftermath. This suited him very well. Nothing more would be required of him. He asked her what her business might be, not really believing that she had any.

'That's under wraps at the moment,' she said. 'I'd need to form a company and find sponsors, of course.'

'I had a most interesting working life,' pursued Mrs Lydiard. 'I was secretary for many years to a very important cancer specialist.' She mentioned an eminent name. Bland was surprised, but on reflection decided that something must have occupied her time, since she had done such an effective job in disposing of her husband and children.

'I'm afraid I don't hold with conventional medicine,' said Miss Gibb. 'And I'm glad to say it's nearly had its day. In the future the accent will be on natural healing. That's the area I'm interested in.'

'My employer saved many lives,' said Mrs Lydiard. She looked at the girl intently, as if wanting to tell her that wear and tear were also natural, that there is such a thing as stealthy degeneration, that the enemy might strike at any moment. She forbore to do so, from either good breeding or contempt for the girl's youth. There was a very slight alteration in the atmosphere. Bland sensed it, but also felt himself to be unaffected. The spectacle was too intriguing. He understood, in a brief illumination, the monstrous egotism, the pure solipsism of the artist.

'More champagne?' He saw that they had nearly finished the bottle, although Mrs Lydiard was still toying with hers. 'Or shall we go? It's only round the corner,' he told Katy.'

'I hope so,' she said. 'I certainly can't walk far in these.' She indicated her frail black sandals.

'Not far,' he assured her, wondering if he would have to take her arm. The idea pleased him; he felt stimulated. 'Not far,' he repeated. Or was it the champagne? Not a bad idea to have a glass or two in the evening, but then one would have to finish the bottle. Unless one invited someone round, of course.

The walk to the restaurant was accomplished hesitantly, as if the two women were in need of his support. They walked slowly, more slowly than was necessary, out of deference to the girl's clattering sandals. Yet she was sturdily built, he had noticed, was surely no stranger to exercise. He thought the performance exaggerated, yet he remained amused by it. What she expected to gain from this unimportant evening, apart from a decent meal, he had no idea; her preparations had seemed excessive, but perhaps she looked beyond her two companions to further adventitious acquaintance. Perhaps all young women today did this, as if to show themselves, suitably attired, in a public place were enough. Women were different now, he knew, no longer sitting with downcast eyes, like Louise when he first knew her, no longer attentive to what men had to offer. Indeed the roles were reversed; men now had to prove themselves worthy of attention. At least he did not have to take her seriously. The whole evening had been wished on him, or had he wished it on himself? He no longer knew. He found himself keeping an eye on her, turning back from time to time to Mrs Lydiard, who was having to manage as best she could. He felt he did not have enough energy to contain them both, and wished there were another man in the party, as perhaps the girl had hoped there might be.

Seated, Miss Gibb thrust her hands into her hair and

shook it back from her face. The movement revealed a little more of the white flesh. 'What would you like to eat?' he asked. The look of unselfconscious greed on her face was reward enough for any host, he thought. 'Moira?' For, if only by Katy's decree, they were to be Moira and George.

'Oh, I think a grilled sole,' said Mrs Lydiard. 'I rarely eat much in the evening.'

'I'll join you. Katy?'

'Snails,' she said. 'And king prawns *al forno*.'

They looked at her with respect; clearly an adventurous eater. 'And to drink?' murmured Bland.'

'More champagne, I think, don't you?'

'Moira?'

'Nothing for me, George, I rarely . . .'

'But it's a celebration, Moira!' said the girl. 'And it's terribly exciting! I might be on the verge of a new life! That's something to celebrate, isn't it?'

'As you like, my dear,' said Mrs Lydiard, suddenly looking old and tired.

'We'll drink to your new venture,' said Bland. 'And you must tell us more about it.' For he still had an almost professional interest in her history.

'I told you. It's under wraps at the moment. But I'm hoping to build on my American experience.'

'And what was that exactly?'

'I was with Howard Singer,' she said simply, putting down her glass as if to mark the significance of the declaration.

Bland searched his memory, but found no record of Howard Singer Enterprises, or the Howard Singer Corporation.

'Who is Howard Singer?' queried Mrs Lydiard.

Katy made a gesture of comical despair, as if she could not credit their ignorance.

'I'm surprised you've never heard of him,' she said.

'He's very well known in the States. He has one of the most famous stress workshops on the West Coast.' Her eyes were modestly lowered, as if in anticipation of their reverence. An aromatic plate of snails was put in front of her.

'What does he do?' asked Mrs Lydiard bluntly.

The eyes flew up again. 'What doesn't he do? Shiatsu, Vibrasound, Tantric Massage, Reflexology, Chakra, Crystal Therapy, Essential Oils – that's my particular speciality – Flower Remedies, Colour Counselling – you name it.'

'Sex therapy?' suggested Bland.

'Of course. An enormous number of people are on the wrong track, you know.' Most of them, it was implied; possibly all of them, in Singer's estimation.

Bland could see this man, this Singer, clearly a charlatan, bronzed and smiling, with very white teeth, and a Hawaiian shirt disclosing abundant grey fuzz. He added a pony tail and an elephant hair bracelet, as he neatly dissected his fish. Waves of garlic drifted across the table. Mrs Lydiard, he surmised, was not enjoying her dinner. He on the other hand was having a better time than he had anticipated. He refilled Katy's glass, and said, 'And that's what you'd like to do, is it?'

'I've heard of those things,' said Mrs Lydiard. 'It's what they call New Age, isn't it?'

'Brilliant, Moira! I knew you'd be open to ideas. I think it's wonderful when people like yourself keep up with the times.' She meant old people, clearly. For a moment or two her temper seemed uncertain; anger, it appeared, was never very far from the surface. But Bland was more interested in the voice, which had again become patrician, although it had previously been a hybrid mixture of English and American.

'I think I'd rather trust my doctor . . .'

'Yes, I do too,' said Bland, thinking of his cache of sleeping pills.

'You'd be wrong! Massage could help that leg of yours, Moira, and I'm sure all your pills haven't.'

Yes, he thought, she was clearly angry, although they had gone out of their way to humour her. Feeling reckless, he suggested, 'And I suppose the first step is to get in touch with the child inside you?'

'Within. We say within.'

'Within,' he concurred.

He was beginning to enjoy himself, although all appetite had left him. Mrs Lydiard too seemed depressed by her fish. However, Mrs Lydiard's expression of other-worldliness, and her apparent decision to rise above whatever she deemed unworthy of her notice, could, he decided, be put down to a feeling of exclusion. It was clear from Katy's animation, her self-absorption, her very greed, that she had little time for elderly ladies beyond the sudden absent-minded smiles she aimed in Mrs Lydiard's direction. Mrs Lydiard, possibly not a good judge of character, was not as foolish as she seemed, he thought. Simply, she had rejoiced in his invitation, had enjoyed adorning herself, and was now as disconcerted as a girl to be relegated to the sidelines, when the evening had promised nothing but pleasure. There was indeed something combative in the atmosphere. Maybe women always felt like this about other women, he thought, particularly when a man, however negligible, manifested a degree of interest. Not that he was interested. Amused, rather. He smiled to himself. At least he had the good sense not to feel smug.

He found the girl beguiling, largely for her adroit shrewdness and for her very genuine silliness, of which she was unaware. As to her 'work', Bland reflected that to be very good at something inherently stupid was not necessarily a mark of high intelligence. On the other hand, to make a living out of it, as he did not doubt that she might, would be no mean achievement, would, in addition, argue superior business sense. He wondered about her relationship to the prestigious Singer, of whom he had never heard. Acolyte, clearly, since the man was evidently something of a guru, and possibly, no, probably, more. Despite her relative youth she was obviously experienced, more experienced than either of her fellow diners. He had not forgotten the sudden shock of her appearance, when she had manifested herself – there was no other word for it – at his door. Now that a range of natural expressions had taken over her appearance was less decisive, although the manner in which she had ingested her terrible meal compelled the attention. She ate daintily, but with ruthless efficiency, the moisture glistening on her mouth. He put her age at about twenty-nine or thirty. When she reached middle age the plumpness round her waist and hips would be difficult to shift, particularly if she ate as undiscriminatingly as she was doing this evening.

'You are so right', pursued Mrs Lydiard, who was nothing if not socially responsible, 'to want to start your own business. The future belongs to the self-employed. Otherwise one gets such a shock when one is obliged to retire. Didn't you feel that, George?'

'I've hardly had time to get used to it,' Bland replied.

'I was bereft,' she added. 'Positively bereft.'

He was beginning to understand Mrs Lydiard. She did not miss her children, let alone her husband. She missed her employer, who had seen her through so many happy days in Harley Street, for whom she had dressed so carefully for so long, and whose presence at her side on such an evening as this would have made her impervious to any slight. She was not entirely baffled by the turn things had taken; she could see that on this particular occasion she was being treated as a makeweight. At the same time she was as fascinated as was Bland, whom she clearly thought ought to know better, by the girl's crude charm, and longed to be included in what Katy termed her celebration. If the occasion warranted it – and she still had some doubts about this – she wanted to join in. Bland, watching her, when he could spare some attention from Katy, reflected that the girl possessed an unusual gift: she brought everyone to the brink of bad behaviour, simply by dint of behaving rather badly herself. One vied for her attention; one raised one's voice; one exaggerated one's own presence. However much one longed to maintain one's usual standards, within a few minutes – half an hour at the most – this was mysteriously no longer possible. Mrs Lydiard, he could see, was eager to make amends for her momentary disloyalty, if not quite ready to desert her other convictions, conventional medicine retaining the priority. He himself was feeling imprudent, largely because he had discerned that the girl was dissembling. He felt quite kindly towards her, but his judgment, he thought, was intact.

'How did you come to know Sharon?' he asked noncommittally, refilling her glass.

'Sharon?' She was deeply flushed now, eyes and teeth gleaming. 'She was Sheila when I first knew her. Sheila Robinson. She changed it to Sharon because she thought it was more distinguished. Whereas anyone could have told her that Sharon is incredibly naff.'

The vowels had narrowed again, the tone had modulated into a distinguished drawl. Even her expression had changed, had become distant, as if contemplating a little-known human folly.

He noted once again that she had not answered his question. He also noted that although she had had a great deal to drink she was not drunk, whereas he himself was feeling a little warm, a little vague. Mrs Lydiard was rearranging her gloves and her handbag, as if impatient for the evening to end. Gloves, he could hear Katy think-ing: how incredibly naff. Coffee was served.

He signalled the waiter for the bill, looked at his watch, and saw to his surprise that it was after eleven-thirty.

'Forgive me for keeping you up so late,' he apologised to Mrs Lydiard. 'At least tomorrow's Sunday.'

She smiled patiently at him, as if every day were Sunday to her. He collected them both by the door; they seemed to have become bulky and voluminous, difficult to manoeuvre. Just as well I don't have to drive, he thought. Out in the street the clean air staggered him with its purity; he felt grateful for it, humbled by it. Suddenly the evening seemed tawdry, a waste of time and money. He wished that he could have remained on distant terms with Mrs Lydiard, and that this cumbersome girl had never entered their quiet lives. His earlier feeling of licensed irreverence was replaced by a sensation of shame. Mrs Lydiard was silent, whether on her dignity, or wearily aware that any young person, even so marginal a one as this (and what in the end did they know about her?) could turn her into someone of no importance. Mrs Lydiard, Bland could see, felt old. As, suddenly, he did himself.

'Thank you so much, George,' said Mrs Lydiard dis-tantly. 'No, don't come up. I'm quite all right on my own. Why don't you see Katy to her door? I'm sure we're all ready for bed. I know I am.'

'Ready for bed?' queried Katy, amused, as they made their slightly unsteady way up the stairs. 'I'm not. I rarely go to bed before one-thirty or two, sometimes later. I'm at my best at night, do my best thinking then. Howard and I often did encounter work around this time . . .'

'Encounter work?' he queried.

'You know. Question and answer sessions. Trans-actional analysis. Howard has this marvellous technique for getting people to recognise their hang-ups.'

'You mean he sees clients, patients, or whatever, in the middle of the night?'

'Sure. Are you unhappy with that?'

'I would be if it were happening to me.'

'I could tell you a bit more about it if you're interested. Even give you a trial session. On an introductory basis, of course. Are you going in?' she questioned, apparently amazed at this state of affairs. 'You're not going to bed though, surely? If not, I don't mind watching television with you for a bit. You get the really grungy programmes round about midnight. They're the ones I really enjoy. And they're American. Howard and I knew a lot of people in the entertainment business.'

He put his key in the lock of his own door and said, 'I think I'll turn in, if you don't mind. I *am* a little tired now. I only got back from France this morning. Good-night, Katy. Thank you for a pleasant evening.'

Although he was by this time in his own hallway she lingered, watching him. All at once he felt tired of her, inimical to her, as if she were a threat, as if she might destroy his peace of mind, the desperately calm and comfortable life he had fashioned for himself, if she had a mind to. He retained enough self-possession to wish her, once again, a pleasant good-night, once again to thank her for an enjoyable evening. If he overdid it it was because he was unsettled, and mildly ashamed of himself.

'Okay,' she said. 'But remember, if you want to kick a few ideas around, or even share your thoughts, you know where I am.'

He noticed, even in his tired state, that she had not thanked him, had not expressed appreciation for the evening. This was how women behaved now, he told himself. He had little experience of the phenomenon, being cast in an ancient and no doubt false mould of politeness, of smiles and acknowledgments, and dutifully expressed deference towards the masculine gift of largesse. He also noticed that she was utterly unmarked by the evening's excesses. At least, they felt like excesses to him; to her they must seem little more than an interlude. Inside his flat he knew both alarm and relief, as if he had been caught out in some deception. Intellectually, he knew, the evening had been indefensible; at certain moments he had been secretly derisive not only of the girl but of himself. Such an evening could not have taken place if Putnam were still alive, or, if it had taken place, would have been put into context by Putnam's commentary. Putnam had served this useful function, among so many others. He knew that he was not being quite honest with himself: he had been stimulated by the sight of the girl's appetites (for there had been more than one in evidence) and intrigued by her, as if she were a puzzle sent to beguile him in these bewildering days of leisure, this life so free of incident and adventure. He wanted, he thought, to study her further; that surely was allowed. In bed, in the blessed dark, he thought, she is young! All that this implied, all the longing, all the hurt, all the frustrations of his own youth came flooding back as he remembered her flushed cheeks, her decorated eyes. These were the last images that tempted him before he slid into sleep, her cheeks, her eyes, and her gleaming mouth closing on a morsel of nourishment, her scarlet fingertips guiding it steadily towards extinction.

4

'Amazing Grace', droning out of the radio by his bed, alerted him to the fact that it was Sunday. He sat up cautiously: not too bad. On the other hand not quite as good as usual, which was only to be expected after his intake of the previous evening. He looked back on the occasion with amazement: what on earth had possessed him to arrange it? At least he had refused to prolong it; that was one thing saved. But perhaps this too was cause for concern, that he had turned down an opportunity to do what any other man would have done, and by his very action, or lack of it, had confirmed his status as cautiously respectable bachelor, near celibate, and hopeless recluse.

The incident worried him, not, he thought, because he had in any sense desired the girl, but because he despaired of himself. He realised that had he not been aware of Mrs Lydiard's implicit disapproval he would have invited the girl into his flat, not to make love to her, but to find out more about her. She had stimulated his near professional curiosity; he doubted that she was altogether above-board. He retained, for closer inspection, the undoubtedly expensive black silk outfit, toted across continents in a cheap nylon holdall, ready for a fortuitous meeting with a man, even a man as unpromising as himself. But that was wrong too, he thought, as he ran his bath, for the most worrying factor of all was that throughout the previous evening he had not felt noticeably benevolent. What he had felt, he reflected with a slight shock, was young, much younger than his official age (which must be all too apparent to the girl), and open to suggestions, however louche. He had even been willing to engage in a species of flirtation, distinguished only from the conventional kind by the fact that it was a flirtation with the truth. He would get the truth out of her; in this matter he would have his way with her.

Nevertheless he was still puzzled by his own behaviour, which was part good nature, part avidity. His interest had been engaged, and for that he was grateful to her. On the other hand he must be circumspect, more circumspect than he had already shown himself to be in the presence of Mrs Lydiard, who, having taken her leave of them at the lift, had assumed a dignified air, as if dissociating herself from bad behaviour. He must remember that this girl, Katy Gibb, was not being given to him to study, that she had a life of her own, flimsy though it might seem to him. After she had left the Dunlops' flat – for she could hardly remain there after their return – he would never see her again. Therefore it might be wise, as well as appropriate, to give her a wide berth, to treat her as the stranger she both was and was destined to be, and to behave with renewed decorum, as befitted his station in life.

He felt disturbed that anything out of character had ever crossed his mind, then reflected that the provocation had been blatant. This, he thought, was also worrying, but was no concern of his; the girl was young (or possibly not so young), was at a loose end, had perhaps drunk too much, had perhaps thought that this was the way in which she was expected to reward her host for a not very scintillating evening. But at some deeper level he had known that she was angry, with that strange unfocused anger of hers which could be activated by a random incident or circumstance, by something as mysterious as an association formed in her own mind which would remain completely inaccessible to others. He wondered if she had had the benefit of Howard Singer's therapy, or rather of one of his therapies, his encounter work, as she had called it. However bogus the man was he could surely not fail to notice the strange combination of concealment and aggression which even he had isolated. But however complicated her mind appeared to be, Bland sensed that it was closed, uncommunicative, not available for comment, not susceptible to explanation. Hence his strange sensation of alarm as he had slid into sleep the previous night.

He remembered the last conscious image he had entertained: the lips closing definitively over something glistening and defenceless. The image itself had frightened him then and contrived to frighten him now. But there was a difference: now he divined its gross indecency. With a bemused expression, to which he was oblivious, he decided that he had been near the edge. This edge, which he did not and could not define, represented the limit of acceptable behaviour, acceptable not merely to society but to his own internal censor whom, so far, he had done nothing to defy. He was aware that what he termed acceptable behaviour would be a laughable neutrality to others, a hedging of bets, a failure to take advantage of life's opportunities, like the opportunity offered to him on the previous evening. He even felt that he would never gain the upper hand over what was on the whole a limited past and a limiting future until he crossed that same limit, that it might at some point prove crucial to recognise that limit and to decide no longer to respect it, to reach the edge and to behave as if it were no longer there, and in that way to be free. And that certain situations, and certain persons represented that challenge . . . But behaviour is as much a question of habit as it is of principle, and he thought that at his age habits could no longer be broken. He was condemned to be what he had always been; indeed he must be careful, vigilant even, if he wished to remain the same, as he suspected that he did. Why else had he been so quick to recognise anomalies in his own attitude, his very slight cruelty during the dinner, a cruelty which had felt so liberating but which had been followed almost at once by a sensation of danger?

The upshot of all this was that he had better steer clear of the edge if he did not want to ruin the rest of his life, and that he had better accept the fact that he was a dull character who was unlikely to comport himself with dignity in untoward situations. His dignity had been hard won, and he was not about to abandon it now. As the morning grew lighter the very idea of a man of his age amusing himself with a girl young enough to be his daughter seemed grotesque, unseemly; he rejected it utterly. And the girl had been quicker than he to reach this conclusion; hence her anger, both at his amusement and at his belatedly respectable reaction. He must therefore, as the priests said, avoid the occasion of sin, must barricade himself if necessary behind the walls of his accustomed habits and routines. He felt so disgusted with himself for his pitifully sportive impulses that he concluded that the girl deserved better, even if she herself was a complete mystery. Where previously he had been afraid of her he was now afraid for her. All in all it might be better for both their sakes to make sure that each of them stayed out of the other's way.

He went into the kitchen and helped himself to a couple of teabags from Mrs Cardozo's private store, saw that there was nothing to eat, and that he must shop and cook something and generally behave in a sensible manner. The trouble was that he had no taste for it. This new problem – of how to get through the uneventful day – was liable to preoccupy him unless he took violent action. For a variety of reasons he judged it imperative to get out of the house. He seized the tweed hat he wore only on a Sunday, and that only for walking in the park, and made for the front door. His instinct was to shut it firmly behind him, signalling to the world that he was his own man and had done nothing of which he could be ashamed or for which he could be called to account. Then, obeying some other instinct which he recognised as equally strong, he pulled it to with extreme caution, tiptoed past the Dunlops' door, and only reverted to normal speed when he was on the stairs. After all, he reasoned, she was probably sleeping. And it was in both their interests to keep their lives completely separate. At least, it was in his interest to do so. Out in the blessedly normal street he was alarmed by the divagations of his recent thinking. Such speculation was outside his normal parameters. He resolved to put it behind him once and for all.

The park received him into its indifferent embrace. The morning was fine: sun sparkled on dew, on mica. He walked towards the Peter Pan statue and watched the light flashing off the water of the lake as frantic geese and ducks, scrabbling for the food held out by nervous children, disturbed its placid surface. He watched the same thing every Sunday morning, without ever quite thinking it delightful. With the sun in his eyes, and thus almost blind to his surroundings, but sufficiently familiar with the place to assume that the feet pounding past him belonged to men in tight bright clothes, each imprisoned in an equally bright capsule of effort and reward, he made his way towards South Kensington where there would be a couple of cafés open and where he could eat breakfast. This cheered him, as the prospect of a treat, however derisory, usually did. The day was fine, perhaps too fine; such early brightness could not be sustained. All the more reason therefore to appreciate the morning before succumbing to the usual gloom of Sunday afternoon. He kept up a steady and invigorating pace until he was at the bottom of Exhibition Road, by which time the clear skies had already developed a steely glint. This was the way of it on these short winter days; one's craving for the light was only acknowledged in mere snatched moments, such as this. The rest of the time one had to endure the dark as best one could.

Lingering over his coffee, he wondered what to do next, what to do with all the time that remained to him. Christmas, he supposed, was the immediate problem, as it was for so many. He would receive the usual invitations and would be unable to offer the usual excuses, for everyone now knew that he was retired and on his own. He would have to go away, he reflected, although the idea of travelling alone was no longer as pleasurable as it once had been, when there had been so much to come back to. Now the prospect seemed faintly menacing, as if something might happen to him when he was far from help, or as if he might die without anyone knowing. But it would have to be faced, and it might have to be faced immediately. Rome, he thought, or Vienna, for he knew them both well and was at least assured of comfortable hotels. Reluctantly, as if the journey were already upon him, he paid for his coffee and toast, and set out to find a supermarket. He bought lavishly but absentmindedly, thinking he might eventually find a use for all this stuff, the cod's roe and the artichoke hearts and the mascarpone, although he could not quite work out in what context they might be useful. Then, with his plastic bag only slightly weighing him down, he set out for the north side of the park and home.

There was still no sound from the other flat. With the same stealth he closed the door behind him, unpacked his provisions in the kitchen and put them away, simultaneously aware that there was nothing sensible for lunch and that he was anxious to get out of the house again as soon as possible. Again the pantomime of caution, but it was no longer a pantomime, he acknowledged: he did not want to be confronted, detained. Again he was relieved to be out of the building; again he breathed more freely when he was in the street. He would lunch at his club, he decided, and then he would look at some pictures.

This was what usually happened to him on those Sundays not occupied by a ruminative walk to the suburbs. At least, it was the pattern on those Sundays which found him both tired and depressed, as he was now, tired because of the previous evening, and depressed by his renewed consciousness of Putnam's absence. On such a day he and Putnam might have been lunching together, before each of them went off peaceably to their separate occupations, which would in their turn be recounted over their regular lunch on Monday. Thus was an air of purpose given to the longest day of the week. They might not talk again until the following Sunday, but the contact would be unbroken throughout their professional concerns, which often came together when it was a question of entitlements or bonuses. In the office they would lift a brief hand of acknowledgment to each other, but not linger. Thus there was ample material for commentary, which seemed to be, and often was, mutually beneficial. The fact that Putnam would have cast a sceptical eye on Bland's excursion the previous evening was particularly unwelcome, as, for a different reason, was Putnam's absence. With Putnam there was no possibility of making a fool of oneself. By the same token he had often added some depth to Putnam's scathing verdicts. Putnam was a mathematician, of course: one had to remember that. As Stendhal said, there was no hypocrisy in mathematics, which isolated it from most other scholarly pursuits. Nevertheless, although he was without sentiment, Putnam acknowledged Bland's thoughtfulness and respected it. His absence was once again deeply felt.

Art would console him, Bland decided. That was art's business, after all, and he, it seemed, was in the business of being consoled, or at least of needing consolation. On this particular afternoon, the weather already dull, the streets empty, he suspected that at the end art would fail him, as perhaps it failed others, since the physical body in its extremity would be oblivious to the blandishments of paint on canvas or fine words on paper. Particularly to paint on canvas, which would appear, he feared, as a symbol of vanity. What then to hang on to? Since religion was closed to him, apart from a modest belief in a general good, he supposed that he would have to store up as many images as his memory, in those last days, if it were still intact, could play back to him. He had decided at some point that those memories would be visual, since his gifts of observation were acute. If he could recapture a corner of a Rubens landscape, say, or a vase of flowers by Odilon Redon, he thought he might be happy. Or as happy as his slightly melancholy temperament would allow him to be. It was just that, although the pleasure was great, sometimes the task seemed a little too conscientious, as if it were a preparation for death itself, as if death were just around the corner, as perhaps it might be. Sometimes these Sunday excursions were undertaken with a slightly heavy heart, as a poor man might go to his bank, to see if there were anything left.

But once inside the Royal Academy he was joyously divested of misgivings and hesitations, as he realised, with great good fortune, that he was to be afforded an unexpected treat: the Sickert exhibition. After no more than two minutes in the first gallery he surrendered to a general atmosphere of wit and pungency, of visual panache and overriding affection. There followed a passage of time in which time was almost forgotten, as he wandered round the galleries, completely absorbed in a world of beery gaslit pleasure, where men in ill-fitting tailcoats belted out low-grade songs, their teeth spotlit, their uplifted hands a smudge of pink, and where the respectable poor, bowler-hatted, leaned down from the gallery to catch every nuance from the distant performer on the stage. He saw St Mark's, sombre under a greenish Venetian sky; he saw Dieppe, brushed broadly in chalky pinks and mauves. He smiled, as did others near him, as chunky Tiller Girls took a curtain call in a blur of red and blue, and he realised that art was not always solemn, and could even – heretical thought! – be viewed as entertainment. Perhaps all artists, even the most exalted, were in the entertainment business. This he promised himself to think about.

Just as this vivifying idea was making inroads into his consciousness, and just as he was circling the galleries once more, two of the images reminded him suddenly and painfully of his earlier home and of earlier, humbler associations. One was the front of a shop called *Dawson Bros*, its windows filled with white hats as vibrant as a flock of seagulls. The other was a glum view, completely without incident, of a tube station with the name *Whiteleys* plumb in the centre of the canvas. Simple scenes, contemplated without comment. Here was a man who loved cities, he decided, and even their inconsequential outcroppings: not only Venice but Whiteleys. And once again, by some trick of the dim gallery light, he felt like a boy in new long trousers, anxious to avoid the discordant slumbers of his parents' Sunday afternoon, but not quite assured, greeting the street, as he had done that morning, in a spirit of timid gratitude, and gazing in shop windows until it was time to turn reluctant footsteps homeward. And it had never ended, this feeling. *A Few Words*, he read in his catalogue, and scrutinised a picture of a shifty-looking man making an excuse to go to the pub: that was his father all right, except that his father had been spruce, jocular, had made no excuses, and was expert at being drunk and not showing it. His mother had been Dorothy, his father Clive: that, he thought, placed them perfectly. As he turned to leave, feeling now very weary, he paused to admire the shadowy violinist plying his trade in some French café, where the ladies leaned their hats together in conversation. He read the title as *O Nuit d'Amour*, the title of the tune, he supposed. All at once the events of the previous evening, and his morning reaction to those events, were present in his mind, and once more he was reluctant to go home.

He stumbled slightly in the now dark afternoon. He had, he realised, been out all day and must have been on his feet for most of the time. A cup of tea seemed the obvious priority, and for that he might as well call it a day and go back to the flat. A taxi, sailing slowly by in the strangely silent turning by the Ritz, stopped with a creak of brakes. Bland turned once more to his catalogue, unwilling to relinquish those images of urban vitality as the Sunday gloom began to close around him. What a cove, what a card, he thought to himself, lost in admiration. His calf muscles ached: he had difficulty in disengaging himself when the taxi drew up outside his building. A few lights were on, but not many. He could see a light in the Dunlops' flat and reminded himself once more to be cautious. But he was too tired now to disentangle the thoughts that had plagued him in the morning, and was simply grateful for the dull warmth of the lobby, and the fact that there did not seem to be anybody about. He had half expected to be ambushed, either by Mrs Lydiard, or more probably by Katy Gibb. He had no idea why these people should have a claim on him, yet they had seemed to be in no doubt that access to him was henceforth to be unlimited. He suddenly desired not to know them, not to know anyone, in fact, to be left alone to read and to look at pictures, to make the best of his solitude, even to find pleasure in it, above all to be free of the conflicting demands of both his conscience and his desire. Such poor desire, he thought, fluctuating all these years, though never entirely sunk, hardly the desire of late twentieth-century man. That too was said to be unlimited, although he doubted the truth of such an assumption.

He felt younger than his age, but it was the memory of those adolescent Sunday walks, brought to life so vividly by the pictures he had just seen, that now preoccupied him. *Ennui*: that was it, both the best-known image and the aptest description of his earlier condition. He had been so lonely then, so unprepared to face the world! Even friendship would have made demands that he could not satisfy. At home there were the argumentative parents, and he could not be sure whether he loved them or not: that had been his torture. When he had started work, after his one year at the university, he had been surprised by the varieties of friendship on offer, and only later did he interpret this as ordinary goodwill towards himself, whom he had considered beyond the range of human sympathy. His spirits had begun to improve, but by this time he was preoccupied by his mother's deteriorating condition and had to hurry home to care for her on those evenings which he might otherwise have spent at concerts, at lectures, or even in the library. The early death of his father, of a heart attack at the races, and losing, as usual, had affected his mother to an extent which had surprised them both. After a lifetime of disaffection she had decided that she could not live without him, and consequently cared no more for herself. It was all unnecessary, even provocative, and again his feeling for her verged on sheer dislike. But he had been patient, and loyal: at least he had been that. Simply, such patience and such loyalty, deployed at a time of life which should be characterised by spontaneity and excitement, seemed to have impeded the full flowering of his vitality, so that ever since he had been cautious with his feelings, preferring affection to love, and fearing disorder above all else.

'Excuse me, sir,' said Hipwood, leaning confidentially over his desk. 'I wonder if I might have a word?'

Reluctantly Bland retraced his steps. He had been about to get into the lift. The stairs had seemed too much of a challenge.

'What can I do for you, Mr Hipwood?'

They were Mr Hipwood and Sir: thus were the social distinctions honoured. Hipwood wore a navy blue uniform, and appeared, from his handlebar moustaches, to have had a background in the armed forces, albeit a distant one. He controlled an extensive network of cleaners, car washers, newspaper delivery boys, and odd job men. Thus most of the tenants were in his debt and were resigned to being so. He was in his way a powerful man, reporting to the managing agents rather more of what went on in the building than it was his duty to know. Bland suspected that Mrs Cardozo, who was one of Hipwood's protégés, told him exactly the facts as she knew them of his habits, expenditure, quantity of drink imbibed, scale of gratuities, number of visitors etc., though as her speech was so heavily accented, and as she was given to odd bursts of on the whole benevolent hilarity, it was questionable that her information was of any great value. Bland disliked Hipwood, who smelt powerfully of some sort of unguent and of the extra-strong mints which he sucked between bursts of ostentatious activity.

'It seems, sir, that we have an intruder in the building.'

'Oh, really?' said Bland. Normally he would have been mildly interested, but by this time he only wanted his cup of tea.

'A young woman.'

'Oh. I see.'

'Came in yesterday morning, when I'd just nipped out the back. Thought I hadn't noticed her, but I had. I didn't say anything. But the point is she's still here! She hasn't come out again! And where is she?'

'I think I can explain, Mr Hipwood . . .'

'It's more than my job's worth to countenance this, sir. I'm in a position of trust here. People rely on me for their security. I can't let them down, now, can I?'

Bland had heard this speech many times before, usually at the approach to Christmas, when Hipwood would reiterate his loyalty and devotion to whomever happened to be in earshot.

'She's a Miss Gibb, a friend of the Dunlops. She's staying in their flat while they're away. And she's quite above-board, Mr Hipwood. In fact, if you'd been on duty last night you'd have seen her come out to dinner with Mrs Lydiard and myself.'

The mention of Mrs Lydiard's name calmed Hipwood slightly, but not for long.

'I haven't seen her today, sir. You would have thought she would have come down, introduced herself, so to say. After all, that's what most people would have done.' And have handed over a token of their appreciation for his vigilance, Bland was given to understand. This sort of behaviour would not be within Katy's sphere of understanding. Her attitude to Hipwood would have been that of a person of high regard to an indentured servant, the attitude all the tenants were so scrupulously careful to avoid.

'And Mr Dunlop said nothing to me about it before he went away,' Hipwood continued. 'I find that odd. He's usually so careful, especially about his own affairs.' Bland was given to understand by this that Tim Dunlop was mean.

'It was all fixed up in America, apparently. They all met up in New York, and Mrs Dunlop invited Miss Gibb to stay in the flat.'

He was well aware that matters had not been so clear-cut or even so straightforward, but, faced with Hipwood's insistence, and by now seriously tired, he was suddenly on Katy's side.

'It's the responsibility, sir. Put yourself in my position. There was that business only last month, that other intruder.' Anyone not known to Hipwood personally was termed an intruder. Bland had heard this story too, more than once. He took out his wallet, extracted two ten pound notes, and handed them over.

'I'm sure this will take care of any inconvenience,' he said. 'And of course I'll keep you informed if I hear anything further from the Dunlops.'

This cleverly implied that he had already been in touch with them. It occurred to him to wonder why he was being so devious, but the main priority now was to put an end to Hipwood's complaint. He had done this too precipitately, perhaps had not thought matters through. But did any of this really concern him? Was it right that he should be waylaid in this manner? His tactic was crude, but it was effective. Hipwood subsided, and retreated once more behind his desk.

It was only when he was in the flat that Bland reflected that he had been a fool, had in fact made a monumental blunder. How would his largesse look to Hipwood, who would lose no time in leaping to conclusions? No doubt the Dunlops would be taken on one side as soon as they returned, would not even be allowed to put down their bags before Hipwood requested a word. And he, Bland, would be forced into more explanations on behalf of a person who so singularly forbore to explain herself. He poured water carelessly into the teapot, splashing and scalding himself in his agitation. When the doorbell rang his heart sank. It seemed a matter of self-preservation to delay answering it until he had made the tea.

She was back in her jeans and T-shirt, which now, he saw, were not perfectly clean. There was no sign of the previous night's seductress. The princess had turned back into a scullion, or at least the sulky creature, half girl, half woman, whom he had first encountered. The change interested him: he thought that, unobserved, when not on public display, she might be a slut. This somehow was acceptable, for reasons he was too tired to go into. Yet her bearing was quite queenly, almost authoritative; she entered his flat as of right. She sauntered, looked about her, seemed inclined to examine his possessions, yet desisted out of boredom, or indifference. Bland had an involuntary memory of a woman he had once half-heartedly courted. Edwina Sutton had denigrated everything and everyone, though she was neither clever nor amusing. 'Neither clever nor amusing' had been his mother's verdict on anyone she disliked, which was nearly everyone still browbeaten enough to visit the house: the phrase had remained with him. When Edwina Sutton had come to his flat in Baker Street, and had picked up and put down his precious books with a gesture of impatience, he had conclusively decided that they were incompatible. Thereafter, when he ran into her he greeted her cordially and professed himself to be overwhelmed with work. She was not deceived, but was too languid to challenge him.

This girl was not languid, although like himself she appeared to be at a loose end. Unfilled time, he sensed, would not make her restless, would not drive her out into some unremarkable activity, as was often his case. She would wait for some way of occupying it to present itself; how else to account for the fact that she had apparently been waiting for him all day? The mere fact of her turning up at his door filled him with foreboding, together with the disagreeable memory of his recent donation to Hip-wood. Yet there was nothing remarkable about her, apart from her assurance. In her tired clothes she seemed confident, even slightly annoyed with him, as if he had let her down in some way. She made no effort, and continued to make none, waiting for him to give an account of himself, of his absence. Her feet, once again, were bare. He noticed that she had painted her toenails. This evidence of her day's activity was not impressive, yet he found it pathetic rather than exasperating. She appeared to have washed her hair again; there was a faint smell of lemons. He could think of nothing more depressing than what must have been her empty afternoon. At the same time, and overwhelmingly, he wished she would go away. 'Nightclub queen', another derogatory locution of his mother's, came to mind. He had an image of a nightclub, in the daytime, the lights out, the doors open, the staff clearing up. Just why this came to him he was unable to say.

With a start he came back to the present. He was aware of extreme fatigue.

'Hallo,' he said, with as much joviality as he could muster. He sounded like his own father, he thought with disgust.

'I thought you might have looked in, to see how I was,' she said, but without the smiles of the night before. Once again he felt vaguely cornered. 'I tried you earlier,' she said, 'but there was no reply.'

'I've been out all day,' he said. And then, lamely, 'I went to the Royal Academy to look at some pictures.'

'I wish you'd told me you were going. I'd have come with you. I love art.'

He noted that art was not granted a capital letter by the curiously antagonistic way in which she mentioned it. In this way it was accorded a lower status than her other pursuits. Again she was angry; again he seemed to be the cause of it, or perhaps the reason for it. But he thought it went deeper than that, went back a long way, and he sensed something enthralling there, some secret history that it might be his task, and his pleasure, to uncover. He felt a flicker of genuine objective interest: this was more

70

like the old days, when it had been his job to assess individuals applying for promotion or for a transfer within the firm. Always he had managed them gently and kindly, yet his word was law. Perhaps if he employed the same skills there might be a way of reconciling this girl's unspoken but insistent demands with his own peace of mind, which was apparently under attack from this very quarter.

'I've just made some tea,' he said. 'Would you like a cup? Unless you've already had some. It is a bit late, I suppose. I hadn't noticed.'

'Tea would be fine,' she said.

When he carried the tray from the kitchen to the sitting-room he found her on the sofa, her arms spread along the back, her right ankle resting on her left knee. Again he noticed the beauty of her feet.

'And what have you been doing today?' he enquired heartily, handing her the tea. She detached one arm from the back of the sofa to take the cup from him.

'I've been asleep most of the time. I'm still jet-lagged. And I went to bed too early after that dinner. I should have stayed up, really. You should have made me stay up.'

'Well, you can please yourself, of course, but it was pretty late for me. And for Mrs Lydiard. We're not as young as you are.' Again the distasteful note of false jocularity. How he hated this! He wanted her to go away; he wanted to be alone. He even wanted the second cup of tea that she was now drinking.

'I expect so,' she said, and lapsed into a brooding silence.

It was a relief when the telephone rang. He glanced at his watch and saw that it was six-thirty, the time when he usually rang Louise. But it was Louise herself on the line. He heard her placid 'George?' with relief, with genuine pleasure.

71

'Two minds with but a single thought,' he said. It was sometimes a relief to fall into clichés with Louise. 'I was about to ring you.'

'I just wanted to let you know that I'll be in town tomorrow. I'm spending the night with Philip and Sarah, and I thought I'd do some Christmas shopping.'

'Splendid,' he said. 'When shall we meet? Shall I take you to lunch? Yes, that would be best. Why don't you come straight here from Waterloo? We'll have coffee and decide what to do with the afternoon.'

'Yes, lovely,' she assented. 'I thought I might find something for the children in Selfridges, if we've got time . . .'

'Louise, I really want you to see the Sickert exhibition. You can do your shopping in Lymington.'

'The trouble is, they like these electronic games.'

'I should have thought Philip could have supplied those.'

'Yes, isn't it funny? He says he has enough of them at work, he doesn't want to hear them at home. That's why it's so difficult. And they've already got their bikes . . .'

'Louise, I'll have to ring off. I've got a visitor. I'll see you tomorrow.'

'All right, dear.' He was softened, as always, by her mild endearment. Such pliancy, such docility! It was at times like these that he remembered why he had so nearly married her, and why in the end he had decided not to. Perhaps there was no need to marry her. The relationship had always lacked urgency, even at the beginning. They had felt like two members of an endangered species, huddling together for mutual protection. And even after all these years something of that feeling remained.

He put the receiver back on its rest, and turned to the sofa, where Katy Gibb continued to watch him calmly.

'Another busy day tomorrow,' he said, again with that

awful note of jocularity. He was wondering whether he would ever get rid of her.

'So you won't be around again,' she observed. 'What a pity. Never mind. I might give Moira a ring. Have you got her number?'

He wrote it down for her, watched her insert the piece of paper into the pocket of her rather too tight jeans. 'Well . . .', he said.

'You want me to go,' she stated. She made it sound ungracious, as perhaps it was. 'I had hoped we could talk a few things through. About my plans, and so on. But it's okay; another time.'

Having posed this interesting proposition she got to her feet, twiddled her fingers dismissively, and walked to the door.

'Plans?' he said. 'That sounds most interesting. You must tell me more.'

Her answer was to twiddle her fingers again, and to leave. There was something inexorable about her departure. He felt as if he had been dismissed.

His evening was discordant. She had made it appear that she needed his co-operation in some way, or that she was about to divulge some information about herself which would make it imperative for him to approve the plans of which she had spoken. But what were her plans? And why had he not probed a little further? There was precious little to go on so far, only her vaguely asserted intention of starting up her own business. But her own business doing what? As far as he could see she was disastrously unqualified, and, in addition, the business and commercial worlds were in the grip of a recession which some were calling a slump. Who would put up the money (which she had said she needed) for a dubious enterprise based on some bogus import from California? No matter how many credulous people she might attract, the whole idea was shaky, evanescent. She would need premises; she

73

would need staff. He shook his head. Even with the most magnanimous of sponsors he did not see how it could be done.

Of course, it was all nonsense, he thought later, as he was preparing for bed. There would be no sponsors and no money; he ought to have seen this before. And she had no money of her own; that much was clear even from so short an acquaintance. Her presence in the Dunlops' flat was unexplained and was likely to become a problem, if it had not already turned into one. The memory of the twenty pounds he had handed over to Hipwood made him curse under his breath. None of this had anything to do with him! He only wanted the freedom to enjoy the rest of his life, or whatever of it was left. That was what he had wanted so passionately when he was young, when he was younger than that girl. But then he remembered how it had been to be so hemmed in and frustrated, and realised that the girl – whom he still thought of as the girl – was probably enduring the same restrictions as those which now came back to him with astonishing force. Young people, he thought, should not be so confined; it did them no good in later life. All at once he felt a powerful sympathy for the girl, marooned in that alien flat, and unable to get out of it, and with nowhere else to go.

For himself he felt only sadness, the sadness that seemed to hover like a shadow over the end of every day. To be young, to start again! But this time to be different, to be selfish, to be obdurate! One paid a heavy price for behaving well. This freedom of his was illusory, based on honourable retirement, it was true, but a poor facsimile of the real thing, which belonged to the fleet of foot, the light of heart. And it was too late even to feel anger, he thought, for anger had turned to sorrow. He felt such a constriction of the heart that he thought he might weep. Without Putnam, or even the office, to restore his self-respect, he was lost, his life mere boredom. Struck by this realisation he lay wide-eyed for a good part of the night, without a thought for lost rest, but with a desire for change that obliterated or subsumed all other desires, both those he had forgotten and those which burned in his consciousness, as if he were St Antony in the desert. The events of the day seemed to him curiously significant. He thought that they marked some sort of turning point, the true meaning of which would be revealed to him when time had run its course.

5

'Halloa!' shouted Mrs Cardozo from the front door: her usual greeting. 'Good morning!' he shouted back, then went into the kitchen to prepare her coffee. So this was to be retirement, he reflected, tea with this one, coffee with that one, and none of it of his own choosing. But she was a cheerful, if noisy woman; he responded to her cheerfulness, and tried to rise above her outbursts of song and the ribald attitude she chose to take with regard to his puny arrangements. She frequently protested her loyalty to him; he in his turn was unwillingly dependent on her, and submitted with good grace to the half-hour which was set aside for coffee and conversation, although he did not always attend too carefully to what she was saying, having heard most of it before, and able to tune in to any new proposition as and when it came along.

She was married to a hospital porter who was always on the verge of losing his job. The reasons for this were mysterious. Bland had heard, on more than one occasion, an account of the machinations of the department in which he worked, and had tried to disentangle them, but without success. He had met the man once or twice when he had come to collect his wife; he had seemed decent and sensible, if anything more amenable than his riotous partner. Bland had offered to put in a word for him, if a personal reference were ever needed. Mrs Cardozo had dismissed the suggestion out of hand, not, she assured him, because she believed him to be without influence, but because she considered her husband a waste of time, a lost cause, like most men. Her view of Bland, whom she saw as a wealthy ninny, as she did most Englishmen, verged on the irreverent, sometimes the incredulous. Bland had learned to put up with this. Fortunately her contempt was largely reserved for her husband, to whose misdemeanours she alluded at some length. Gusts of laughter concluded this exchange, always the same, after which she would consent to rise from the table, turn on both taps and the radio, and begin her work. Bland, who found her heavy going, and something of a liability, consequently overdid his concern for her well-being. He thought it impolite to leave the flat when she was there, although the noise pursued him from room to room. On days like these he pitted himself against *The Times* crossword, forcing himself to finish it against the odds: the discipline, he thought, was good for his soul as well as his mind.

Today was to be Louise's day, so he dressed carefully in his grey suit, mindful of his appearance, as she always was of hers. They had graduated to fine clothes after paltry beginnings, although in those early days in Reading she had always contrived to please him, in her simple blouses and her pleated skirts. She dressed, as he thought, politely, and he, as a man of his generation and his class, considered politeness a virtue. Her only coquetry was her shining hair, which always had a sweet powdery smell, as if she had just emerged from a warm bathroom. They had met when they were both eighteen; he was a student, just beginning at university, and she was a clerk in the local branch of Lloyds Bank. Greatly daring, he had asked her out one day, and was much encouraged by her placid consent. She had seemed neither alarmed nor intrigued by his invitation, thus conferring on him a feeling of assurance, for he had been more nervous than he had allowed her to see.

She lived at home with her mother, as he did: their lives exactly mirrored each other's. After that first visit to the cinema, at which decorum prevailed, they had taken to walking together on Sunday afternoons, which they soon agreed was more enjoyable. Her life was an open book to him, as his was to her; the thought had early occurred to him that he might marry her. But he was tied to his mother, who was deteriorating rapidly, although at that stage the decline was general, non-specific, and characterised by increasingly sarcastic behaviour and a refusal to do anything for herself that could be undertaken by her son. He sometimes thought that this was deliberate, as indeed it might have been. He was too young, and too inexperienced, to recognise its morbidity.

He remembered with shame his first attempt at hospitality. He had decided to take Louise home to tea, knowing that her excellent manners would protect them both. It was a Sunday afternoon, for by this time they always met on a Sunday, walking if it were fine, going to the cinema if it were wet. His mother, whom he had informed of this event, had declined to honour the occasion with any sort of preparation, had in fact remained in her chair with a quizzical expression, as if Louise were being presented at court. After Louise's desperate pleasantries had finally petered out, and silence threatened to immolate the entire occasion, his mother had finally given tongue. 'I hope you can do something with that son of mine,' she had said. 'He's been a baby far too long.' He had known what she had meant, and blushed. Louise's hand had stolen into his, and he had loved her for that gesture, and for her simple sturdiness on his behalf. He had thought then, and he still thought even now, that her archetypal simplicity contained seeds of greatness of which she was entirely unconscious.

In fact Louise and he had become lovers some six weeks previously, in a borrowed flat, and for the space of a single afternoon. The event had been mutually satisfactory; they were content to postpone further explorations until they had achieved a better time and place. There had been a simplicity about that too, a lack of urgency which he found more acceptable than the more torrid conception of desire to which his youth entitled him. He was staid by nature, and fortune had provided him with an appropriate partner. She was calm, unflustered by his advances, which she reciprocated with a pleasure which he knew to be real, for she could not dissimulate, and this was another of her very real virtues, more precious to him then than his mother, squinting through her cigarette smoke, could ever appreciate. Since, on that one and only occasion on which they were to meet, it was quite clear that no attempt had been made at hospitality, Louise had said she must leave: her own mother was alone, and she liked to keep her company. Her thanks were profuse, and were lazily accepted, as if a favour had been conferred. He had burned with shame, but there was one consolation: with Louise he would never lose face.

Recklessly he had walked her to her door; recklessly she had invited him in. A small grey-haired woman had greeted them with some astonishment, but had agreed to make tea. She also decided to make them a sponge cake, for which they had to wait in embarrassed silence, while whiskings and whirrings seeped through from the kitchen. But it was a day for embarrassment, which in his mind was always connected with Reading, as if the emotion were Reading's gift to her sons and daughters. Bland had praised the cake too effusively, and had found himself gazing into a face as calm and as colourless as a nun's. A small grey eye had viewed him without indulgence. Mrs Wilson, who had drunk no tea herself, had taken the tray back to the kitchen and had stayed there, ostentatiously tactful, or perhaps genuinely indifferent to his presence. Louise had followed her shortly afterwards. Bland heard the words, 'Is he still here?' Then Louise returned, looking unhappy; he had taken her hand and kissed her, then, since it was expected of him, he had left. The incidents of that afternoon were never referred to again. To do so would have been to question their status in the world, their very identity. Without words they consoled each other as best they could.

He almost loved her, and would have married her had she been slightly but essentially different. He thought that she probably felt the same about him. Each was too loyal to admit that something else was desired, something less sedate. Louise, for all her placidity was a healthy woman, while he himself was bruised with unassuaged longings. Yet they were undoubted allies. Prepared for disappointment, they nevertheless made the most of their friendship, which became, and had remained, a civilised and affectionate affair, an affair of long walks, teas in distant hotels, discussion of the week's news. Looking back, Bland found their innocence honourable. In those early days they were able to confess freely to each other their obligations towards their less than accommodating parents. They found comfort in their occasional intimacy. They progressed from the borrowed flat to a small hotel, then to a larger one, and after his mother's death and his removal to London he had got in touch with her again, thanking her for her kind letter of condolence, and explaining that the events of that last year had been so sad ('sad' was the most neutral word he could find) that he had not been in touch, but that he longed to see her again. When could they meet?

By that time he was installed in the flat over Baker Street Station, and their meetings were frequent and easy. They had continued to come together until she had announced that she was getting married. By that time they had both come up in the world, but although free, had become trapped within the framework of their early relationship. They had continued to meet until she removed herself to Lymington and her awful husband. At least he thought of him as awful, having been introduced to him when the three of them met, not entirely by accident, at a concert at the Wigmore Hall. Tall, bony, and already nearly bald, the husband-to-be, a retired doctor, had given him a quasi-professional handshake – brief – but said little. Bland, who had not expected to like him, found him worse than expected, and prepared to wash his hands of the whole affair. But his heart was sore at the prospect of losing Louise, and in the end it had proved impossible to break the thread that bound them together, time, in this instance, being on their side.

Shortly after their son was born the husband had become some sort of an invalid, and had eventually died. This had not affected Louise unduly: by that time she had a son, a house, and a social position. He supposed that she had always been conventional by nature, for which he did not blame her; he was conventional himself. When a daily nanny was installed she resumed her visits to London. There was little love-making by this time, although no opportunity was wasted. She was quite calm about this, suffered, or appeared to suffer, no guilt. Curious, he had questioned her. 'After all,' she had replied, 'I knew you before I ever met Denis.' He was given to understand that this, in her eyes, validated an *affaire* which had never, technically, been an infidelity. Women, he thought, were sometimes more ingenious than men.

And ever since, the telephone calls had continued, still banal, but with a deep peace about them which comforted them both. Each, by this time, felt related to the other, bound by a common inheritance. The calls were perhaps more satisfying than the occasional meetings: their conversations were by now so schematic that they were almost abstract, each pursuing a familiar line of thought. In a way he loved her still, could not imagine her out of his life. Sometimes, when tidying her hair in his bedroom, she said, 'Shall we?' But he knew from her rueful smile that her heart was not in it. They had both aged, perhaps prematurely. There was no compulsion now, nor was there any need to explain, to make excuses. When he took her down to catch her taxi back to Waterloo his kiss was warm and loving. It was a blessing to him to know that she felt the same.

It had seemed that he could manage without marriage. From this he deduced that he was meant to be solitary, had always remained, and would always remain, the same. Solitude, which occasionally baffled him (how had it come to this?), felt familiar. As he made his way up the social and professional ladder, away from the greater solitude of his youth, he embraced what was probably freedom, or rather liberty, and this, he thought, had always been his greatest wish, his need. Away from his contentious parents, away from his love for Louise, away from modest single-bedroomed flats to his present almost superfluous comfort, in an enviable position, a few minutes from the park, he had embraced each change with ardour, but not, he thought with satisfaction. The finer rooms, the larger windows, seemed to him part of a predestined flight, in the course of which he had obeyed impulses which he did not appear to generate of his own free will. He failed to supply the enthusiasm which should, ideally, have come from others. Carefully ordering carpets, curtains, wall-papers, he had arrived at a passionless good taste which was tolerable when he returned to it in the evening but oppressed him rather in the light of every day. Now there would be time to spare, and he would have to find some accommodation with his surroundings, or else some new interest to take him away from them, so that after an interval, repeated daily, he could feel once again a mild gratitude that his money had enabled him to live in such easeful splendour.

The internal telephone rang. 'Mrs Arnold is here, sir,' announced Hipwood. He approved of Louise, who in her turn knew the ropes. She always had a word with Hipwood, enquiring after his health; she even sent him a Christmas card, although Bland had told her that this was not necessary. She made a point of presenting herself, lest Hipwood should assume the worst. Bland knew that he did this automatically, but it was part of Louise's curious innocence to believe that it was up to her to make people think well of her. In addition to this, she had, in recent years, taken on the mantle of a country gentlewoman, accustomed to receiving respect and acknowledging the obligation of being gracious in return. Sometimes Bland thought that if she were a little more devious she might be better company, but he knew that nothing would change her now, any more than he could change himself. His very slight boredom, he knew, came from lack of change, and the prospect of the long day ahead, together with their almost formulaic greeting, threatened to depress him. This had been the pattern of their relationship: an atavistic closeness, formed when they themselves were almost embryonic, balanced by a divergence of tastes which the passing years had only emphasised.

'Well, dear,' she said predictably, as he opened the door to her.

'Well dear,' he replied, ushering her into the sitting-room. After these preliminaries he thought he could probably foresee what the rest of the day's conversation would be. Louise would talk about her grandchildren, in whom he took not the slightest interest, and he would make appropriate noises, diverting her attention from time to time to a sight, a sound, which he thought would please her: the nearly tame blackbird that lingered in the tree outside his window, a child's face glimpsed for a second amid the hurrying crowds. He preferred anonymous children to those who came complete with a set of parents: anonymous children belonged to everyone. Louise, as usual, would ask few questions, leaving his inner life undisturbed. They were most in harmony during their habitual long silences. It was silence rather than dialogue, the silence of things unsaid but understood, which had confirmed their original unity, and Bland now looked forward to those intervals, on which he knew he could count, and in which he could recapture their earlier closeness, so essential to them both and yet so familiar that surely a very slight feeling of tedium was forgivable.

Nevertheless, he was pleased, as always, to see her. She looked well, in her forest-green suit, with the Hermès scarf he had given her the previous Christmas. 'Comely' was the word he would have chosen to describe her. She had the unsurprising good looks of a healthy woman who was now able to care for herself, to shop selectively, and to visit the hairdresser twice a week. Fine mild eyes beamed from under unreconstructed brows: a discreet pink lipstick enlivened the still girlish mouth. She had never been a beauty, but had always contrived to be pleasing. Now the gaze was kindly but frank, as if there were no longer any need to be modest, and the hair was carefully coiffured in a style appropriate to the older woman. Her figure, slight in his day, had in fact filled out considerably, although her legs had remained slim. She took a pleasure in her appearance, which he thought reflected her pleasure in the life she now lived as a contented widow in a small town where she was well known and well liked. Yet he knew that her visits to London, and to him, were part of that pleasure, just as they had become part of that agreeable well-run life. She saw no anomalies in their long history: in her view it had always been meant to continue, and indeed to end like this.

'We'll have lunch round the corner,' he said, already in

a hurry. 'And then I want you to see the Sickert exhibition. It's quite exceptional. I saw it yesterday and I can't
wait to go again.'

'Whatever you say,' she replied. 'But you will remember that I want to go to Selfridges, won't you? I told you
about the present situation, didn't I? And I want to look
at curtain material. That blue in the drawing-room faded
quite badly last summer.' ('Drawing-room', he noted.)
He made a noncommittal noise.

'And yet it was such a good colour,' she went on.
'Perhaps if I got a darker shade . . .'

'Shall we have a quick lunch first?' he said impatiently.
'Then we can go straight to the exhibition. You can do
your shopping afterwards, and come to me for tea.'

'Lovely,' she said. 'As long as you leave me plenty of
time.'

She snapped shut her powder compact, retied her scarf,
and announced herself to be ready. They walked com-
panionably round the corner to the Italian restaurant,
where he was well known, and ate, as always, veal. 'Nice
to see you again, sir,' said the waiter. Of course, there
had been that dinner the other night. He smiled. The first
of the silences installed itself, and was prolonged until
they had drunk their coffee. 'Lovely,' she repeated. It was
so easy to give her pleasure, he reflected; that had always
been part of her charm. It may even have made him a
little lazy, as if he might have preferred more of a challenge: more foreplay, he privately termed it. Yet he knew
that a more difficult woman would have defeated him,
might entertain him initially but would baffle him and
leave him bereft, if not positively damaged. With Louise
he was safe. That too was part of her charm. It was a gift
for which men were nearly always grateful. And if they
sometimes grew discontented, feeling in themselves an
unused store of curiosity, they eventually grew resigned
as time and age did their inexorable work. That was why

old married couples seemed so contented, he thought: they had bowed to necessity, which in their case was not the mother of invention, but its opposite. They were like survivors of a war, grateful for a comrade in adversity, grateful too that hostilities were at an end, and that a peace treaty had been signed and witnessed.

After that, Bland thought, most men would have the delicacy to keep their disappointment to themselves, as he did now. The day seemed to have become dusky very early, although it was only just past two, and the crowds in the streets, surely more numerous than usual, impeded their progress. In the taxi she asked him about his Christmas plans. He answered her abstractedly, remembering only that he had meant to go away. 'I was thinking of Rome,' he said, only half believing in the project. 'I shall be alone this year,' she told him. 'They're all going to Sarah's parents. I thought of a cruise, but I hate travelling alone.'

'Maybe we could go together,' he said moodily, aware that the onus was now on him to express enthusiasm. A sudden shower of rain spattered the window of the taxi: he felt glum. 'That's why it got so dark,' she observed. 'Maybe it'll clear up now.'

But the day became slightly more melancholy, and the pictures did nothing to cheer him. He gazed conscientiously at the images which had so delighted him on the previous day, and did his best to point them out to Louise, but he seemed to have lost the thread, and the crowds got on his nerves. Louise laughed dutifully at the Tiller Girls, but seemed untouched by Venice, by Dieppe, and by the comic tragedies so slyly indicated by the droop of a moustache, a head propped up by an exasperated hand. He would have to come back another day on his own, he decided; maybe he was tired. He steered her thankfully towards the exit, and put her in a taxi to Selfridges. He would walk back, he told her; he would see her later.

Alone he took a deep breath, glad of the respite. Yet I am always glad to see her, he reminded himself. Perhaps I am not quite myself, burdened with all this new leisure. Yet he knew that was not the cause of his malaise. He felt himself to be like one of the failures in the pictures, seedy, tetchy, graceless. He was glad of the dark afternoon, so that he could no longer catch sight of himself.

By contrast the flat seemed almost welcoming. He opened a window on to the darkling sky, leaned out, and breathed deeply. He was, he supposed, prepared for the evening, which would be long. Unwilling to pull curtains, he remained leaning on the window-sill, aware that for a man of his age such a brooding position was ridiculous. When Louise's steps could be heard in the quiet street, and he could just make out her form advancing confidently towards him, he retreated into the room, and put the day to rest.

Later it became better. As they sat together, all the lamps lit and the tea-tray between them, he felt as fond of her now as he had always been, and ascribed his earlier disaffection to some passing physical cause. He always loved her most when she was about to leave, when the end of her visit was in sight. Then it seemed to him imperative to arrange a further meeting, for she was in a sense his lifeline, even though he had grown as used to her as a child is to its mother. And she was always pleased to fit in with his plans, or even to suggest a plan of her own. He liked to look at pictures and she at gardens: they shared and shared alike.

'I'll ring on Sunday, of course,' he said.

She looked at her watch. 'I've still got a few minutes,' she said. 'There's your doorbell.' They looked at each other in amazement, as if the world had suddenly discovered the fact of their careful liaison.

'I'm not expecting anyone,' he said.

87

'Well, you'd better answer it. What a shame. Well, I'll leave you to them, whoever they are.'

Bland opened the door to Katy and Mrs Lydiard, whom he saw to be burdened with expensive carrier bags. Mrs Lydiard looked excited and a little dishevelled: behind her back Katy made a small face, her eyes rolling upwards. 'We've been shopping!' exclaimed Mrs Lydiard. 'We've been frightfully extravagant, I'm afraid.'

'Well, you have, Moira. I haven't bought a thing. But I do have this lovely scarf that Moira bought me,' she added, in response to a sharp glance from Mrs Lydiard. Bland noted that they both smelt of the same asphyxiating scent. He also saw that Katy was not particularly impressed by her gift, saw this as soon as her eyes took in the Hermès silk square that Louise was tying round her throat. He also noticed that they were both tremendously dressed up. Katy, in particular, in a suit of tangerine-coloured wool and soft fawn leather boots, looked somewhat older than she had on previous occasions, and he was obliged to revise her age upwards. Today he would have put her at thirty-three or four.

He introduced them. Before he went into the kitchen to make fresh tea he had time to note that Katy had ignored Louise's outstretched hand and, putting her palms together, had bowed her head in an Indian greeting. Repressing laughter that threatened to become unmanageable – the first that day – he was glad to make his escape, if only for a few minutes.

When he returned it was to find Louise and Mrs Lydiard deep in conversation, delighted to find interests in common, and also perhaps to indulge in the sort of pleasantries they both best appreciated. 'I do believe appearances are so important,' said Mrs Lydiard, whom Louise had evidently complimented on her smart navy blue jacket. 'At my age one dare not let one's standards drop. The change can be seen immediately.'

'I do so agree,' Louise enthused. 'Although it's more of a struggle in the country than in town. People don't seem to bother so much. I have to go quite far afield to find something suitable. Or just that little bit out of the ordinary, you know?'

'Have you considered colour counselling?' asked Katy, who had so far contributed nothing to this exchange.

'Why no,' said Louise, surprised. 'I don't think we have it in Lymington. Is it very expensive?'

'Louise,' he said. 'If you're going to catch the six-thirty . . .'

'Oh, I'll catch the next one,' she said, loosening her scarf. 'Of course you don't have to worry about such things yet,' she said to Katy. 'You're young! And very pretty,' she added, though with some reserve. 'I wonder we haven't met before. Are you a new neighbour? I do think these flats are so comfortable . . .'

'Katy has been living in America,' said Bland.

'Oh, you're American!'

'Not really,' she said, her voice distant and aristocratic. 'Of course, I've lived all over the place. We were an army family.'

For some reason Bland saw an army camp in Germany, on the outskirts of Hannover or Paderborn. He saw dismal married quarters, a young and downtrodden wife, an army sergeant father, sitting down to his evening meal with khaki braces over a khaki shirt, a pretty child hushed into silence while her father ate, and then alternately petted and chastised. He saw all this quite clearly, and knew that although it might be a fantasy it was a fantasy very near to the truth.

'And where is your father stationed now?' pursued Louise. Mrs Lydiard was leaning back in her chair, a smile on her face. She glanced at Bland, triumphant, with a look implying shared intelligence.

'My father's dead,' said Katy.

'Oh, I'm so sorry, my dear. I didn't mean to pry . . .'

Bland could almost hear Katy say that that was exactly what Louise had meant to do. But there was no malice in Louise; he if anyone knew that. And the question had been innocent enough.

There was a brief silence. 'Well,' said Louise finally. 'I must be on my way. I could just make the six-thirty. So nice to have met you.'

'I must be on my way too,' said Mrs Lydiard. 'This has been most pleasant. Thank you for tea, Mr Bland. George, I should say. Perhaps you'd like a glass of sherry one evening? I'll give you a ring. Goodbye, Katy. Remember what I told you.'

But he was not immediately to learn what this was. He supposed it to be some well-meaning but irrelevant advice about finding a job while making plans for the future. In any event, by the time he had taken Louise down and put her in a taxi, his train of thought was broken. He was surprised how the day had fatigued and irked him, and looked forward to being alone. There had been a surfeit of women. Louise's last words to him had been rather tiresome, he thought. She had remarked on what a strange girl Katy had seemed, whereas Bland had wanted to savour this strangeness on his own. How had George met her? Had he known her long? There was a slight reserve, again, in her manner of asking these questions, not quite looking him in the eye. Then, with a sigh, she had turned to him and put up her face for his kiss. 'Until Sunday,' she said. 'Until Sunday,' he replied. And on Sunday, he reflected, as he went back up the stairs, there would be more questions. And the answers, he knew, he would keep to himself, if indeed there were to be any answers. For Katy was his own private research project, the findings of which he would keep in the equivalent of a locked file, inaccessible to prying eyes.

He mounted the stairs wearily. The open door of his flat

seemed unattainable. Just as he prepared to lock himself in for the night the door of the Dunlops' flat opposite to his own opened to reveal Katy, two patches of red flaring on her cheeks, her anger this time spectacularly in evidence.

'Is anything wrong?' he asked.

'I was getting a lot of negativity back there. I could feel my stress levels going up.'

'We are too old for you,' he said gently. 'Of course you find us tiresome. You should be with people of your own age. There's very little to interest you here. My friend was merely asking a few polite questions. You shouldn't let them upset you.'

' "I don't think we have it in Lymington," ' she minced, ' "is it very expensive?" '

'What did you expect?' he asked. 'These things are for smart young women, not elderly widows.' But she had perhaps been looking for a consultation, he saw, since that was apparently how she earned her living, and if she had hoped to capture Louise, with whom she was barely acquainted, as a client, then she must be seriously short of money. He remembered Mrs Lydiard's expression, the satisfied expression of one who has given good advice and was not in a position to have it rejected. No doubt she had paid for their lunch, in the course of which she had poured this advice into Katy's unwilling ear.

'Was it Mrs Lydiard who upset you?' he asked. And did she buy you that terrible scent in an attempt to win you over? For he could see it now: Katy's attempt to annex Mrs Lydiard as a useful ally, followed by her discovery that Mrs Lydiard had no intention of letting herself be annexed. No doubt the giving of advice was Mrs Lydiard's weakness. That it was probably good advice did not make it any more palatable. Rather less, in fact. He supposed that it had had something to do with money. Mrs Lydiard's suspicions were therefore not too far from his own. It was an unwelcome discovery.

'I have plans of my own,' she said grandly. 'I have only to make a few phone calls to set up interviews with some of the most important people in the alternative health field.'

'Then that is what you must do, obviously. Why not do it tomorrow?'

'I hardly think I need any advice on a matter which I know like the back of my hand. In my business it's all a matter of personal contacts. I don't suppose people such as yourself would understand that.'

'No,' he agreed, thinking back to his own working life, which had proceeded along the most conventional lines. It had been his destiny to be a company man: he thought of himself as an office boy, even after multiple promotions. Without the company, he thought, he was dying of insignificance. He had been popular because he was blameless; perhaps he had not been valued, as more eccentric or rebarbative characters not infrequently are, but he had been respected, and that respect had been precious to him. The office had represented peace, good order, a place in an acceptable hierarchy. It had also represented work, a work that included judgment, a weighing up of facts on which much depended. He did not believe that work could be done other than in a sober fashion, at a desk, within regular hours, which would keep one in one place, and accountable. He did not believe that work was a matter of activating a few contacts. Perhaps actors or journalists lived like that, he thought, but for most people going to work meant just that, going to where the work was, putting in a day's best effort, and then coming home, on the bus or in the train, as others did. And home, at the end of the day, was perceived anew as a reward, the goal of one's hopes and ambitions.

At least he supposed that ambition came into it. He had had none himself, a fact which had made him trusted. To be accepted was his reward, and he had wanted no other.

Putnam had been the same, and that, in turn, had cemented their friendship. And now it was all gone, all the safety and the pleasure of his working life, his working friendships, and here he was, at the end of an apparently pointless day, having this otiose conversation with a complete stranger, although one for whom he felt mildly sorry, and who had the trick of engaging his curiosity, partly in default of anything more serious, and partly because his professional instincts were not quite dormant, because he saw her as mildly sociopathic, and he wanted to follow the case, as it were, to its conclusion.

'I like your suit,' he remarked temperately.

'This?' She kicked at the full orange skirt with the toe of one soft kid boot. 'This is Sharon's. I always wear Armani myself. That black thing was Armani. Though I have to say her taste has improved since I knew her.'

'When was that?'

'Oh, ages ago. We go back a long way.'

'You didn't see her in America, did you?'

'I might have done. Why are you asking me all these questions? Why is everyone so interested in my affairs all of a sudden?'

'I don't think that Sharon knows you're in the flat.'

She shrugged again. 'Actually she always said that I could stay with her when I was in town.'

'You'd better tell me the truth,' he said.

She looked bored and impatient, as if he were importuning her, as perhaps he was. Her cheeks were no longer an angry and, he thought, rather splendid red, but mottled pink and white, as indecisive as her mood. He thought she was uneasy, as well she might be, but what struck him as significant, as it had done in previous conversations, was her inability to answer a simple question, as if evasion were a technique practised for its own sake, one of Singer's techniques, no doubt, but one which never incurred the risk of bringing the practitioner within dangerous distance of the truth.

'The truth?' she said, as if giving the lie to his conclusions. 'As I said, we go back a long way.'

Again he admired the ease with which she had evaded his question.

'When did you last see her?'

'Oh, now it's times and dates, is it? If you must know, we used to share a flat. In Muswell Hill.'

'And more recently than that?'

'I went to her wedding. When she married that weed.'

'Tim?'

'Tim. Though I advised her against it, of course.'

'Of course,' he said, reflecting that she was not only antagonistic to women, but antagonistic, on principle, to the men they married. This made her antagonistic to nearly everyone, a fact which he had picked up on earlier. Her attitude to men was predatory but hostile, and if he were to judge by her behaviour, hostile to himself. But no doubt she despised him for being old, while at the same time making a mental note of his attributes. He was tired of this game, which was not entirely a game. He felt foolish, not merely old, but almost in his dotage. To engage himself further would be unseemly: he was not, and could not be, in a position of trust or responsibility. He must shed these pompous illusions. At the same time he noted that his recent interrogation, which she now had a notion of having passed unscathed, had brought a healthier colour to her cheeks, as if she had been expecting a punishment which had not been meted out. Again he had a vision of the army sergeant, perhaps a man of uncertain temper, alternately cajoling and slapping, even beating, perhaps more than that . . . He felt pity for her, felt a warmth towards her, felt the beginnings of a need to protect her. From this standpoint he could see that Mrs Lydiard's complacent advice, made no doubt with the best of intentions, but insensitively, gratingly, might have brought the girl to the point of open rebellion. But now she was mollified, even smiling. Her smiles were rare. Somehow he had earned this brief indulgence. He received it gratefully. Then, feeling ridiculously rewarded, almost embarrassed, he wished her goodnight. 'Sleep well,' he added.

She unwound herself from the door-jamb. 'See you tomorrow,' she said.

In his bedroom, his fortress, he brooded slightly as he eased his shoes from his feet. He cautioned himself conscientiously against anticipation of further indulgence. All this must stop, he thought. He wished that the Dunlops would come home and take Katy Gibb off his hands. For she did seem to be on his hands. It gave him something to think about, of course, and since the problem would ultimately prove to be self-limiting, he could see no harm in that. The Dunlops would return, and she would leave, and he would be alone again. Here was the position at its most stark. His last thought on the matter, before preparing his evening meal, was that there must be no damage. His role was to help, as it had always been. He sighed, as if life were suddenly a burden to him, and as if he hoped, for a brief but illuminating flash, that help, or at least relief from age, from loneliness, from sadness, might be visited on him, unexpectedly, gratuitously, and without his having earned or even understood the reason for it.

6

Nevertheless he seemed to have passed some sort of test, to judge from her appearance the following morning just as he was leaving the flat. He had only to open his door, it seemed, for her to open hers. He did not want to see her, felt if anything irritated by her apparent availability. He himself had been relatively occupied, had felt that he had made an auspicious start to the day. Quite a few people had telephoned to invite him to various Christmas activities. He had successfully turned down the Hardwicks' kind invitation to their dog- and grandchild-ridden household for the Christmas weekend, but had noted down in his diary two drinks parties, and lunch with a former colleague, at Wilton's, on the Wednesday of the following week. He had maintained, without too much difficulty, a façade of good cheer. 'Fine, fine,' he had heard himself say no less than four times. 'Yes. Keeping very busy. Sometimes I wonder how I made the time to come to work.' This was greeted with dutiful laughter. It was the recognised formula for putting the enquirer at ease.

And indeed, in the light of a sunny morning, he was enjoying one of his brief moments of satisfaction, although he knew that it was likely to prove brief. He had not been forgotten: he had the proof. After Christmas it would be his turn to be gracious. He would make contact with those old friends with whom he had temporarily lost touch; he would invite the Hardwicks to dinner, or perhaps the opera; he would give a small drinks party, or maybe not such a small one, for now he had the time and the leisure to think about such things. In the past the few parties he had given had been a success, although he found them a terrible strain. Hipwood, at his most officious, had been co-opted as footman, a temporary position for which he was handsomely rewarded, while Mrs Cardozo had supervised the caterers in the kitchen. Bland himself felt absurd on these occasions, which were the very obverse of the intimacy which he craved and only rarely achieved, except with Putnam, to whom he felt he ought to excuse himself the following morning. 'People expect one to entertain,' he would say, to which Putnam would inevitably reply, 'More fools they.' Yet Putnam turned up faithfully, in much the same spirit as that in which he might attend a niece's wedding: stoically, determined not to spoil the celebration, yet withholding judgment, mindful of pleasures elsewhere. Now that Putnam was gone Bland felt he might shoulder the burden once again, perhaps more at ease now that that ironic eye was no longer there to watch him.

Perhaps Putnam had been too caustic, he thought, but on the other hand how tonic his asperity had been! Putnam never 'entertained', but was merely happy with his own chosen company. Bland was perhaps more sensitive to social pressures. There had been no chance of his making a fool of himself while Putnam was there to provide the necessary judicious checks. Not that he had ever been in much danger: it occurred to him now to wonder why he had not been more extravagant, more excessive. If he thought about it, casting his mind back over the past, it was to conclude that he had known too few women, unlike Putnam, whose activities in this respect appeared to be seamless. He never discussed them, and out of discretion Bland had done little more than refer to his own holiday adventures, those conversations struck up over café tables in Paris or Geneva or Florence, and concluded some time later (but not too much later) to everyone's expressed satisfaction.

In his glancing references to those liaisons Bland implied more than the truth, which was that for him these had been abortive friendships rather than physical episodes, that it had been the search for companionship which had prompted him to proffer the cigarette lighter or to pick up the fallen newspaper. To make love to these strangers – initially such a pleasing idea – fell somewhat short of what he had desired. He would have preferred, he sometimes thought, to continue to sit in the sun with the charming partner of the moment, to learn something of her life, and her satisfactions or dissatisfactions, rather than to escort her, in the fullness of time (usually a day or two), to his hotel room, or, if he were well known in the place, to a smaller, more discreet hotel in a more distant part of town.

Always on these occasions he felt a faint preliminary disappointment that it was all so easy, almost affectless. He felt that he was doing what was expected of him, what was expected of any man in his situation. It began to seem like a duty, rather than the pleasure he had originally envisaged. The story of his life, he thought, soberly retying his tie afterwards. He always longed to be out again in the sun and the clean air, with his partner clinging to his arm in a semblance of friendship, as if she were – at last – rather more than a willing accomplice. He supposed that some basic physical hygiene was involved in all this: in any event he always slept better afterwards. But he paid dearly for his moment of intimacy, which always occurred at the beginning of the encounter rather than in its aftermath. His subsequent estrangement puzzled him.

What was missing? It had all been quite agreeable; no feelings had been hurt. He could not quite analyse the desolation which frequently descended upon him, coinciding usually with the end of the holiday, and therefore easy enough to account for. If put to the test he would have said that he was after friendship, that he had made a friend and simultaneously lost her by the very act of making love to her. He did not wonder whether his love-making had been at fault. Pleasure had been mutual and had been mutually expressed. He had not failed his partner. If he had failed anyone, he thought, he had failed himself.

Immediately after such encounters he felt weary of their opportunism, their predictability. But the women seemed well disposed and he would in any case have revised his strategy had they not been, settling back, with some disappointment, but also with some relief, into his true character as a dignified if somewhat wistful English gentleman. At least he supposed he was a gentleman: he was certainly gentle, if sometimes concerned that he did not always act like a man. This worried him, until he sat back with a sigh and transferred his attention to the pleasing holiday sights before him. A companion would have been pleasant, but the companionship to which he had access was not fulfilling. He was unlucky, he supposed, in harbouring inchoate wishes which never found their exact equivalent in one other person. Yet he had no doubt that many other men found themselves in the same predicament, and he pitied them, and himself, for that loneliness that no amount of recreational sex could assuage.

All this was now, perhaps fortunately, in the past. There would be no more adventures in foreign cities, and if he were to proffer a cigarette lighter over a café table in the future it would simply be a courtesy from one stranger to another. He had imagined that such an evolution would bring a deep peace. That it did not he put down to the anxieties of approaching age, which, he was beginning to discover, banished peace almost as effectively as adolescence had done. He was astonished by the gusts of longing that frequently swept over him, when he awoke in the morning, for example, or in the middle of the night, when the news from the World Service failed to keep him company. He forced himself to think of all the solitaries listening to the radio when they should be sleeping, mariners, night watchmen, invalids, but failed to find comfort in the knowledge that others were awake. His sleeplessness seemed to confine him to a ghetto, in which the forsaken, the forgotten, and the unsatisfied were his fellow inmates. It seemed to him that women in these situations could not possibly experience the same degree of loneliness.

Nights such as these left him momentarily broken the following day, and he was almost glad that he no longer had to go to the office. If he wished he could take a siesta, and having once surrendered to the temptation found the habit quite difficult to break. He got used to sleeping, sometimes heavily, in the afternoon. He found himself looking forward to this sleep, lunching early if he were at home, taking a taxi back if he were lunching at the club, eager, almost, to reach his dusky flat, whose steady warmth was so unlike the radiant heat of those distant days in foreign cities, when adventure beckoned, or rather seemed to beckon . . . These days he crammed his activities into the morning hours, planning and timing them as if they were real obligations. His shopping, a visit to the London Library, perhaps an hour at the club, were enough to make him feel as if he had been active, as if he deserved to take his rest. Later, becalmed by the heavy sleep which obliterated the afternoon, he would go out for the evening paper and for whatever purchases he might need or have forgotten in the earlier part of the day. He preferred his street in the dark, when the lights came on: he liked to see people about their business, something he had failed to take in that morning. He looked forward to his peaceful evening, reading, listening to music, watching television. Sometimes it seemed to him that he only came to life in the latter part of the day, before, with a sigh, he was obliged to prepare for bed and for a night which would inevitably be, if not sleepless, at least disturbed.

He recognised the signs of age, both in his largely pointless activity and his totally unearned inactivity. All he could hope to do was to keep them to himself. Yet it seemed to him sad that the fire should have quite died down, leaving him inert, a man without impulses. Sometimes he wondered whether he were dead already, until a transient pleasure recalled him to life. His days were pleasant; even this particular day was pleasant. The sun was high in a clear sky; it would be a crime to stay at home. He would go to the London Library; he had a fancy to read Mauriac again, as he had in the years of adolescence. Then he would lunch at the club. He sighed a little as he made his plans, all too aware that many men might envy him. He was not quite reconciled to this limbo of a life and wondered if anything could restore him to some semblance of feeling, or whether he had said good-bye to feeling for ever.

Leaving the flat with as much goodwill as he could muster, he was not best pleased to see the Dunlops' door open and Katy Gibb appear. He had been profoundly submerged in his thoughts; for a moment or two he looked at her with no sense of recognition. This morning she was dressed in black trousers and what looked to him like a very expensive black cashmere sweater. He was jolted back into the present. The sweater, he reckoned, was Sharon's. He looked for, and found, the bare feet, and prepared to exert even more goodwill than he had thought would be necessary. A quick greeting, and then he could be about his own affairs.

'Good morning,' he said. 'I hope you slept well?'

'No, I didn't,' she replied. 'You wouldn't find me up at this hour if I had.'

'I should have thought that half-past nine . . .'

'But then you go to bed so early, don't you? Don't you get bored doing that?'

These questions were accompanied by a confident half smile, as if she were prepared for them to be friends.

'You'll have to excuse me,' he said. 'I've got rather a busy morning.' He groaned as he heard himself uttering this lie, but felt it necessary to stock up with half-truths in order to protect his time from what he suspected might be frequent incursions.

Her answer was to step across the landing on her bare feet, and to bestow on him the same luminous gaze with which she had favoured him at their first meeting. He had to admire her newly washed hair, still faintly damp, from which rose a lemony smell of shampoo.

'Only if you're making a cup of coffee, I don't mind keeping you company for half an hour.'

Sheer exasperation, and also the masochistic thrill of succumbing to her will, a will turned idly in his direction for want of something better to exert itself upon, led him to fling open the door, rather harder than was necessary, and to usher her into his sitting-room.

'Coffee or tea?' he asked her shortly.

'Oh, tea! And perhaps toast? Toast would be magic!'

She appeared to be dreamily relaxed, a fact which perplexed him, when she had previously been so much on her guard. He supposed that the few words they had exchanged on the previous evening had been sympathetically received. He had said or done something right.

'I take it you haven't had breakfast,' he said.

'Oh, I never eat breakfast,' she replied, still dreamily. A few minutes later he watched her spreading honey on her buttered toast. 'I'm usually out to lunch, and by the time I've got up and had my bath and dressed there's no time. You know how it is.'

She managed to include him in her intimacy, or rather in the intimacy of her morning activities. He studied her covertly. She certainly appeared scrubbed, burnished, as if her efforts had been extensive. Her cheeks were pink, and although she wore no make-up he was being given to understand that he was seeing merely the empty canvas, that when the invitation to lunch was received she would transform herself, as she had done on the day of their first meeting, when she appeared so startlingly changed into a woman of mysterious significance. He preferred her, if he had a preference, as she was. There was something appealing about her, although she was far from being a beauty. The mousy hair was straight, the eyes, of an indeterminate greyish blue, rather small. The skin, however, was perfect, smooth, and with a sheen that broadcast messages of health and youth. In black the body showed to its best advantage, although that little roll of flesh on the stomach might be troublesome later on.

'Are you going out to lunch today?' he asked.

'It's too early to say, really. My friends are never really around before ten or half past. I'll make a few calls later on.'

'Do they work, your friends?'

'Some do, some don't. Most of them don't need to.'

'What will you do when the Dunlops come home?'

She shrugged. 'Go and stay with somebody else. I've got masses of invitations. I've only got to pick up the phone. You're not worried about me, are you? There's no need, you know. I'm feeling very good about myself, very positive. I'm in the moment, you know?'

'Is that what they say in California?'

'Self-actualisation is what Howard taught me. It means affirming the essential self. That's why it's so important to walk tall and think positive and get in touch with your feelings. And tell the world how great you are!'

He thought that if all Howard Singer's acolytes spent their time telling each other how great they were then no information of any importance was ever likely to be exchanged. This seemed to him an excellent idea for keeping people happy on a fee-paying basis, providing that those people were rather stupid or lonely or at least susceptible in the first place. And it was no doubt Howard Singer's business to tell them how great they were, so that they could then impart the information to others. He imagined a playground filled with adults in leisure wear, all self-actualising obediently until the end of the session, and no doubt begging to come back at midnight to have any residual doubts taken care of in one of Howard Singer's encounter hours, those hours when the truth could be shyly told (and who knew what truths were told then?) before the burden of self-affirmation had to be taken up again in the light of common day. Was Howard Singer up to this? he wondered. How did he fare, with his all-purpose cheeriness, if someone were addicted to truth and anxious to pursue it?

'What happens if someone has a real problem?' he asked. 'Supposing someone comes up with something like incest? Or vampirism?' This last was an attempt at a joke. She did not smile.

'We get more eating disorders than incest,' she said.

'And what does he do for those?'

'He holds them.'

'Holds them?'

'Surely you've heard of holding therapy? If someone's been on a binge he just holds them and lets them cry.'

'And what good does that do?'

'It enables them to get in touch with their pain.'

'And with the child inside? Within,' he corrected himself.

'That's right. And it works.'

He doubted that. He thought it might work for half an hour, but would not bring about transformation. And surely transformation was what these people wanted? It was, he realised, what he himself wanted, as had been promised in those fairy tales which he had read as a child and of which he retained an awed perception. The sadness of those stories! Those boy woodcutters, those little mermaids – how they suffered! For his father had shown a rare spark of intelligence and had presented him with the stories of Grimm and Hans Andersen instead of the contemporary fables for which he had clamoured. And the sorrow of those mermaids and woodcutters had corresponded to something sorrowful in his own nature, so that he was emboldened to feel that his own sadness was legitimate, and that it was but a prelude to that transforming stroke of benevolence or good fortune that would enable him to accede to a happy end. That happy end had never come about. Nevertheless he still believed that it might, or even, at a pinch, that if he waited he would be rewarded, at last, in a way not yet foreseen. He felt a powerful anger against Howard Singer, who pursued a lucrative trade, and who denied his patients even a transforming vision. With him it would be all acceptance and understanding: he would understand every aberration, whether he really understood it or not. He had met this attitude in some of the younger women in his office: an assumption of all-round emotional proficiency. It was the new creed, it seemed. At the same time he cherished a headline he had savoured in the evening paper: 'Women take up Boxing to beat Stress'. As if only by knocking hell out of someone could they get rid of the overload caused by too much acceptance. How did Howard Singer get rid of his stress? Did he run therapeutic punch ups with his patients, some of whom he must surely loathe? And was this girl, who somehow came to be in his flat, although he could hardly understand how or why, really as stupid as her conversation? He noted in passing that she was at least not actually lying or evading his questions, as she usually did. No doubt she thought she was making him privy to a great deal of useful information. He felt a surge of annoyance, so powerful that it took him by surprise.

'You'll have to excuse me,' he said. 'You caught me just as I was going out.'

'What time will you be back?' she asked.

'I have absolutely no idea. Was there something else. . . ?'

'I just thought, if you're around this afternoon, and if I'm not doing anything . . .'

'Of course. Of course you thought that.' This sounded harsh to him, though she appeared not to register the snub. 'Why don't you come in for a cup of tea?' he said. 'Not before five, though. Now I really must go.'

'All right, all right.' She put up her hands in a propitiatory gesture. 'I've got things to do myself, you know. I'll see you later, then.' She turned to go, though she did not seem in any great hurry to leave. He had time to admire her rather pronounced hips in the tight black trousers. Her movements were slow, and, he thought, exaggerated. He could feel his irritation rising. The mere sight of her now was enough to annoy him.

Fuming, he ran down the stairs. It was nearly eleven o'clock, and as far as he could make out the rest of the day was compromised. Why had he sacrificed it? He walked at an unusually fast pace, down Kendal Street – *his* street, he reminded himself, just as the flat was *his* flat, owned and paid for – into Connaught Street and across the Edgware Road, not slackening his speed until he was in Upper Berkeley Street and making for Selfridges. He had planned to do his shopping and then go to the London Library, but now it seemed more urgent to get his books first, as if laying them up would protect him in some way from inane encounters of the type with which he suddenly seemed threatened. He felt a heightened disgust with himself for giving in so spinelessly to the girl's suggestions: she was apparently unaware of his reluctance, or had decided to ignore it, although when it suited her she was quick to take offence, her drawling intonations, assumed for the occasion, expressing a wealth of upper-class distaste. This was bogus, he knew, and probably she did as well: those wealthy friends of hers, in whom somehow he did believe, having proved themselves useful models, would have contributed this much if nothing more material.

The mystery of her resources, or of her currently resourceless state, continued to preoccupy him. He knew that few people of her age, or her presumed age, took work as seriously as he did himself. Work for him had done duty as an alternative life, one which he was now obliged to register only as a memory. There was no reason why a young woman should devote herself, as he had devoted himself, to life at a desk. He had a notion that, apart from the barbaric nature of her discourse, she was shrewd, and would make a success of her flimsy enterprise, if it ever got off the ground. She had, in addition, already formed a fairly accurate idea of his own resources and capabilities. He had no doubt that she had earmarked him for future use, in which case she had made a grave mistake. He was not so stupid as to take her on trust or to tolerate any demands she might make of him. No doubt she thought to seduce him into this. He was, however, impervious to whatever charm she possessed. Such charm was calculated, far too calculated, blatant even, a studied mixture of the worldly and the juvenile. Even her name – Katy – was deliberate. He had noted in his odd excursions into the modern world, how many tough determined women reduced their names to diminutives, as if to disarm the opposition, or to reassure themselves as to the lovable nature of their true characters.

What he felt, apart from the automatic response of pure observation, and an almost impersonal appreciation of salient characteristics – the flawless skin, the unexpectedly adult hips – was an overpowering anger which surprised him. It was not merely that she had disrupted a day which had been harmlessly dedicated to his own concerns. It was not merely that she polluted his ears with an unbroken stream of jargon. It was not even that he suspected her of deceit and duplicity. His feelings, suddenly gigantic, struggled for expression. What he felt, quite simply, was a desire to wring her neck. But even that would not do, was too formulaic to contain an anger that was becoming enjoyable. Wringing her neck, or wreaking some physical damage on her, would not settle the matter. What he suspected now, and it made his heart beat faster, was the fact that in visiting some kind of violence on her, in actually manhandling her flesh, he might experience a powerful erotic satisfaction. In an unwanted moment of lucidity he recognised that he had hit on some truth that he had long hidden even from himself. What he felt now was interesting, exciting, disturbing, distasteful even. He felt that approaching her, for whatever purpose, would involve a recklessness, a heedlessness, an antagonism or at the very least a hostility, the factor that had always been missing in his too correct, too considerate love-making. His lifelong affection for Louise, his friendships, sentimental or carnal, with other women, had been all too anodyne. This would be different. The knowledge hit him like a stone hurled by an unseen assailant.

For a brief moment he was afforded a glimpse into the heart of hedonism, something ancient, pagan, selfish. He saw it as movement, headlong rush, carelessness, the true expression of the essential ego. It would cause fear and damage to those who opposed it, for it was without fear of damage itself. Few were brave enough to accommodate it, although to taste it was addictive, Dionysian. Certainly a man of his age, and his character, would do well to shun it. Yet what he had seen, or felt, did more than enchant him: it entertained him. To live like that would be to know true freedom, freedom from another's cares, or rather the cares that others imposed on one and which called for the exercise of forbearance, restraint, even virtue. To be done with all that, and all that it entailed, would be to be at one with the gods, those ancient heedless gods, with their complicated and demanding private lives and their imperviousness to punishment. Dead, they merely took their place in the galaxy, which was perhaps how human life too should end, instead of miserably seeking repentance, crawling on one's knees to an unforgiving deity, a deity still suffering its own pain, and enjoining others to suffer in emulation. And the damage that he had longed to do: no one said that it had to be lethal. It had simply to be the full flowering of his own instinctive joy, too long repressed, too long feared, and at last acknowledged.

Of course, it was all quite reprehensible. There was no need for this to be known, he assured himself, striding down Bond Street in the light of a cruel and all too brief winter sun. He could keep this unseemly intelligence to himself. He was a civilised man: he did not rape and pillage, and his aggressive impulses, which were never very strong in the first place, had been bred out of him. He could utterly disguise the fact that he disliked and possibly desired this girl, though desired in an ambiguous and radically destructive way. He was not a monster, and although he had this peculiar and unsought reaction, which he was sure other men had entertained, there was no question of his acting upon it. Indeed, looked at in the light of this involuntary vampirism (strange how that had come up earlier), the girl now seemed pathetic, a victim, with her airy Californian make-believe, unprotected, even, transparent in her pretensions, a psychological amateur by comparison with the swamp into which he had so suddenly and amazingly fallen.

He had never used a woman for his own purpose and would not now do so, however willing Katy had initially appeared to be. Her willingness had nothing to do with his current feeling. Of course he pitied her, unknowing as she was of his secret desires. He even felt pain, as he thought of her, idle, in the Dunlops' flat, her possessions in a nylon hold-all, her empty pretensions left floating on the unsympathetic air.

His earlier fear of her, which must have been fear of his own buried impulses, had entirely vanished. He felt shame, certainly, but also some of that exquisite sorrow that was the obverse of desire. He even felt sorrow for that young woman, so gamely repeating her mantras in an uncaring world, and marooned in a dark London flat, waiting for a turn of fortune to release her from whatever difficulty had brought her to this place, unheralded, unexpected, and, apart from her own quick but clumsy thinking, without support. He breathed more easily: he was sorry for the girl. He was glad to have got that settled. Were it not for the residue of that pity he would have dismissed the matter from his mind altogether, shaking his head indulgently over the memory of his earlier lawless impulses. Yet, he now discovered, even that pity contained an erotic twist, which, when consulted, brought a flush to his thin cheeks.

Walking purposefully down Duke Street, and ignoring the picture dealers' windows into which he usually peered, he felt as if he had emerged from a long sleep, and was half afraid that this might be the truth. Yet he also felt a vigour which was not unpleasant; he felt like a man again, could hold his head up and stare boldly at the young men whom he passed in the street. In the London Library an acquaintance told him how well he was looking.

The poor girl was coming to tea, he reminded himself. This fact was somehow more important than his progress along the upper floors of the Library. He removed his books from the shelves with a negligent hand: he scarcely now remembered which ones he had wanted to read. Since she was greedy he would feast her: he would cram her mouth with sweetness. This too had its erotic appeal, which he suppressed. He would have a quick lunch at the club, then buy a cake at Fortnum's, and walk back while the sun still laid its illusory light over the city streets. He could foresee the later hours, when that sun would dwindle, turn red and opaque, and finally disappear altogether in the early dark. He would be at home, eating cake. The idea had its childish charm. Altogether this was a day of surprises. There would be no need to take a nap this afternoon. He had never felt so wide awake in his life.

The faintest hint of his habitual melancholy reasserted itself that afternoon, as he sat in his chair, waiting for her. He thought it ridiculous for a man of his age to spend his time in this manner. Yet what am I to do, he thought, with the time that is left to me? Why not simply divert myself, as harmlessly as I can? No harm: that was what he had to bear in mind. None of it was entirely appropriate, and that made him uncomfortable. To an unsympathetic eye he would appear weak, pathetic, even more bereft than his prospective visitor, on whom he had earlier lavished such feeling. Only her animal presence, he knew, could bring him back to life. As he arranged his cake on a plate, a pang of sorrow caught him unawares. He felt sorrow for himself. I must beware of pity, he thought: it is pity that has to go. But in those few moments of waiting it was sadness that gained the upper hand, as if after the orgy of his earlier impulses.

Once she was in the room, however, sorrow and pity

gave way to the usual exasperation. She had made up her face and drenched herself in the obnoxious scent she had somehow acquired in the course of her shopping expedition with Mrs Lydiard. She looked homelier than usual, or perhaps she had let down her guard: she prowled about the room, inspecting his possessions, turning up the lid of a cigar box, twisting round a vase to inspect it, humming slightly under her breath.

'Oh, do sit down, Katy, and have your tea,' he said, aware that the visit was going to be tiresome, wishing now that she would hurry up and go, leaving him alone with Mauriac. 'Look, I bought you this cake.' He could hear himself, sounding ridiculous. Extreme control would be needed if he were not to become bad-tempered.

'Good heavens, you don't expect me to eat anything made with white sugar, do you? Besides, I'm on a diet.' She pulled aside her sweater to reveal the waistband of her trousers, which she had eased with a small but ragged slit. The side seam, too, had been loosened. He saw a roll of milky flesh, which seemed momentarily repellent.

'At least sit down,' he repeated. 'I can't talk to you if you're moving about all the time.'

Still humming, she returned obediently to his side, drank her tea, and wiped her glistening lips on her napkin. In this gesture he thought he could see the whole of her childhood. He wondered which one of them would break the silence.

'Do you like this room, George?' she said finally.

'It suits me pretty well,' he replied. It was comfortable, if impersonal. He was modestly proud of it.

'It looks like a window in Peter Jones.'

He felt pained: it was from Peter Jones that he had bought most of the furniture. A large sofa, striped in green and coral pink, flanked by two tables bearing lamps made out of Chinese vases, with coral pink shades, stood against the only wall not covered with bookshelves. Two wing chairs, covered in the same green and coral pink material, faced the sofa, at right angles to a brass and glass coffee table. The carpet was green, the curtains again striped. Peter Jones had supplied metres and metres of the fabric and had had to re-order. Eventually it was completed. He had felt relieved rather than gratified. The effect was soothing, perhaps gloomy on a dull day, but its underwater calm suited him.

'It's boring, George. It wants livening up. It's too careful. Now, if you were to throw a few cushions around, or change the curtains . . . At least you could move that desk. It could go somewhere else, away from the window, for instance.'

It was not a desk but a delicate little writing-table, an early twentieth-century imitation of a traditional style, with slender legs and a brass rail round the top, a reproduction, but a faithful one. It had been made by a diligent craftsman and was too fragile for much use. He kept a spare cheque-book in the single central drawer. Heavy-duty correspondence took place at a larger and more important desk in what he called the study, a small dark room overlooking the back of the building. The virtue of this piece was aesthetic. He had bought it at auction and had instructed Mrs Cardozo to be careful when dusting it. It lived its own delicate life in a corner, almost protected from use. He regarded it as he would a picture, an object of virtue. It gave him pleasure to contemplate it.

'It's near the window because it's near the light,' he said mildly.

'Well, you can have a lamp, can't you? I'm going to try it over there, opposite the door. No, don't bother. I can manage.'

'I'd rather you didn't touch it, Katy. I like it where it is.'

'Now don't say anything, just wait.'

With unsurprising vigour she manhandled the little

table across the room into the opposite corner, where it abutted on to a bookcase: a biography of Picasso slumped heavily against its fellows, precipitating a slow waterfall of paperbacks onto the carpet. Above the top shelf a lamp juddered on its base.

'There! That looks better, doesn't it?'

'I don't really think it does, you know.' Only a dissolution of his character could have permitted this, he thought, reminding himself that he could restore order once she had gone.

'Oh, you! You're just used to it where it was. Change is growth, you know. How can you grow unless you change?'

'I don't know that I want to. I found growing up rather painful.'

'I'm not talking about growing up. I'm talking about personal growth. Good heavens, anyone can grow up! Personal growth is quite different.'

'I don't think anyone can just grow up. It's not as easy as you make it sound.'

She ignored this. 'Personal growth needs assistance. It means sharing. Is there anything you want to share, George?'

He contemplated her, sitting on the carpet on one of his immaculate cushions. He did not feel like sharing. He felt, once again, like colonising, appropriating, cannibalising. He felt like violating. The very banality of her presence, and of her remarks, released once again those murderous impulses which had troubled and invigorated him earlier. At the same time the very openness of her face, turned to him with an expression of unusual friendliness, disarmed him. But she thinks that I am the one she has disarmed, he thought: she has decided that I am in the bag. Hence her confidence. He found all this unbearably sad. The modulation of his feelings, from antagonism and hunger to melancholy and defeat, surprised him. I am no longer up to this, he thought. I am in a minefield. I am thirty, no, forty years too late. I should have felt all this as a young man, when there was less time to reflect. And now I am old, and this wretched girl is young, and for all her talk of sharing, lacks even the faintest idea of what is going through my mind.

'Shall we have some more tea?' she said. 'Shall I put the kettle on?'

He glanced elaborately at his watch. 'Good heavens,' he said. 'I had no idea it was so late. I'm afraid I've got to be going out.'

'Anywhere interesting?' she asked.

He no longer thought such questions bizarre. 'Not very,' he said. He thought he might take a therapeutic walk, through the hurrying home-going streets. He was anxious to be alone.

'Well, if you must.' The drawl, the disdainful expression were back in place.

'And I dare say you have things to do yourself,' he said gently. If only he were not aware of her vulnerability!

'Yes, well, as you know, I've got a business to get off the ground. In that sense I'm always busy.'

For an instant he wondered if all this were true, whether in fact she was more straightforward than she seemed. She had a certain authority, and, although she was an intellectual lightweight, a certain power as well. He could see her exerting that authority over a team of young women, and even over susceptible young men as well. She might, if fortune smiled on her, become London's equivalent of Howard Singer: there were surely plenty of troubled people who would be delighted to be told how great they were. Yet the auspices did not seem favourable. Her very idleness, her willingness to visit him, betrayed a time spent less in planning, in organising, than in waiting. And her visits to him were no doubt less than innocent. The time would come when she would mention once again her search for sponsors. But he was more experienced than she was. He would be equal to her there.

He had thought of himself as a man afflicted with lucidity. For this reason he could no longer hide from himself the fact that she inspired in him an intoxicating mixture of antagonism and longing. The urge to dominate her, in some nebulous and unformulated fashion, returned to him in her absence, only to evaporate once she was actually in his presence. That presence was ambiguous, disconcerting, as disconcerting as the hitherto unknown range of feelings that surged over him when she was no longer there. Her actual, rather fleshy form, and the face that could take on many disguises, caused him to feel pity, even despair. Once the door had closed behind her, and the inevitable blankness of her absence had been registered, he reverted to the faintly lycanthropic character who had been revealed to him only that morning. He turned his mind to this character from time to time, as other men might turn to pornography. All this could be quite harmless, he thought, as long as he could keep it to himself. He had only to exercise his higher consciousness for the temptation to disappear. And the temptation, he noted thankfully, was cerebral rather than physical. Not once had he actually contemplated any kind of physical approach. He was quite safe on that score. Like Swann's Odette, she was simply not his type.

On the whole it might be better if she went away. Or if he did. He thought again of Rome, reviewed the arrangements to be made, and once again postponed the idea. He could always get a single flight. Louise, he thought, had not taken the plan too seriously: she would not be too disappointed. And if she were she would forgive him. He had not abused her eternal forgiveness in the past, keeping in the back of his mind the fact that he had shown magnificent forbearance in relation to her marriage. Though shocked, he had been dignified. In fact it had not been too difficult. She was dear to him, but he no longer felt for her that sharpness of desire that had lent such urgency to their early meetings. Then it had been unbearable. But by dint of agreeing with her on nearly every subject, by dint of approving of her, and admiring her, his desire had lost its edge. She was still in many ways his ideal. His word for her was 'decent', and her decency had never quite lost its appeal. But by that very virtue she had banished that sensation of danger which the fact of nearing the edge of unacceptable behaviour had always imparted to him. Now he appeared, for whatever reason, to be rather near it once again.

His life, in retrospect, seemed very long and quite uneventful. Yet it had been occupied with struggle, with the no doubt modest but nevertheless taxing struggle of finding a place for himself in the world. This he had managed to do, and the result was now revealed to him as unsatisfactory. How else to account for these primitive emotions which had suddenly come to the fore? Perhaps he was merely undergoing a period of change: Howard Singer would have talked him out of it, or through it, as they seemed to like to say. He grinned as he thought of himself in a support group, although he knew that such things existed, and were even patronised by redundant executives. He isolated the word redundant, and resolved to think further along these lines. There was no reason why he could not deal with his own malaise, if that was what it was. He was not totally without understanding.

He manoeuvred the writing-table back to its original position, trying not to notice the very small scratch on one of the legs. His possessions, his surroundings, suddenly bored him: for a moment he failed to care what would happen to them. If he were to leave they would wait patiently for his return, and if he failed to return they would not in that event disappear. The knowledge that they would survive him, outlive him, shocked him slightly. It was only just that they should suffer some infinitesimal damage, just as he seemed to be suffering, so that time passing should be equally demanding of them all.

7

By the light of the following morning – a lucid white winter light that seemed to banish the dark more effectively than on previous days – his state of mind seemed to him rather more puzzling. Reprehensible, certainly, but also uncharacteristic. He hoped that he was not about to deteriorate into a waggish old man, physically harmless, but given to questionable fantasies. He greeted Mrs Cardozo with more than usual warmth, made coffee for them both, then told her that he would be out for most of the morning. Space and distance were what he needed. He decided to take a walk.

By 'a walk' he meant not an obedient peregrination of the park but a sortie into a relatively foreign landscape, or what he thought of as foreign, remote streets of small houses, which enclosed lives at which he could only guess and which continued to exert a strange fascination on him. Whereas the streets of European cities were familiar, and no longer occasioned any shock of surprise, these closed silent little houses, facing each other imperviously across wide blank streets, thrilled him with a mystery of real strangeness. They were the stuff of his Sundays. In the fading light of a suburban afternoon they had often seemed to him to be deserted, uninhabited, so still were they, so undisturbed by any sign of life. He had been born in such a house, but in another town, where afternoons seemed to stretch into infinity, and where only a rare passer-by had hinted at a human presence. He had never been back, but occasionally his own comfortable metropolitan life seemed to him an aberration, as if he were still a stranger, a newcomer, unused to the assumption of urban prosperity which had apparently settled on him without his quite understanding whether this was allowed, or whether he had done anything to deserve it.

On this fine white morning he crossed the park, in a hurry to reach the alien but mysteriously familiar streets, no longer interested in the raw space which enveloped him. He came out into Queen's Gate, yet the buildings here were too lofty, too impersonal to suit his mood, and he paid them little attention, only vaguely aware of their architectural interest. He felt still a slight vulnerability, the residue of dissipating energies. He thought he would make for Hurlingham, which he had once investigated on a particularly bleak Sunday, as if under an enchantment, his steps ringing out on the empty pavements. It must have been all of a year ago, he reckoned, for the shop windows had been full of sad decorations left over from Christmas, and now it seemed to be Christmas once again, for there was a tree outside the hospital in the Fulham Road, and more trees on forecourts and in car parks. And on florists' stalls, among the azaleas and the poinsettias, soon destined to wither in the heat of Christmas fires, the first frail daffodils, the pots of closed green hyacinths, and, paper white, the heavenly narcissi, not yet scented, but just showing their orange hearts.

He was soon eased and tranquillised by the steady progress of his feet, yet his mind was not quite under his control, as he liked it to be. He was still subject to strange tides of feeling, having now to do with memory rather than with his new preoccupations. For a surprisingly vivid moment he was back in the past, and inhabited by the

strange complex of emotions which overtook him whenever he thought of his mother. This memory was quite
specific, and though it seemed abrupt he thought there
must be a connection somewhere if only he could trace
it. So powerful was the memory that it seemed to him
that he was a boy again, or rather a young man, living
unwillingly at home, and subject to the pains of home,
which now overtook him with astounding force. If life
were to be lived backwards in this way, as it seemed to
be, then age was to be dreaded, for reasons which had
nothing to do with whatever the future had in store for
him.

His small stuffy bedroom in his parents' house had
looked out onto a patch of garden, which he now saw in
almost perfect detail. An equally small top window let in
a breath of mild air and a smell of grass. At some point
his mother had decided that it was dangerous to leave this
window open, although there could be no possible threat
of an intruder, since the only way into the garden was
through the house. Every morning, after he had left for
work, his mother would go into his bedroom and close
the window. Every evening he would open it again.
'Mother,' he had said. 'Please leave my window open.
The room gets so stuffy.' But she took no notice. As she
grew older, sicker, more disaffected, she would not only
close the window, and keep it closed all day, but would
linger in his room as if to defend her action against all
comers, and in particular against her son.

When he returned, heartsick, from the cardboard box
factory, in the evening, his room would be not only stuffy
but filled with his mother's stale cigarette smoke. The fact
that she had been sitting there filled him with alarm. He
knew that she never looked at his books, his scraps of
writing, for she was genuinely uninterested in him, and
this he had come to accept as normal. It was, rather, the
fact that, too late, she was attempting to make contact

with him, when all he desired was for her to accept that he would ultimately leave her. He pictured her, alone in the otherwise empty house, drifting dumbly into his room, shutting the window, and then sitting there for perhaps half a day, her purpose already forgotten. By that stage her speech and understanding had been slightly affected, although it took him a long time to realise that she was a little deranged. In the end, out of pity, he left the window shut, hoping to pacify her. His nostrils had retained the characteristic smell of that room, compounded of toast and cigarette smoke, the smell of an airless life which he had thought would haunt him for ever.

It still haunted him, but in random flashes, vivid pictures of the past, visitations, when he was all unaware. For the rest of the time he was free of it, and comfortable in his latter-day transformation. But, to judge from his recent epiphany, what had not disappeared was the powerful feeling of protest against the hand which life had dealt him, and the oceanic desire for validation, for dominance over whatever resistance might be put in his way, even if it were no more than a token, a suggestion, a provocation. The most unnerving aspect of the previous day's insights was that this excitation had surged up again, out of nowhere, out of the past, and that the feeling had attached, almost at random, to another human being, to the girl, Katy Gibb, who, as far as he could honestly see, posed no threat to him at all.

Yet, looked at rationally, his mother, whose sly invasion of his territory had first aroused this feeling, had posed no threat either, for although she might not love him, as he thought a mother should love her son, she had certainly wished him no harm. But wait, he thought suddenly, she was in my room when I was not there, when nobody should have been there, when the room should have been empty. And in the same way, or in a reflection, the merest adumbration of the same way, Katy is frequently in my flat when I do not want her to be there. He felt a shock of horror at the thought that she might be there in his absence, or rather – and this was closer – as if she intended to be. This of course was ridiculous, impossible, yet the shock was salutary: he had traced his combative thrill, with its undercurrent of grandiosity, to its source. He was defending his territory. It even seemed permissible to defend it by aggression (if that was what he had felt), should a direct threat arise. It could not arise; of course it could not. But if it did he was prepared, again with that same relish, to oppose it.

He had reached Eel Brook Common, and his tension was beginning to dissipate, as if he had come to grips with a hitherto insoluble problem. He raised his head and addressed himself to the tall idiosyncratic houses leading off the green. He attempted to regain an air of bracing certainty, a pantomime which had served him well in the past, but an area of vulnerability remained. Never to feel safe, never to feel free! Yet he had satisfied his conscience, had remained with his mother to the end, though the end had been as graceless as his own feelings. After her death he had felt momentarily delivered, and the moment had lasted long enough to get him to London. It was only lately that his early years had invaded him once again, as if the secret of his liberty had been discovered, and discovered to be undeserved, without foundation, illusory.

He had it in him now, with his unfortunate sentimental education, to contemplate Katy Gibb calmly and without rancour. He saw her as infinitely disadvantaged. He was not unaware of her desire to appropriate some of his money, but he was genuinely sorry that her designs were so apparent. He was, in a sense, grateful to her for this. There was not the slightest danger that her efforts would succeed: he was hard-headed where money was concerned. He had had too little to start with, and felt that what had come to him was so excessive that it must be carefully husbanded, as if it still belonged to somebody else. The idea of Putnam's money going to some flimsy enterprise was outrageous, absurd. He had made a careful will, so careful that he had left himself few funds to play with in his lifetime. Most of the money would go to Louise, whom he hoped, indeed knew, would outlive him. By his own standards he was a wealthy man, yet he spent nothing. This continence almost amused him. His wants were few and were easily satisfied: books, modest travel, appropriate disbursements to various charities. The idea that he might squander what he possessed was profoundly shocking to him. Therefore he was well defended.

But deprived of his money, or to put it more politely, of his help, the girl's situation would be desperate. Her smart friends, the ones she got to invite her to lunch, would have long ago got her measure. He, if anything, had been rather slow on that score. She would move on, of course, eventually: something told him that she would not wait for the Dunlops to return. And it was winter, and she only had a few possessions in that nylon bag, presumably the vaunted Armani outfit she had worn on the night of their dinner. Everything else had been appropriated from Sharon's wardrobe. Why could he not dismiss the thought of her? He saw her as he had first seen her, scowling and unfortunate, until she had turned that suddenly languorous gaze on himself and onto Mrs Lydiard. And from that moment on it had been an astonishing performance. He had an inkling of astonishing performances given in other settings, in other parts of the world, wherever there was an audience to be vanquished. But the performance was not quite astonishing enough, and an acute observer would always be able to see through her, as Mrs Lydiard had done. Initially charmed, Mrs Lydiard had soon seen sense, and had vanished from the scene. He supposed he should telephone her. On the other hand he did not particularly want to listen to her strictures. He did not feel able to discuss Katy with Mrs Lydiard, or indeed with anyone but himself.

He was by this time nearing the end of New King's Road, entering the suburban – or should it now be urban? – heartland. He admired the straight abrupt little streets, with the strange Greek sounding names – Elthiron, Guion – and the stucco-fronted cottages, now home, no doubt, to the relatively rich and famous. He heard sounds of furious activity from a school playground and looked at his watch: twelve noon. He would go on to Putney Bridge, he decided, and then take a cab home. The sounds from the playground dispersed, and suddenly he was in the midst of children, streaming along to the bus stop, warm, impervious to the chilly air, excited, shrieking. End of term, he supposed. How strong they were! They looked mythical in their confidence, a future race of giants. How would life deal with them? Their energies made him feel tired, or maybe the walk had tired him. Munster Road. Why name this road in Fulham after a town in Germany? Again, and unbidden, there rose in his mind an image of khaki uniforms in the smoky light of late afternoon, the warrior's return to army quarters, and the blonde child dodging her father's hand . . .

He found a café, sat down gratefully, and ordered coffee and a ham sandwich. The ham came in half a baguette and was very good, as was the coffee. Through the misty window he contemplated the houses which had initially seemed so mysterious to him: now they felt overwhelmingly familiar, as if he had spent half a lifetime in this place. He sat for perhaps forty minutes, then, as the café began to fill up, got to his feet, and went out to look for a taxi. By the time he got home it was nearly three, and he was in need of a rest.

Sleep claimed him swiftly, and just as swiftly relinquished him. In his first conscious moments he heard the sound of the doorbell, and sat up, quite fully alert. Smoothing down his hair, he crept stealthily into the hall and stood for a moment, listening. A murmur of conversation alerted him to the fact that this was probably a harmless invasion, Hipwood with a parcel perhaps, carol singers, or some such. With a sigh of relief he opened the door, to face Louise, in a smart black coat, accompanied by a child of about six.

'Louise!' he exclaimed. 'But it's not Sunday!' This was ridiculous: she never came on a Sunday. Nobody came on a Sunday. Sunday was for telephone calls.

'Hallo, George, dear,' she said. 'I know we're unexpected. I didn't tell you I was coming because I didn't know myself until this morning. Sarah's got the flu, so grandma's holding the fort. And Stuart had a dentist's appointment. This is Stuart, by the way. Philip's boy.'

Relief made him exuberant. 'Come in, come in! What a pleasant surprise! Dentist, eh? Poor fellow. Nothing wrong, I hope?' He bent down to the child, who stared back at him impassively. 'Would you like a drink, or something? I've got some Bovril somewhere. Would you like that?'

'I don't give a bugger,' said the child.

'Stuart!' warned Louise. 'The school,' she mouthed at Bland. 'Stuart's picked up some *very* silly words, I'm afraid,' she added in her normal voice. 'Sensible people don't use words like that.'

'Dad does.'

'Well, he shouldn't! We shall have to tell him off, shan't we?'

'What about this Bovril?'

'I think he'd rather have a cup of tea. They drink a lot of tea, though I'm sure it can't be good for them. Would you like a cup of tea, Stuart?'

'Yeah.'

'It's all right, dear. I'll make it if you like.'

'No, no, you sit down. I'll do it. And I've got a rather good cake. From Fortnum's. Would you like that, Stuart?'

The child considered, then nodded. Louise was already removing her coat. Suddenly the flat seemed full of a not unwelcome animation. Lifting his cake from the tin he reflected that it would not be wasted after all. The thought gave him a disproportionate pleasure.

In the sitting-room Stuart perched moodily, swinging his legs. Not an attractive child, Bland thought. Louise, on the other hand, was looking her best, her grand-motherly rôle giving her cheeks a faint flush, her excellent legs covered in fine dark stockings. His Hermès scarf was laid carefully on the back of a chair. She had time to think of that, he noted gratefully. He did not doubt that it was kept in a drawer from one year's end to the next. It was for her placid appreciation of his thoughts and gestures that he loved her.

The boy, pacified with cake, had stopped swinging his legs. Louise ate daintily. Another thing he loved about her: there had never been any nonsense about dieting, or refusing the good things of life. They both enjoyed them too much, had too much for which to be grateful. They were alike in that way, as in so many others.

'Can I have the telly on?' said Stuart, tea over.

'No, you can't. You can look at this book if you like. Look at the pictures. But be very careful: those pictures are precious.'

He handed him the stories of Hans Andersen, with the Arthur Rackham illustrations. He had found the book in a second-hand shop in Paddington, and had marvelled that it had escaped unnoticed. The owner had asked a modest price. Bland had wondered if he knew how much the book was worth. He had salved his conscience by paying something over the asking price, and had sped home with his treasure safely hidden in his briefcase. He felt it to be in the nature of an heirloom, something retrievable from his sorry childhood, an act of loyalty to his largely unloved father. When he had opened it, in the flat, he had been moved. He had been unable to linger long over it. The emotions it had brought forth were still too raw.

'You can read the stories, if you like,' he said.

'They're about fairies,' said the boy uncertainly.

'They're about children, like yourself. Do you like the pictures?'

'Yeah. Yeah, I do. Can I keep it?'

'You can't keep that one, but I'll tell you what I'll do. I'll try to find you one of your own.' He had in fact seen a copy, at a vast price, in a shop in Sackville Street. He would telephone as soon as they had gone, and ask them to post it direct to Stuart. There need be no inscription. He did not think the occasion warranted any sentiment. 'You'll get it through the post. It will be a Christmas present. Will that do?'

'What do you say, Stuart?'

'Thanks.' He was, Bland could see, reluctant to tear himself away from the strange, hypnotic, almost frightening images.

'I'll write down Philip's address and telephone number,' said Louise. 'Perhaps you'll give me a ring later, if you've a minute.'

'How long are you staying?'

'Not long, dear. All being well I could be home by tomorrow evening. I hate being away from home now, don't you? I love my home, although I didn't like the house when I first saw it. Well, we ought to be going. Stuart, do you want to . . . ?'

'Okay.'

'I'll show him where it is. Then I think we might treat ourselves to a taxi. All the way to Clapham! What do you think of that, Stuart?'

Her guilelessness was infectious. Even Stuart, who

probably took a taxi to school when his mother's car was out of commission, smiled. There was something protective in the smile. Louise was a woman who invited protection, all the more so since she was not obviously in need of it.

'I'll ring,' he said, kissing her.

'Yes, do, dear.' She hesitated. 'I enjoyed meeting that Mrs Lydiard,' she said. 'And that friend of yours.'

He was startled. 'Katy Gibb? She's no particular friend of mine. In fact she's not a friend at all. She's staying in the flat opposite. She'll be gone soon, I dare say.'

A very slight look of reserve crossed Louise's face and vanished. 'I found her rather tiresome,' she said.

'Oh, she is.' But once again he was weakened by a sense of pity.

When they were gone, in a flurry of scarves and instructions, he washed up the cups, then put the book away. He did not open it; he felt sure that he would find a sticky thumb print on one of the pages. He would look for another copy, not only for Stuart but for himself, a private copy, to be kept safe, far from depredations. He ascribed to the book feelings which it could not possess, which were in fact his own. He telephoned the shop in Sackville Street, gave his instructions, and asked them to find him another copy. 'As soon as you can,' he said. 'I'm not worried about the price.'

He left the door on the latch and went down to thank Hipwood for getting Louise's taxi. A favour of this sort always necessitated a brief conversation: it was Hipwood's due. They discussed Christmas. 'I shall probably be away,' said Bland. 'But I'll let you know in good time. And of course I'll see you before I go.' This meant that an offering of a pecuniary nature would be handed over. Hipwood was on his dignity. 'And of course I'll keep an eye on things, sir. Nothing much gets past me, you know.'

'We are all in in your debt, Mr Hipwood,' said Bland, as he always did on these occasions.

'Thank you, sir,' said Hipwood gravely.

He reached his door without mishap, but as he was about to close it the door of the Dunlops' flat opened to reveal Katy Gibb, dressed in jeans and a red sweater, her feet bare.

'Hallo, hallo,' he said, his voice breezy. Once again the actual sight of her affected him with prickly exasperation. 'How are you today?'

She ignored this and remained leaning in the doorway. After a few seconds she unwound herself, a sensuous movement, he noted, and one which showed off her figure to its best advantage.

'Aren't you going to ask me in?' she said.

'Well, I am rather busy,' he countered, his heart sinking. 'I've got some rather important letters to write.' All his excuses sounded false to him, as indeed they were.

'I would have come across earlier,' she said. 'Only I saw that friend of yours going in.'

'Your friend' would have been more polite, he thought, and then remembered that Louise had used the same words. To each antagonist the other had become 'that friend of yours'. On the other hand, why refer to her at all? And why had she seen Louise entering his flat? Did she spend her entire life watching and waiting? Why could she not go out like other people? He doubted whether she had voluntarily left the flat since the day of her arrival. Yet she did not have the pallor that characterised those kept at home through illness or disability. She looked healthy, her cheeks flushed, although he noticed a small sore blooming at the corner of her mouth that had not been there before.

'Are you eating properly?' he said sharply.

'Oh, I don't eat much in the daytime. Most people eat too much anyway.'

'What *are* you eating?'

'There's masses of tins. Stuff in the freezer. Don't worry, I won't starve.'

'Don't you think that's a little irresponsible? Those tins belong to the Dunlops.'

'You are funny, George. If those people came to my door I'd let them have everything I possessed. That's what friends are for. But perhaps I'm just like that. If the Dunlops want to visit me they can take what they like. I won't start counting.'

'And you think they might visit you? In California? You'd better come in, by the way.'

'Sure.'

'But I thought you wanted to stay here? And start your business.' It was abundantly clear that neither of them believed any longer in this hypothetical business, but he thought it only polite to pretend that he took her seriously. Besides, he was interested. It was like a detective story, or a novel by Henry James. Fate had brought this enigma to his door, and he could not easily dismiss it. In any event, he reminded himself, he had nothing better to do.

'I want to talk to you about that,' she said, installing herself in the armchair so recently vacated by Louise. 'I need some advice. A man's advice. Someone who knows the business world.'

'I don't know anything about the business world,' he said. 'I was in Personnel.'

'Oh, PR.'

'Not exactly.' He was deeply annoyed. 'I was responsible for hundreds of people, and not only in their working lives but sometimes out of working hours as well. I arranged their appointment, or their transfer, or their medical retirement, or their disability allowance, whatever was necessary. I've worked closely with people throughout my career.'

'Excuse *me*,' she said. 'You forget I know a bit about people too. I've been working with an expert. With *the* expert, you might say. But I suppose you're not quite in touch any longer.'

She arranged herself in her chair, her right ankle supported on her left knee, her plump crotch closely outlined by what appeared to be a newish pair of jeans, unlike the ones in which she had presented herself on the day of her arrival. These were clean, and much tighter. Sharon's again, he supposed, but this now seemed to be taken for granted.

'Young people like you wouldn't understand how I gave my life to that company, and was glad to! I suppose you find it strange that I turned up every morning at the same place and did my job for more years than you've probably spent in this world. Could you do that?'

'I doubt it,' she said. 'I'm more the creative type.'

'So there's no point in trying to make you see how satisfying it is to stick at one thing, to *work* at it, rather than go around looking for favours.' This seemed to him unnecessarily severe. He hurried on, hoping that she had not taken offence. He seemed to have summoned up, rather against his will, an idyllic picture of a lost paradise, in which he saw himself eternally walking to the office on a sunny morning, his briefcase in one hand, his neatly rolled umbrella in the other. How he had enjoyed these gentlemanly appointments! And when he arrived, always on time, his secretary was ready for him, with a cup of coffee, and his opened letters. He had obeyed the rules, had used no stationery for his own correspondence, had made no unnecessary telephone calls. There must still be some of his own headed paper in the top drawer of that big desk which he had relinquished so mournfully. It would be used for scrap, of course. By somebody else, his successor, whom he thought might do the job well, but not as meticulously, as painstakingly as he had done it for thirty years. Thirty years! He had been a model employee, and he was not ashamed of the fact, although he had few extravagant skills to show for it. Life now seemed to be infinitely more complex than life in the office.

But how to explain to this chit of a girl, with her nonsensical talk, the charm of a regular job, and a job of some responsibility, interviewing nervous young men (but they had become more brash as time went on), explaining retirement entitlements to men as old as himself, with whom he deeply sympathised, and whom he treated more gently than the hearty sweating young applicants. And the incidental charms had not been negligible, saying to this one go, and he goeth, sending that one to do the photocopying . . . And always the sterling friendship of Putnam in the background, Putnam who viewed the whole thing with a more ironic eye, including his own assiduity, but who never confessed, in an unguarded moment, that he considered the whole enterprise faintly ridiculous. That was a mark of respect, he knew. Putnam, for whatever reason, had respected him. That was what had made their friendship so precious.

But was it ridiculous, he thought? Or rather, was I ridiculous? It hardly mattered when Putnam was there. The contrast between then and now, between matters of some concern and this ridiculous, this truly ridiculous, conversation, was almost too painful for him. Briefly, he shut his eyes.

'I feel sorry for your generation, really,' said Katy Gibb. 'The war must have ruined your chances.'

'I was a child in the war,' he said stiffly. 'It is not exactly a burning memory. Besides, I didn't live in London then. Reading was pretty quiet.'

'Well, of course, I wasn't born,' she said, spreading out her hands in a pretty gesture.

'I feel sorry for you, then. You missed the Sixties. You just inherited the fall-out, without having any of the fun.'

He remembered himself and Louise, marvelling at the pageant of the King's Road in those far-off days – and they too were sunny in his memory. He remembered nothing of the politics of the time, only those sunny Saturday afternoons, spent strolling at their ease, until it was time to go home and probably to bed. Then Kennedy had been shot, and shortly after she had married, a late marriage, when he had had in the back of his mind the idea that the danger was past, that she would not now leave him, but that there was no need to marry her himself. People did not get married in the Sixties: he had thought that this suited them both. But Louise was more practical. Sauntering through the crowds on sunny weekend afternoons had not satisfied her as it had satisfied him. She had found this man, this Denis Arnold, and she had imperturbably decided to marry him, although he was deeply unattractive and not even very pleasant. But he was a doctor, albeit recently retired, and perhaps a little innocent snobbery had entered the calculation. She was tired of working: she wanted a child. Bland had known this, but had not known how great was her need. His ignorance was genuine: afterwards he had reasoned that most men were the same, shying away fastidiously from a woman's needs and functions. He had been desolate, bewildered, when she had removed herself; he had also been on his dignity. He had not got in touch with her until he heard of her husband's death. He had paid his visit of condolence, had seen the child, whom he could never have accepted as one of his own. That had been a significant reaction. It was at first pity which led him to telephone her, and shortly afterwards the Sunday calls had become a matter of routine. Now when they met there might have been no intervening marriage, nothing to spoil their almost childlike friendship. It had become a sort of marriage in its own right.

He supposed that this invasion of his thoughts by the past was one of the symptoms of ageing. There had been the incident of this morning, the memory of his mother, so vivid, so uncomfortable. Otherwise, he thought, age had spared him most of its indignities. He tired easily, but he could always rest. That was one of the blessings, he supposed: age bestowing the time to rest, along with the aching bones and the suddenly drooping eyelids. He found that talk tired him more than activity: this morning's walk, for example, had merely left him with a rather pleasant desire to sit and listen to some music, whereas this girl's presence irritated him to the point of madness. In fact he could hardly bear to pay her any attention, seated as she was in that immodest manner in Louise's chair, and apparently prepared to stay until she judged that he had listened with due care to her propositions.

'I know nothing about business,' he said shortly. This was not quite true; he knew how organisations worked, but thought that this knowledge was hardly relevant to the matter in hand. 'And I doubt if you know much either.'

'I don't,' she replied. 'But that's exactly what I'm looking for, don't you see? After all, I'm the potential, aren't I? I'd be the investment. It's sponsorship I need. I'll supply the expertise. Don't you worry about that!'

'And what expertise would that be?'

'Anything you care to mention! Aromatherapy. Aerobics . . .'

'My dear girl, we are in the middle of a recession. You can't honestly believe that this is going to catch on . . .'

'Of course it is! Health is very big news! How many people do you know with a personal fitness trainer?'

'Not one,' he said.

'Well, I know six or seven,' she finished triumphantly.

'All friends of mine, all young people, men as well as women.'

'You mean they pay good money to be exercised, when they could just as easily go for a brisk walk on their own? For free?'

'I'm afraid you just don't understand the modern ethos, George. One gets at the mind through the body.'

'I dare say little has changed in that respect.'

'Yes, but now there's much more stress,' she persisted. 'These days you have to call in the experts if you want to keep out of the hands of the doctors, and all those filthy drugs they pump into you.'

'Actually, doctors don't do that.'

'Oh, come on, George. Everyone knows what harm modern medicine can do.'

'I never heard of any. But this is a silly argument. What you want to do, if I can get this clear, is educate the mind through the body. Or shouldn't it be the other way round?'

'They work in harmony, of course,' she said pityingly, as if dealing with a lesser intelligence. 'That's what I want to do, yes.'

'Well, I can't understand why you need my advice.'

'I need premises,' she said. 'I need a place where people can come. Well situated, of course. A flat would be ideal. How much would one like this cost?'

'More than you could afford. More than I could afford now. You surely weren't thinking . . . ? No, I'm sure you weren't. In any case what money I have is all tied up.' This was relatively true. 'I believe there are certain government schemes, training schemes, and so on. There may even be grants. Although I doubt if you'd be considered a high priority.'

Indeed, never had she seemed a lower priority than she did now. Her face had fallen. She had not been excessively friendly when she presented herself after Louise's departure: the mere fact of Louise had activated her reserve of anger. He was ashamed to note that he felt quite frightened of her. She was all blind will, it seemed, and not particularly discerning. Her needs were taken to be obvious: she implied that she had no time to waste on pleasantries or even on preliminaries. Like all those who look to others to fulfil their requirements, however absurd, however outrageous, she was disproportionately annoyed when such help was not forthcoming. And she possessed several useful techniques, including a drawling distaste for anyone who disappointed her, and an ability to take offence at an unsuspecting criticism. Those who were lured into thinking that she was at home with the truth could find themselves excommunicated from her presence by virtue of an unpopular opinion. Friendship could turn to enmity, and no doubt already had; he wondered, for example, whether she and Sharon Dunlop were currently on speaking terms. It appeared to be up to him (or down to him, as she would no doubt say) to sort this out, just as it appeared to be his business to extract some grain of truth from her increasingly blithe remarks.

However, as always, his sense of pity was aroused. And also his sense of shame, for it seemed to him that his remarks had been too harsh, or rather that she was not constituted to face the truth, preferring always a cloudier version of events, and a solipsistic one. He may have seemed brusque, peremptory, for how else to account for her downcast features, her sudden withdrawn sulkiness. The interview had started badly, he realised, because she had seen Louise leaving the flat. But why should Louise not have visited him, and what right had this girl to be displeased? She was jealous, but he thought that she did not like him. It was not affection that inspired her jealousy: it was a global resentment that included both himself and Louise. It was in fact a mystery to him that she had no affections. He had never seen her so clearly: a waif, a victim, but the kind of victim that criminals are said to be by kindly probation officers, who will look into their backgrounds and produce a culprit in the form of anyone who may have exerted a bad influence in the past. He realised that he was dealing here with a special case, and that he would do well to tread carefully. He had no doubt that she possessed weapons superior to his own. And he had no idea when she would decide to use them.

Now, however, she was merely morose. But she cannot have believed that I would simply hand over a sum of money, he thought. At any other time he would have felt aghast, indignant. Now, once again, in that moment of having his worst fears confirmed, he felt sorry for her. He had taken away her last hope, illusory though it had been. Her hopes were not his responsibility, he reminded himself. Nevertheless, he had been instrumental in disappointing them. She might even now be wondering why Howard Singer's creed had so woefully let her down. She had told him how great she was (but had omitted to tell him how great he was), and nothing had happened. Nobody had believed her. Perhaps nobody ever had.

He studied her, in her would-be seductive pose. Now that both the anger and the pity had been registered he was able to ignore them both. He saw her hand go up and pull gingerly at the sore on her mouth.

'Did you have any lunch?' he asked.

'A tin of sardines.'

'I thought you people believed in a healthy diet. Fresh fruit and vegetables, and so on. There's a perfectly good shop downstairs.'

He suddenly thought, but that is what the rich say to the poor. What is happening to me? Why this desire to protect her? She is quite unworthy. All at once, seeing her sitting there, obstinate and defenceless, he felt a pang of something quite unfamiliar, quite expansive, quite inconvenient. He felt a lightness, a sense of empowerment; the past seemed to him constricted, constrained, his years of work merely unenterprising. It was not quite a moment of illumination, but it nearly resembled a transformation of some kind. He wanted to study the girl further, to keep her near him, to see if there were any worth under the nonsense, to get to know her true nature. It seemed important to him to make her grateful, even to make her smile. At that moment it seemed to him imperative not to disappoint her.

'How would you like to spend Christmas in Rome?' he said.

8

The idea that he might be approaching some new and strange experience excited and alarmed him. The effect was to keep him in his chair, long after she had gone, eyes wide with surprise. To begin with he attempted to suppress the idea that he was fascinated by her, as if it could be dismissed by an effort of will. It would mean the end of everything, the end of George Bland whom everybody knew and accepted without much thought. But perhaps that was the pity of the thing, he reflected. He was not loved, not particularly valued. Perhaps Louise loved and valued him, but Louise would have to go if he married Katy. The possibility was enough to envelop him in a scalding blush. For he might marry her, he thought: that would solve her problems if not his. From this new and admittedly shaky vantage point he saw himself as a man who had always been in favour of marriage. He would no doubt, he thought, have married Louise had she not deserted him and married Denis Arnold.

This reasoning at last proved untenable, and some part of his lucidity reasserted itself. Marriage instantaneously became out of the question. In any event he doubted whether Katy would even consider it. He was a man of sixty-five and she was a woman in her thirties. She would, in her words, consider marriage to a man such as himself incredibly naff. He was made of conventional material: that was all there was to it. But he reserved enough judgment to see the affair for what it was, and for what it would be. Her obvious immaturity he was inclined to view with some indulgence. Besides, he credited her with a great deal of primitive common sense. She had, after all, engineered the strange situation in which he was apparently imprisoned.

After half an hour he abandoned the idea of marriage, embarrassed for having even considered it. Reason told him that he could not expect her to be faithful to him. It did not matter: her attraction for him was not physical, and he doubted whether he would ever make love to her. Truth to tell, he did not see her body as having any power over him. She was of another generation, and thereby removed from his expectations. These days he was relieved that there was no one to witness his own physical changes: the spreading calloused feet, the slightly bent shoulders, the irrelevant penis. He could no more think of undressing in front of her than he could of exhibiting his gracelessness in public. For she would not be kind.

What really tempted him – and he was surprised by the force of this temptation – was the idea of jettisoning his careful tedious life and of surrendering to the idea of venality, vulgarity. The descent might prove irresistible; certainly the idea was proving companionable. And it was as an idea that he welcomed it, for he knew that it was mind and not body that was thus engaged. He would take a perverse joy in letting her ruin him, or perhaps not quite ruin him, for it would be his pleasure to tempt her and tease her, to withhold his favours while she fretted and sulked and pitted her wits against his. For he would win. And it would be entirely within his gift to gratify her, all the time amusing himself with her stratagems. He saw their association in terms of wicked joy for himself, of pleasurable reward for her. At the same time, by deploying his own stratagems, he would be keeping in check those more painful feelings that he had for her, the pity and the sadness which he could not obliterate. The pity was for her, the sadness for himself. He hardly knew where these feelings came from, yet somehow, in the midst of this strangeness, they continued to keep him company.

She was a lost girl: that he knew without a doubt. So alien was her past that he could not even see into it, beyond his own wayward imaginings. He could only suspect the abused or at best neglected childhood, for she did not have the sunny assurance of one who had been loved. Happy families, he thought, tended to infantilise their offspring, sometimes for life, whereas she had a shrewdness that spoke volumes. Of her later life, the life beyond the army camp in Germany which he had envisaged for her, he had no idea. Possibly a further posting with the father whom he saw as irate; Cyprus, perhaps, or Aden. At some point she would have left home, never to return. She would have gravitated to the city, have made contact with those she spoke of as her friends, although they were not much in evidence, and at some point got to know Sharon Dunlop, then Sheila Robinson, and moved into the flat in Muswell Hill. There would have been boyfriends, lovers, many affairs; he had no illusions on that score. It was no doubt in the wake of some unhappy experience that she had gone to America, and, as luck or ingenuity would have it, had fallen in with Howard Singer. He was beginning to feel grateful towards this man, whom he hated so intimately: at least she would have found a semblance of human warmth in his coterie or coven, and perhaps have earned enough to remain solvent, though on present evidence that seemed unlikely. If she were as destitute as he supposed her to be then his affair was well aspected: he would represent her last hope.

The apparent ease of the thing repelled him, but that,

he told himself, was because he was unused to this sort of satanic planning. He felt torn between the man he had always been and the more adult version of himself that he was planning to be. It was time to join the real world. His past life now seemed drained of colour, as if an automaton had performed those duties in which, until recently, he had taken such a pride. Those days at the office, so comforting because so familiar, so unsurprising, now appeared to him to be ludicrous, almost grotesque. He had been a man in the prime of life, and he had subjected that manhood to an anaesthetic of routine and small indulgences. Even the one love affair of his life was in some ways the equivalent of the office, a safe haven, something – ah, that was it – which brought retirement as its natural conclusion.

And now that he was officially retired, retired in the eyes of the world, he would be expected to take his leave with the same discretion. Those who had known him would soon forget him. There would be no malice in this: he had reached the age of separations, when generous curiosity is replaced by self-absorption. It would be assumed that he had remained the same as he had always been. And in a sense this was true, for he had never, until now, claimed any part of the world for himself, never acted out of character, never committed a folly, never unexpectedly disappeared . . .

And now he planned to disappear, and the plan was to be entirely his own. It had come to him without warning, when he was thinking of other matters, in particular the routine simple matter of Christmas hospitality. Maybe the prospect of this had been the unconscious spur to his change of mind and heart. Mind rather than heart, he assured himself: yes, definitely mind. The whole thing had the attraction of a logical process, except that the logic was Mephistophelian. The beauty of the plan was that each would think he had the best of the bargain. As for the forfeit, that would no doubt fall due eventually. The prospect did not alarm him, perhaps because he had reached an age when debts are called in, when one surrenders bodily vigour to the inexorable demands of time. Time gave one an initial endowment which it then progressively cancelled, and Time's ally, Nature, equally progressively imposed humiliations. It would not be the same for her: she would become impatient, rebellious even. It would then be his pleasure to tempt her back into a good humour, to devise for them both some exquisite diversion. For he could afford it, a reflection which somehow brought no gaiety. Nevertheless his money would enable him to retain control of the situation, for his mind, which would be so pleasantly exercised, would not lose sight of this important advantage. It would, in a sense, be an intellectual diversion for him, one in which he was assured of the upper hand.

And yet, at this point in his reasoning, the old vulnerable sadness stole over him, and he was forced to admit to himself that part of him loved her, and that what he loved was that unprotected untutored anticipation in her that corresponded to the infinite longing which he knew himself to possess. It hardly mattered that her anticipation was for an illusory material success, whereas his was for some aspect of life which he hardly knew, not satisfaction so much as an emotional gratification which he had thought, somehow, always, to be out of his reach. It would be a way of cancelling at last that childhood self which so obstinately persisted, for there would be no opportunity for childishness in the life that he was currently devising. He would live on his wits, quite as much as she would.

He saw himself on the balcony of a foreign hotel, in a lightweight suit, waiting for her to return from her morning's shopping. They would travel widely, constantly, never staying for long in any one place, for they would be an ambiguous couple. He would make no attempt to conceal his age, would no longer raise a tired smile when porter or concierge referred to her as his daughter. She would deceive him, of course, but that would hardly matter. The pain of the thing would spring from an incompatibility which his mind alone could not overcome, so that at the end he would be uncomforted, an old man in a lonely bed, not because she had a young lover – that he could accept – but because the sadness had become impervious to whatever release she could offer. She would ultimately represent frustration because their separate disappointments had failed to annul one another, and each would be returned to a solipsism even more dangerous than the solipsism that had gone before.

He thought too that he loved her for her silent scowling face, the face of an unhappy child, and of a powerless one. She did not always show that face, but it persisted behind the seductive smiles with which she had favoured him from time to time. She had shown him that face at their first meeting; she had shown that face to Louise, who had subsequently pronounced her to be rather tiresome, a mild form of condemnation entirely in keeping with the mildness of Louise's character. Katy, he thought, would be a formidable enemy to another woman. He wondered about her mother, who had left so little feeling behind. Not a strong character, he supposed, dismissed by the child, who favoured the irascible and seductive father. Thus, even at a young age, she would have set out to flatter and to placate. It was clear that she had not succeeded. There was an aura of failure about her which did not deceive him. For a woman in her thirties (for it seemed to him now that she must be all of thirty-five) to dress like an adolescent and to have no home was surely evidence of a curious formation. He was fascinated by her failure, which he felt as though it were his own, and he longed to protect her from further knowledge of it, just as he hoped to exchange his own vulnerability for something harder and less costly.

He would take her abroad, he thought: indeed, he would have to. He could hardly imagine them living in his flat, although that was what she wanted. He knew very well that she planned to turn his sitting-room into some sort of treatment area; he could see his furniture receiving the libations of her essential oils. No doubt, in his dotage, he would be given a white jacket and put on duty at the door. That was what she wanted. Whereas he proposed to give her another life altogether, and which she would accept, but perhaps restively. They would travel, live elsewhere, a perpetual elsewhere. He saw, from his imaginary balcony, a red sun sinking over palm trees, and realised that this was an image which had confronted him during his recent sojourn in Nice. Such a little while ago! He looked round the room with a start: had it always been so dark? The lamps seemed weak and dim against the encroaching blackness outside the windows. In a moment of panic and exaltation he thought that he would be pleased to leave all this behind. They would follow the sun, perhaps never coming home. They would, in effect, have no home, apart from the temporary homes offered to all rich travellers. And having no home they would have no responsibility, and thus gain a kind of freedom. He could offer her freedom if nothing else, although he did not think that freedom was what she wanted. What she wanted was her own way, and satisfaction for her blind frustrated will. She would not find it, any more than he would. But perhaps it would take her a long time to find out, and perhaps by that time he would have learned how to let her go.

He realised with a start that it was very late. He had not eaten, nor did he want to eat. This surprised him: he normally had a healthy appetite. But the whole day had been surprising, starting with one set of reflections and

146

ending with another, surely the most inapposite he had ever entertained. Through them all ran a connecting thread, if only he could understand it. On the verge of his new life he was surprised by regret. He urged himself forward out of his chair, stumbling slightly with cramp, and poured himself a glass of whisky. He drank it standing at the window, gazing at the lights opposite. When he had first come to London he had fantasised about the happy families behind the lighted windows; on summer evenings he had strolled through squares and terraces, casting wistful looks into basement kitchens. On those occasions a curtain drawn against prying eyes had felt like a snub. He was past all that now, he told himself; he was beyond envy. Perhaps his own rise to security had blunted the eagerness with which he had sought images of happiness. He had done without them now for a very long time, but perhaps that time was past. Now he would have to do his best in a completely uncertain world, and he needed more whisky to ease his passage. For a difficult moment he was almost ready to turn back.

For this was not the pilgrimage for which his early readings had prepared him. This was not a venture undertaken in innocence. He was behaving like the lewd greybeards in Tintoretto's *Susannah and the Elders* which he had seen in Vienna. Susannah, with braided hair and pearl earrings, sits plumply in the foreground, while the sneaking elders, in the grave robes of seniority, peer from behind a convenient palisade. But in this instance there was no victim either. This perplexed him: he had detected a logical flaw in the proceedings. If he could not deceive himself as to either his motives or hers, did this not argue a cynicism with which he was unfamiliar? He would have to rely on his own restlessness, his own small rebellion against decorum, and – more reliable, this – his own desire to possess some of that life of which he had for too long remained in prudish ignorance. He would turn his back on that life, he resolved, and poured himself more whisky. His muscles lost their tenseness, and for a moment innocence appeared as something one relinquished with childhood, with the notion that virtue was rewarded. Or should be. He was getting muddled now; it might have been a good idea to have eaten something. It was even too much of an effort to go to bed. It was very late when he eventually managed it, leaving his empty glass, unwashed, for Mrs Cardozo to exclaim over the following morning.

When he eventually surfaced from a sketchy vivid sleep he felt tentative, even frightened. But he was visited with a determination to go through with it. Something, however, prevented him from making his decision known to anyone. Besides, there was only Katy to whom the decision was relevant. He dressed carefully, aware of the cold on his shrinking flesh. His mild hangover seemed to have produced a semblance of physical decline, so that he viewed his body with more than usual distaste. Normally he accepted it without much question; it had seen him through life uncomplainingly and was still functioning in a manner which he found acceptable. He brushed the hair which still covered his scalp adequately, if not copiously, and examined his face in the bathroom mirror. He felt curious, as if he had never seen this face as an outsider might see it. It was, like the rest of him, unremarkable, though he now saw that the eyes wore a puzzled pleading expression. He hoped that this was not habitual. It was, he decided, a resigned face, and the idea that he might have gone through life looking resigned strengthened his determination to change his outlook to one of joyous determination, or at least of voluptuous brooding.

Dressed, he decided that he could still pass muster. He had not put on weight, and his slight stoop was only noticeable when he was very tired. He had always taken the trouble to look decent, and his clothes were in good order. He thought, however, that he might treat himself to some new shirts, perhaps a pullover or two. He might think about ordering a lightweight suit for that journey to the sun. The obligatory panama hat, which he thought might suit him rather well, could be left until later.

All at once his calculations fell away, and he thought of her simply, not seeing why he could not love her as any man might love any woman, or as a mature man might love a girl to whom he wished to extend his protection. The idea contained its own very different temptation, access to a world of sweetness, of shared company, of lifelong conversation, and other delights. The real triumph would be to pierce her carapace of worldliness and to convert her to the same simplicity as that which now flooded him with longing. He gazed out of the window into the cold winter sun, dazzled by this imaginary paradise. He felt it a tragedy that he could only approach it as an unbeliever, an infidel. In a moment or two his ineradicable lucidity told him that Katy was not a candidate for this sort of transformation. She was too earthbound, too greedy. He remembered how her face could be transformed by greed. He would have to rely on that greed if he were ever to conquer her.

With a sigh he relinquished his vision. It might have been the supreme emotional adventure. As it was, he would have to make do with the merest approximation, while she might not even have access to a transforming fantasy. She would remain rebarbative. He would always be on the verge of losing her. He would never know peace, never earn the right to relax in her company. Within a very short space of time she would cease to enjoy herself. She would never be grateful to him. All this he knew. Yet at the same time he knew a weird excitement at the thought of her captivity.

He left the flat, descended the stairs, and stepped out into the freezing air. A winter sun was just piercing the frost and fog; it was a fine winter's day, the sort of day on which he would normally have taken a long walk. How distant those humble promenades now seemed, how obsolete! They belonged to a life in which no greater pleasure could be expected. The passing of that life had now to be endured. His course was set on a different and more problematic path: satisfactions would not be guaranteed. The almost unbearable truth of his present situation faced him in all its simplicity. He was only incidentally planning for the future. What he was really doing was correcting the past, rewriting his own history. His life had taken him in a direction which had precluded him from reaching other destinations, and he had chosen that life, had willed it even, seeing it as safety, as a bulwark against anxious and chaotic thinking. Now he was in search of uncertainty, before it was too late and he was for ever imprisoned inside the fate he had once devised for himself.

He went into Trumper's and had his hair cut. 'Very sad about Mr Putnam, sir,' said the barber, who had known them both over many years. 'Yes, I find it difficult to come to terms with his death,' he said. He dared hardly think of Putnam's reaction to his present behaviour. But the sun through the window was now strong, and the lotion being patted into his skin smelled sweet, and he was in any case restless. He strolled in the sun to Jermyn Street and spent a not unpleasurable half-hour choosing shirts and looking at ties. He bought coffee at Fortnum's, contemplated lunch at the club, but felt a sudden desire to be at home. But of course, he had to be at home for when Katy called. He would be circumspect, he told himself: he would say nothing of the future. So far only the journey to Rome had been on offer. He would enjoy these moments of preparation, which would be entirely his own. Besides, it would be more elegant to say little: he had his own performance to consider. He bought cheese and bread, salad and fruit. He was aware that he had eaten very little on the previous day, but was too impatient to linger. He caught a cab outside the shop, and was home in fifteen minutes.

He plunged into the hallway of the building: in his imagination he could hear his doorbell ringing. It seemed imperative to reach the flat before she turned away. He was briefly aware of a navy blue figure conversing with Hipwood.

'Good morning, George,' said Mrs Lydiard. 'My word, you are in a hurry.'

'Why, good morning,' he replied, with an air of great surprise, not entirely assumed. 'How are you? Nice to see you. I am in rather a hurry, I'm afraid.'

'I was just telling Mr Hipwood that at least some of us won't be deserting him over the holiday. I am staying put this year. And what about you, George? Any plans?'

'I shall probably be away myself,' he said. 'But I'll certainly be in touch before I go. Perhaps we could meet. Now, if you'll excuse me . . .'

'Any news of our young friend?' said Mrs Lydiard, with a smile. 'I was just saying to Mr Hipwood that the Dunlops should soon be back. Then I expect she'll be moving on, won't she?'

Bland realised that Mrs Lydiard felt an antipathy towards the girl, perhaps merely the antipathy of an older woman for a younger one. All at once he felt an antipathy towards Mrs Lydiard, with her thin-lipped smile from which all trace of good humour had departed.

'I have no idea what her plans are,' he said.

'Have you seen her recently?' she asked, too artlessly.

'Not very recently, no.'

Mrs Lydiard was too well-bred to raise an eyebrow. Nevertheless she managed to convey the impression that she knew what was going on. Behind his desk Hipwood listened impassively.

'Don't be *too* kind, George,' she said. 'Don't let your good nature get the better of you.'

'I don't think it's likely to do that,' he said, jovially. 'Any letters, Hipwood?' Immediately he cursed himself for this crucial breach of etiquette. This was a misdemeanour which would not be forgotten. Only Colonel Crowther, from the top floor, was allowed to address Hipwood by his surname alone, and only because he had been a superior officer in the war. 'Of course, you weren't in the Forces, sir,' Hipwood was wont to remark, when Bland showed signs of not paying quite enough attention. He had always felt admonished, as was the intention. Hipwood was allowed these small incivilities, for reasons which had to do with his supposed surveillance of their welfare. For a quiet life it was wise to play the cards as he dealt them, or rather to agree with everything he said. Bland had always observed these rules. Now he had broken them, and felt appalled.

Mrs Lydiard registered the significance of this episode with an even broader smile. Information was not lacking, she implied, if one were quick-witted enough to receive it. Her disappointment at being excluded from such a promising little threesome, her frustration at not being made privy to a confession of reduced circumstances, on receipt of which she would royally have offered an extremely small token of her favour, changed to satisfaction. No one could call me a prude, said her expression, but I am not a fool either. But then I am not a man. The smile now held a suggestion of moral superiority. Unable to face this, and the fiasco of the whole encounter, the ruin of his relationship with Hipwood, his unmasking by Mrs Lydiard, he chose flight.

'Do excuse me,' he said. 'Some rather urgent business.' Sweating slightly, encumbered by his packages, he was aware that he had cut an unheroic figure. The shape of things to come, he told himself.

He stowed his purchases in his bedroom without unpacking them: he had lost interest in them. Now it was necessary not only to eat, but to have eaten, so that he could clear away all evidence of domesticity and present an agreeable and worldly façade to his visitor – for he did not doubt that he would see her that day. He cracked two eggs and slid them into the pan, contemplated making a salad and dismissed the idea. He ate hastily and carelessly, registering the fact that he was behaving out of character: normally fastidious, he was now febrile. Seated at last in his chair he felt momentarily triumphant, as if the morning had constituted a huge obstacle course which he had managed, against the odds, to overcome. So exhausting were his thoughts that he could no longer exactly determine to which point they had led him. Somewhere in the distance, from the floor above him, no doubt, he could hear the theme music from the afternoon repeat of *The Archers*. If it were not yet two o'clock, he reckoned, he might allow himself a brief nap. Sleep would expunge his confusion. Afterwards he would be calm, with just that air of amused tolerance which would become him in the afternoon's encounter, an encounter on which he depended to advance his plans.

He came to with a jolt, and with a feeling of panic. The room was dark: he must have slept for more than an hour. He looked at his watch and saw that it was nearly four, and that he had slept for nearly two hours, a sleep so profound that he was bewildered, not knowing what had caused it. He took this to be a sign of age, this sudden and unheralded descent into unconsciousness, and this flustered waking. He got to his feet and stumbled slightly: the ache in his calves was more pronounced today, and he thought of torn ligaments, which would effectively immobilise him, or even a thrombosis, no doubt to be expected. Would she care for him in his infirmity? He thought not: she would gleefully see the occasion as one she could turn to her own advantage and would make her escape, safe in the knowledge that he could not pursue her. Now more than ever it seemed to him imperative to exert some influence, before time could damage him more than it already had done. He felt lost, unequal to the inevitable struggle for dominance. For a moment he would have abandoned the whole plan had he not been faced with the immense problem of how to live his life without her. He felt cold, and wondered whether he had caught a chill. Then he realised that the room was cold. He hobbled over to the radiators and felt them: lukewarm. Normally he would have called Hipwood on the internal telephone and asked him to investigate, but his recent lapse seemed to have precluded that possibility. He switched on several lamps, hoping to create an illusion of warmth. He hoped that the air of discreet luxury, rather than the substance of it, might disarm his visitor. He himself was resigned to discomfort until he was safe in bed, as he momentarily longed to be.

Her presence was necessary to displace his anxiety, and also a faint sensation of horror that he had moved so far from his normal moral position. He was a mild man (too mild, he thought), a moderate man, one who observed the courtesies of that undemanding life which he had once so treasured. Now he was attempting recklessness, and the attempt disturbed him. But recklessness has its own momentum, and he could no longer see his way out of it. Besides, it toned him up, he thought, thinking of his agreeable morning, and ignoring his recent sleep. In fact it was necessary to ignore this if he were to regard himself as capable of any kind of enterprise, especially one which comported distance, and constant travel, and an amused forbearance. He banished the thought of how he must have appeared, and would appear, to an unfriendly eye, his hair dishevelled, his body slack, his mouth open. Extreme vigilance would be the price of his hoped-for liberty. Yet part of him knew that age and tiredness would claim him, for he had always been able to recognise the inevitable. But he could fight it, he thought. The image of Putnam, dying, in the ultimate disorder of physical dissolution, came to him, and he resolved, once again, not to wait for that dissolution, which would surely come, but to enjoy what life was vouchsafed to him until that moment. He would be able to foresee that moment, he thought, and if he still had the courage, and if he were not still enamoured of his life, he would take his pills and make an end. And truth to tell his death could be more efficiently handled by a hotel than if he were to attempt it in his flat, where he would be discovered by Mrs Cardozo. That was not to be envisaged. He had always enjoyed stories of stoic deaths, particularly of Socrates drinking his hemlock, while discoursing to his followers. Surely that was a death to be emulated. And might not such a vision strengthen him just when his body was becoming weaker, and when regard would no longer be paid? He saw himself, quite clearly, dying alone, having made his preparations. He would lie down one afternoon, thinking to take a nap, and all at once knowing that he could no longer sustain this immense adventure he had brought upon himself. He could see the sun, always the sun, sinking outside his window: he could see himself disposed in an orderly manner, upon a foreign bed. The vision made him lonely. But he supposed that death was always lonely; that was why people feared it so. Yet his death would not necessarily be lonelier than that of others. In any event there was no outwitting it. And he still had some remnants of decorum, although he seemed entirely to have lost his dignity.

He went into the bathroom and splashed his face with water, brushed his teeth, added a discreet drop of Eau Sauvage. The bathroom was colder than the rest of the flat. He thought perhaps that he needed a cup of tea: he could always make fresh when Katy turned up, as he did not doubt that she would. Indeed her presence now seemed not only inevitable but entirely natural. She would be in the flat, washing her hair, or painting her nails, and when she was sufficiently bored, or when she judged that it was time to return to the attack she would saunter across the landing and ring his bell. He was surprised that this had not already happened, yet glad that she had not seen him at his disgraceful worst. He made and drank two cups of tea, which warmed him slightly, then went back to the bathroom, and brushed his teeth again. He warned himself against displaying too much eagerness. The mirror showed his features contracted into a slight rictus. He concentrated his efforts on correcting this, smoothed his hair, patted more toilet water into the skin of his neck and the underside of his jaw, then sped to the kitchen to refill the kettle and prepare the tray. He wondered whether to ring the bell of the Dunlops' flat, but decided against it: it was important to keep the upper hand. But he could not stop himself from crossing the landing to listen for a sound, and when he heard none crept back to his flat in case he should be discovered. At last, unable to bear the suspense any longer he crossed the hall and rang her bell. The bell echoed into silence: no one came. He retreated once again, and sat in his own silence, faced with the unthinkable possibility that she might have left. At last, perhaps half an hour later, he heard her key turn in the lock of the Dunlops' door. He rushed into the hall, overwhelmed.

'Hallo, there,' he said, sounding, he thought, not too nervous. 'I was just making a cup of tea. Can I tempt you?'

She dropped the key in her bag, turned slowly, and surveyed him from a distance, as if she could not properly concentrate on his presence. She was wearing the orange suit and was fairly heavily made up. Her hieratic look was

156

in place, and he had no doubt that her speech would be disdainful. This was what he was up against, her gift of removal, of closure, as if she suspected him of unseemly curiosity, or as if he were someone whom she could hardly remember, someone whose interest in her life and her movements was quite out of place. She no longer sought his approval, no longer attempted to stimulate his curiosity. Some interval had taken place, some intrusion of an alien life into the life which he had flattered himself he knew so well. She seemed unwilling even to answer him, let alone to enter his flat. He thought it a pity that her actual words were so at variance with her appearance; had she remained silent she would have subjugated many a stronger man, and a younger man, than he had the good fortune to be.

He felt weak, excitable, as if his entire future rested on this one encounter, or the exchange that was bound to take place. He cautioned himself to stay silent, as silent as she was, but the urgency of the task was almost unbearable. He had, literally, to subdue another's will, something he had never done in his life. His entire *raison d'être* had been respect for others: never in his life had he acted on a rebellious impulse, never responded to criticism (though there had been little enough of that, or maybe he had been unaware of it), never attempted to enforce his own point of view, his own methods, his own beliefs. His life had been soft-spoken, and he supposed that this was the way in which he had become so dull. As a schemer he was untrained. All he had to go on was the extreme restlessness of his present state, which surely indicated that the time had come to be decisive. His desire to be urbane, amused, had evaporated. Somehow the power had passed from him. In that same instant he saw that she was the stronger.

In that split second he had time to admire her gleaming mouth, her suffused cheeks. She looked more adult, more her presumed age. She looked preoccupied, or rather as if something pleasurable had recently taken place. He felt her arm brush against him as he stood aside to let her enter, smelled her scent, which today was slightly altered by something earthier, as if she had been in the presence of someone smoking a cigar.

'You look as if you've been out,' he said jovially. 'Anywhere exciting?'

'Yes, well, I do go out occasionally,' she replied. She wandered round the room, lingering over his appointments, testing the weight of the curtains. Once again he felt a healthy touch of irritation. This would save him, he thought. At the same time he was extremely curious as to where she had been. It was proving more difficult than he had anticipated to attract her attention. While he fussed with the cups and saucers she stood with her back to him, gazing out of the window into the early dark.

'Do come and sit down, Katy. I'm afraid it's not very warm in here. Something's gone wrong with the heating.'

'I'm not cold,' she said absently.

He tried again. 'I rang your bell earlier. You must have been out for a good part of the day.'

'I went out to lunch,' she said.

'With your friends?'

'With *a* friend. This really nice guy I met. Someone who might be able to help me set up my business.'

His heart sank. 'How very fortunate,' he managed to say.

'Well, not exactly. He can't put up the money. But he can introduce me to some people who might be able to. The main thing is that he seemed to believe in what I want to do.'

'And you still want to do it?'

'Well, of course. How else am I going to look after myself? If it's set up correctly the place could be a gold-mine.'

He reflected that this was quite possibly true, and conceded that she was merely being sensible in contemplating her long-term security. Ah, but he was going to take care of that! Yet it seemed important not to unveil his plans for her all at once. In any event she seemed preoccupied, was not playing the part that he had written for her.

'The big problem is having to find premises,' she continued. 'When you work from home it's important to have a good address. I did think of going into partnership in a clinic, but now I realise it's a flat I want.' The remark hung in the air.

'Have you heard from the Dunlops?' he asked eventually.

'No. No, I haven't. Why, should I have?'

'I rather thought they might be on their way home.'

'Nothing to do with me.'

He stared at her. 'But you're still in the flat! How are you going to explain . . . ?'

'I don't have to explain anything, do I? I should have thought you were the one who had to do the explaining.'

'Why?'

'Well, after all, you gave me the keys, didn't you? I couldn't have got in without them, could I?'

Thunderstruck, he gazed into her pleasant smile. She was sure of herself today, having undergone one of her lightning transformations. The tones were normal, friendly, above all reasonable. There was no hint of effort.

'You mean, they don't know you're here? That you didn't see them in New York?'

'I might have done.' She wandered over to the bookshelves, pulled out a couple of volumes, and stood leafing through them. Immediately he realised that if the Dunlops had consented to her staying they would have contacted him, at least left a message on his machine. He was utterly, crassly, at fault. How to explain to the Dunlops? But any explanation would be worthless. The important thing was to get away as soon as possible, and to take her with him.

'What do you do with yourself all day, George?' she queried, removing books from the shelves and replacing them rather carelessly.

His eyes on what she was doing, he replied automatically, 'I read a lot.'

'Here?'

'Here or in the study.'

She turned to him and smiled broadly. '*What* a lot of wasted space,' she said. 'Well, I must be going. Thank you for tea.' Her tone now was mildly condescending.

He could not help it. 'Have you thought about my suggestion?' he asked.

'What suggestion was that?'

'Rome. For Christmas.'

'Well, that rather depends.'

'Depends on what?'

'On whether I can get my business set up first. Whether I can find a base, and start planning.'

She circled the room once more, looking about her with a speculative air. Leisurely steps took her to the door. With a swirl of orange skirt she turned to face him, and lifted up her hand in a mock salute.

'Byee,' she said.

After she had gone, leaving the smell of her scent in the now freezing room, he sat down dumbly, trying to think of what he would say to the Dunlops. They would never forgive him, of course. He would have to move. He felt the creeping sadness again, as he contemplated being forced out of his home. It was against his nature to abandon anything. He could perhaps face this if he were not alone. And there was still a chance, he told himself. For although she would take everything and give nothing, he still had the upper hand.

Some time in the night he awoke from a dream in

which he had lost a set of keys and was locked out of his flat. I lack company, he thought, and saw Putnam's face, as it had looked on the day before he died. What am I doing? The question was so unanswerable that he broached his secret store of pills, took two, and lay rigid, waiting for sleep, which eventually came, heavily, at dawn. For the first time in weeks the reassuring tones of the shipping forecast fell on deaf ears.

9

He waited for her now with joy and pain. For two days
there was no sight of her, nor did he hear her go out and
come in. It occurred to him to wonder what she did with
her time, since she had so little to occupy her, and no
picture presented itself to him other than that of totally
absorbed preoccupation. He had thought that women no
longer lived like this: according to the propaganda they
were all juggling at least two jobs, while effortlessly
satisfying their husbands at the same time. Whereas Katy
seemed to do nothing except wash her hair and paint her
nails, like an old-fashioned courtesan. He supposed that
one should include her intense scheming as something of
a professional attribute: he did not discount this, but rather
respected it, since his own projects involved a certain
amount of concentration, and events had proved to him
how extremely tiring such concentration could prove to
be. Behind his door he listened hard, not quite having the
courage to ring her bell. What he wanted, what he most
imperatively desired, was for her to come to him, in a
spirit of submission, just as in that proposed flight to
Rome the details hardly mattered. Only her assent was
important. He realised, hazily, that Christmas was nearly
upon them, and that he might have difficulty in booking
a flight. That hardly mattered either. The whole enterprise

was to partake of magic: he would appropriate a plane and an empty hotel, his will alone achieving the impossible. And if not Rome, somewhere else would do. All that mattered was his overwhelming wish, and her acquiescence.

He slept badly, waking several times in the night. He heard the news at two a.m. and again at four. One night, on perhaps the third day of her absence, he heard steps on the stairs, and thought that the Dunlops had returned. This prospect so horrified him that he got out of bed and crept to the door. He heard the voices of a man and a woman, but could not distinguish what was being said: there was a sound of laughter, which was abruptly hushed, and a certain amount of fumbling with the key. If the Dunlops had in fact returned they appeared to have got slightly drunk on the plane, in which case they might be expected to come to their senses the following morning and discover that they were not alone in the flat. He foresaw an altercation, a banishment, in which case he would be more than ready to shelter the intruder, although that was not in his plan.

It was only later, when the night was nearly over, that the more likely truth of the matter was revealed to him. Her air of triumph, of condescension, her reappearance in the orange suit when she had last visited him, were almost certainly due to contact with a man. 'A friend', she had said, as women did when it was necessary to dissimulate; in due course 'a friend' became 'my friend', before ending up as 'my partner'. He had always found this irritating; now, in retrospect, he found it unappealing, arguing as it somehow did an appropriation of the hapless male by the female, something his generation could accept only in fiction, and then with suspicion.

Her recent high-handedness, and the noises on the stairs, could, he realised, have only one explanation. A sexual encounter was taking place in the Dunlops' flat, while he himself, technically chaste but prey to fantasies, lingered just behind the door. The symbolism of this did not escape him. Indeed, he discounted it, as being too obvious. Artists had painted it, writers had described it. What he registered now was not the excitement which would have overtaken a younger man but a wistfulness, as if life were a dream, as if bodies, subject to mortality, were obliged to take their satisfaction when and where they could, and as if they were participating in a macabre ceremony which did not seem to have evolved at the same speed as the higher consciousness.

Mere sex seemed to him pathetic in these circumstances, and here the circumstances did not appear to be particularly propitious: hushed laughter, stumbling footsteps, clandestinity. Such encounters belonged to another age, to Louise and himself when young; he could no more claim them now than enact them himself. Any jealousy he felt was for youth, Katy's youth, and that of her supposed partner, and he knew that there was no cure for this. Desire afflicted the old mainly as longing. It was no longer even suitable to dwell on such matters. Sexual speculation, unattractive at any age, was particularly obnoxious when allied to grey hair and waning energy. He crept back to bed, enveloping Katy, her partner, and himself, in the same weary distaste, which nevertheless held at its heart a seed of bewilderment that time had gone so quickly, leaving his own days of vigour so far behind.

After a wakeful half hour he no longer questioned this. He had never desired her physically, he told himself, had wanted only to hold one slim foot in his hand. Nor did his flesh rise at the idea that she might at that moment be making love to someone else. Strangely, she did not excite him. His fantasies concerned only himself, his breaking free, his forthcoming scandalous liberty, denied him all his life. She would be his essential companion by virtue of the fact that he had fashioned her for his wishes, in return for which she would be allowed a freedom of her own. There was no cruelty in this fantasy, or perhaps just a little: there would be no physical damage, no undue influence. There would be no point in forbidding her to take lovers, for she would take them in any case. The lure was not cruelty, but selfishness.

What drew him on, although he was beginning to suspect that he was half mad, was the idea of anarchic self-indulgence after years of duties fulfilled and obligations attended to, an attempt to cancel the obedience of both his personal and his professional lives. He had always been noted for his unfailing sympathy, his consideration for others, but these qualities were not instinctive. They had been acquired at the cost of freedom, of boldness, of true individuality. And all he had to show for these qualities, and for his own laborious efforts, was the money which now waited in the bank until it was time to go to Louise and all the sick children who figured in his will. He would endure until the time came to take his pills, for he did not doubt that it would end in this fashion, much sooner than even he anticipated, if he did not, for once, enact his own desires, all the more imperative an exercise since he was so tardy in recognising them.

The rapidity with which he had succumbed to this particular enchantment seemed to him a proof of its validity. That a man should seek his own freedom seemed to him the most moral as well as the most natural thing in the world. And he had so far experienced only a premonitory glow, the sudden liberating heedlessness that had overtaken him in Bond Street, together with his conviction that his destiny had been revealed to him. In due course he might finally know that euphoric moment which would justify his entire uneventful existence. If this were not quite the happy ending he had been promised, so long ago, it would at least signify a primitive freedom, a moment in the sun, both actual and metaphorical. This moment would be brief: perhaps it could only ever be brief, a subjective illumination that could not outlast more mundane concerns. Those concerns would indeed be mundane, an adroit mixture of cynicism and forbearance, as he sought to indulge and to contain her extravagances. And for this, he thought, he was willing to surrender his lifelong prudence, to discard it as rapidly as a child discards a broken toy, and to begin again, in a far distant place, away from the petty censorship of those who had known him only as a good friend and a model employee. And even if it were madness he would see it through. The pills would be there at the end, however well or badly he chose to live his life.

Compared with the miraculous condition to which he aspired, what did it matter if Katy took a lover, ten lovers, a score of lovers? He would have done the same at her age, had he possessed his present insouciance. As it was, the great enlightenment, the great transformation to which he was progressing, was immeasurably superior in every way to whatever physical tremors she sought and encouraged. With an imaginary future sun in his eyes he could ignore the steps going down the stairs, as he was making an early cup of tea, and the closing of the door, and the sound of the chain being replaced. He would of course never mention this incident, and neither would she, yet each would know that the other knew of it: there might be a certain impudence on her part, a moment of gravity on his, but that was part of the bargain, and he would not be the one to break it. In a sense it would be all concealment from that moment on, all watching and waiting. Yet he felt he had the strength to endure this, for as long as she remained connected to him in the way he had devised.

On the fourth morning life, or a remnant of it, called him outside. The foggy air was not much colder than the air in the flat, for the heating had mysteriously ceased to function. People in the streets seemed to be in a state of abnormal effervescence, pushing wheeled baskets piled high with bags from Selfridges and Marks and Spencer. One woman, with two small children in tow, laughed hysterically as a paper bag containing tangerines collapsed at his feet: gravely he collected the fruit as they rolled towards the gutter and handed them back to her. His expression must have seemed peculiarly withdrawn, for the children, a boy and a girl, nudged each other and giggled, until reprimanded by their mother.

'It's the excitement,' she said, apologetically. 'Off school all day, and they think I've nothing to do but spend money. Oh, well. Wish the gentleman a Merry Christmas, children.'

'Why?' he said, startled. 'What is the date?'

This set them off again. 'December the eighteenth,' she replied. 'Just one week to go.'

This sobered him. He said goodbye, and addressed himself to the business of buying food. He had not been eating much, and only that morning the waistband of his trousers had seemed loose. He turned automatically in the direction of Marylebone High Street and a café he knew there: with breakfast inside him he would be in a better state. The street was busy with shoppers, the shops themselves filled with abundant produce. The contrast between these riches and his own spiritual poverty struck him as ironic. He suspected that he was perhaps not in the best of health, not quite as collected as he would have wished to be. His new Nietzschean consciousness wavered slightly, and for a split second he was willing to call the whole thing off. But this, he knew, was temporary. As soon as he saw her, attempting, as always, to gain her undivided attention, he would be totally absorbed in the exercise. For it was an exercise now, and he did not care to fail.

He was back in Kendal Street by a quarter to ten. In the hallway of the building Hipwood was decorating a discreet Christmas tree. Bland was thankful that he was occupied: he was not quite sure how to repair his recent lapse. All these matters must be resolved, but perhaps not quite yet, on the morning of his departure, perhaps, when money could be handed over and farewells exchanged. He had just made it to the lift, behind Hipwood's back, when he was called to order.

'Your letters, sir,' said Hipwood. 'Late again. New man on the job. Well, I say man, more of a boy, really, with one of those fancy haircuts, if you follow me. Cost a bomb, they do. Still, that's modern youth, isn't it? Three for you, sir, and I had to sign for this one.'

'Very kind, Mr Hipwood. Do I owe you anything?'

'Perhaps you might give this to the young lady,' said Hipwood pleasantly. 'Since you're more likely to see her than I am.'

Bland reckoned that this placed them once more on an equal footing. Hipwood, however, could not resist pressing his advantage.

'Bit of a mystery, don't you think, sir? You'd have thought she'd introduce herself, wouldn't you? And yet before this letter came I didn't even know her name.'

'Gibb,' he said shortly. 'Miss Gibb.'

'Well, not quite, sir. It appears she's a married woman. Bit of a mystery all round, wouldn't you say?'

He turned triumphantly back to his tree. Bland glanced at the envelope, which was addressed to Mrs Kathleen Palmer-Harris, c/o Dunlop. The handwriting was small and difficult, as if the sender were afflicted with cramp, or in the grip of some terrible mental torment. Bland favoured the latter. There was something costive and effortful about the formation of the letters: studying them gave him some sort of respite from the creeping realisation that Katy's life was more crowded than he had recently supposed. Unless 'Palmer-Harris' was another subterfuge, a *nom de guerre* adopted for reasons he could not fathom, although he would be surprised if they were completely straightforward. He was obliged to exercise his brain on every facet of her life, an exercise which gave him no small pleasure. The aristocratic surname was in character, all of a piece with her intermittently high-handed locutions, so disconcertingly introduced when they were least expected, and always, unfailingly, denoting anger.

As for Mr Palmer-Harris, if he existed, Bland imagined him to be a minor personage in this particular drama, a mere spear-carrier. Katy was no more married than he was. Her whole demeanour was that of a huntress, a *fauve*, literally taking her food and her sustenance from others. In all the time he had known her (three and a half weeks, he thought with a pang) she had not eaten a single meal at her own expense. Rather than shop and cook as others did she preferred not to eat at all, until a suitable invitation came along. On that first evening in the restaurant he had thought it curious that she had chosen the most expensive items on the menu: now he understood. The food had to be rich, excessively calorific, so that if necessary two days could be spent digesting it. And then, with a little luck, there would be another restaurant, and another, similar meal. He marvelled once again at her resilience.

In the same way she imposed herself on her friends, moving into their flats and houses whether it were convenient or not. Because she was personable, or perhaps plausible would be a more accurate description, she would always be initially welcome: she could offer gossip, information, the all-purpose enthusiasm of the encounter group. Only her short attention span would let her down. He was willing to bet that, with the exception of Howard Singer's set-up, she had never stayed anywhere for as long as she had been in the Dunlops' flat. How would she greet them when they returned? Perhaps this was not in her plan. Perhaps she had seen in him a last chance, just as he had seen the same thing in her. In which case, he thought, we are probably both mistaken, but because we have no choice we will make do with one another. And perhaps we are both clever enough to get away with it.

Mrs Palmer-Harris, indeed. Undoubtedly a *nom de guerre*. The Kathleen part of it he believed. It went with the army camp and the father in braces. He added a waif-like Irish mother, hardly older than a girl. In which case, what had become of her? The father was dead, she had said. He supposed that the mother had married again and had more children. It was reasonable to conclude that Katy had nothing to do with her. Of all the people Bland had ever known she was the most unmothered.

He ran up the stairs, glad of an opportunity to interrupt her at whatever she was doing. He was also curious as to the state of the flat, for which, he realised, he would have to account. The doorbell seemed to echo into a tense silence. He rang again.

'Who is it?' a voice called.

'It's George. I've got a letter for you.'

'Can't you leave it? I'm washing my hair.'

'I think you'd better look at it, Katy. I'm not really sure it's for you.'

'I'm expecting something. It's probably for me. Just leave it, George.'

'Can't you open the door?'

There was another silence. Then the door opened on to a clearly annoyed Katy, clad in what must be Tim Dunlop's white towelling bathrobe, her hair wrapped in a towelling turban.

He handed her the letter and glanced past her. The atmosphere was disturbed; he sensed the trace of another presence, another odour. The windows, he noted, were steamed up, yet the flat was as cold as his own.

'Is your heating working?' he asked. 'Mine seems to have packed up.'

'Oh, I never have the heating on,' she said. 'It's so bad

for the skin.' She put the letter in her pocket without looking at it. She was clearly impatient, waiting for him to leave.

'The letter's addressed to a Mrs Palmer-Harris,' he said. 'I wondered if it were really for you.'

'Of course it's for me.'

'Aren't you going to ask me in?' he said weakly.

'I'm terribly busy,' she said. The vowels were in place this morning, he noted. She might have been dismissing a tradesman.

'Too busy for a cup of coffee? I was just going to make one.'

'Just for a moment,' she said, crossing the hall after him on her bare feet. In his flat she sat down impatiently, crossing and re-crossing her legs.

'I admit I'm intrigued,' he shouted from the kitchen, spooning out the coffee. 'Is there a Mr Palmer-Harris?'

'Of course there is. My husband.' She seemed disinclined to say more, clearly angered by his questions.

'You're married, then?' He set the tray down carefully in front of her, marvelling at the steadiness of his hands.

'I was. I suppose I still am, in a manner of speaking.'

'How did he know you were here?'

'I wrote to him, of course. Told him I needed money. Don't look so shocked, George. What did you think I was living on?'

'You don't live together, then?'

'Hardly. I divorced him years ago.'

He felt an absurd sense of relief. 'You must have married very young,' he said.

'Very.' He noticed that she never referred to her age at any stage of her life, as if this were to remain a mystery to herself as well as to the outside world. 'I married him to get away from home. And he was crazy about me. Still is, I dare say.'

'What sort of a man is he?'

She made a face. 'Wet. Oh, very pukka, public school and so on. He's regular army, very conventional. I took one look at his mother . . . !' She cast up her eyes. 'I bowled him over. But no, thank you very much. Still, he was good about the divorce.'

'You mean you divorced him?'

'As soon as I saw what life would be like if I stayed with him.' She gave a short laugh. 'Funny guy. I did him a favour, leaving him, not that he agreed with me.'

'Do you still see him?'

'No way. I let him make himself useful occasionally.' She waved the letter at him.

'What is his name?'

'Simon.'

'And you haven't seen him for some time?'

'I didn't say that.'

She had caught his drift, he thought. She knew that he was aware there had been someone with her, and that that someone was not the discarded husband. His heart went out to the poor fellow, who had no doubt been as disarmed as he was now himself. Except that Palmer-Harris had been young, and no doubt innocent, his background and advantages strangely ineffective. He shook his head and studied her. She was conscious of him, rolled down the sleeves of Tim Dunlop's bathrobe and pulled the sash tight, as if to protect herself from his gaze. He remembered Hipwood's knowing eye, ignored the faint warning in his head, then told himself it was too late for ordinary prudence.

'Well, I must be off,' she said. 'Are you going to be here all day?'

'I have some business to see to, but I dare say I shall be in later. Would you like a cup of tea this afternoon?'

For it is to be all cups of tea, he thought tiredly, and no real truths, beyond the one he had learned that morning. Even that was an edited version, which she no doubt thought favourable to herself. The omissions were glaring. What had been left out was the mockery of the man's decent behaviour, her continuing power over him. None of this need be true, he thought, but what is the truth? The truth was that he was in danger of approaching some sort of precipice, and of going over the edge, that the transformation that he sought was somehow linked with this girl, who was until recently a total stranger, and that he was excited – excited as he had never been – by the contest of wills that was being played out between them. He had never been in a more ridiculous position in his life. But knowing, as he now perceived, that his life had been lived without his active participation, without daring, without heat, he was, or seemed to be, committed to this one final act of folly, for which, no doubt, he was overprepared.

'Until later, then,' he called to her retreating back, and shut the door.

The need to get out had become pressing. Because of the wretchedness which had suddenly descended on him he decided to begin the business of clearing Putnam's flat, a task which he had been unwilling to face. In any event, he could not stay at home: he wondered if he could ever bear to endure his habitual claustration again. He went into the bedroom and felt the radiator: still cold. At which point would it be appropriate to mention this to Hipwood, his *doppelgänger*? This was almost a political decision. Yet the sheer added nonsense of this predicament made him impatient. If his will was to be in question, why not exercise it in this useful circumstance? Nevertheless he said nothing to Hipwood, who was arranging tinsel round his tree. His desire to leave the building was too strong, and he almost fled into the street.

Ten minutes' walk amid the Friday crowds, in the damp grey weather, brought him to George Street. Putnam had lived in a subdued, gloomy but respectable building, which, having existed since the 1930s, had acquired a patina of age and sooner or later would without a doubt be appropriated by enthusiasts for late Art Deco. Certain features already possessed a quasi-historical value, such as the lift, which appeared to be composed of bronze glass and sunray ironwork, and the jazz age carpet, in fawn, orange and brown, which lined the corridors. Putnam had appreciated these details, not only for their ugliness, but out of some ancient loyalty to the home of his youth. Bland suspected that this hallowed place had been more humble, yet more dignified, than his own *petit bourgeois* surroundings: he imagined polished linoleum and a brass gong in the hall, possibly the presence of a lodger in a small back bedroom. This had been confirmed, in due course, unapologetically, even with enthusiasm. Such innocence was rare, Bland knew: he thought it a superior quality, superior in any event to his own guarded aspirations.

Putnam had managed to turn his nostalgia into an art form, but never a handicap, or even a joke, and had remained an unashamed populist all his life. The expensive suits, the membership of the Reform Club, had not altered or in any way affected his inalienable simplicity. Putnam would enter a pub, bright eyed, in the sure expectation of an hour's entertainment, although he never drank more than a half of bitter. Bland had accompanied him, protesting, to pubs in the Caledonian Road, in Shaftesbury Avenue, in Pimlico, for Putnam, who came from Birmingham, was an inveterate Londoner. Whereas Bland had sought out the mournful secretive suburbs, Putnam would not move far from the cockneyfied inner regions, and had frequently appropriated Bland for a long walk after work, during which, under the lights of Piccadilly Circus, or Victoria Station, his strange hilarious face would glow with enthusiasm, and with the excitement of the city.

He struck up odd alliances, with paper-sellers, with men and women brooding in cafés, with publicans: he distributed largesse to alcoholics and panhandlers, his vitality increasing with every encounter. Yet in spite of these random friendships, in spite of the women who entered his flat, for however brief a period, he remained prudent, oddly chaste, transparently honest. Every Sunday afternoon he would seat himself in front of his outsize television and watch the film. 'You're sure you won't come out?' Bland would say. 'It's Alice Faye!' Putnam would reply. Or Barbara Stanwyck. Or, treat of treats, Joan Crawford. 'Come back afterwards. I've got some Gentleman's Relish. Now fuck off.'

So they would have their tea, and smoke a couple of cigarettes, and discuss what to do when they retired. Together they were able to disregard their age, holding it, as it were, in common. Within each other's company they had kept mortality at bay. Putnam's slight gangling figure had never shown any signs of fatigue, of wear and tear, which made the rapid onset of his last illness a calculated cruelty. A strange, endearing character, mathematically gifted, yet apparently disrespectful of his gift. After Birmingham University he had been encouraged to stay on and do research, but for reasons which were never fully explained – Bland suspected the poverty of a widowed mother, a suspicion which Putnam later confirmed, in one of those elliptical confidences which, out of a shared modesty, they both prized – had elected to enter the firm in which Bland was already employed and work in accounts. Over the years he had risen to a more exalted position, and was given a pompous title, yet, like Bland, he retained the memory of his apprentice years. It had made their maturity, their shared maturity, all the more secure.

Bland knew what he would find in Putnam's flat, which was complacently hideous. Putnam had maintained, with some pride, that he had no taste: like all his observations this was the simple truth. But this was more than bad taste: this was a courageous stand against beauty, and the obligation to aspire to it. That beauty was truth, and truth beauty, was not apparent to Putnam, who was ever ready to appreciate humbler, not to say crass forms of decoration. He possessed in abundance a variety of objects in inlaid brass – tables, vases, cache-pots – which his grandfather had claimed to have brought back from India, but which were in fact the *nec plus ultra* in Birmingham in the 1930s. These occupied many corners in his sitting-room, which was otherwise furnished with two elephantine sofas covered in rust-coloured tweed, a couple of glass-fronted bookcases, inherited from that same grandfather, and Putnam's own chair, beside which stood one of the brass tables, on crooked ebony legs, bearing an ashtray, a cigar box, and a lighter in the form of a Georgian teapot. In the kitchen Bland knew that he would find a complete range of Fornasetti plates. This proved to be correct. A tea towel, spread over the red plastic washing-up bowl, bore the toasts of several nations under gaily tilted cocktail glasses and beer steins. An ivory-handled knife, bluntly rounded at the tip – another heirloom, no doubt – had been left on the draining board.

The bedroom was more austere, although all the furniture had the streamlined corners, the ovoid ellipses, of Putnam's beloved Hollywood. A low dressing-table, in a pale fudge-coloured material, resembled an illustration of a flying saucer that might have figured in a boy's comic of the 1950s. In one of its three mirrors, Bland knew, he would see reflected a green smoked-glass statuette of a lady with a tiny marcel-waved head, holding up the hem of her skirt in one dainty hand. Bland grinned: Putnam's flat always had this effect on him. He supposed that this stuff, most of which Putnam had bought from a friend who was going out of business, rather hurriedly, it seemed, might be of interest to a collector. It would have to go to auction: he would see to it after Christmas. If I'm here, he thought with a start. He looked round. The rooms returned his glance without adding any comment of their own. If he had hoped for a message, none came through. On impulse he appropriated one of the more hideous vases, put it into a carrier bag marked Augustus Barnett, and took it home.

Closing the door of his own flat behind him he trod on something shiny, a postcard which Hipwood had declined to give him earlier, having no doubt retained it for his own instruction. Bland dismissed the fact; none of these details mattered any more. He turned over the postcard, which showed a turquoise blue swimming pool, with an improbably white hotel in the background, and read the message: 'Returning 22nd. Would you please turn on our heating, which we switched off before leaving? Kind regards, Sharon and Tim.' Bland sank slowly into a chair, his Augustus Barnett bag at his feet. So the coming confrontation would be the final one, he supposed, the endgame towards which all this speculation had been leading. If all went well they could take flight together, for now it seemed inconceivable that she should leave without him, or rather that he should let her go. He now ran the risk of her escaping him, for her husband had sent money, a cheque, no doubt, which she would be unable to cash before Monday. He looked again at the card. 'Returning 22nd.' That was next Tuesday. Today was the 18th, Friday. That gave him a very small margin in which to conclude this venture. They must be gone by Monday at the latest. He ignored the doubts that were slowly filtering into his mind. Why doubt now? Even if they got no further than Rome it would constitute a victory of some sort, a wager won.

He took the vase out of the bag and placed it on top of one of the bookshelves. It looked every bit as ugly there as it had in what Putnam gleefully called his 'lounge'. Bland gazed at it in some perplexity. Passing once more into Katy Gibb's aura had made him nervous, distracted. Putnam receded, his Cheshire cat grin lingering in the room. There seemed to be nothing left for him to do until Katy came later that day. He was too tense to read, could not face composing a meal for himself: his habitual hunger had receded, replaced by a vague emptiness. He wandered into the kitchen and opened cupboards; there seemed to be a great deal of food, but all of it required sustained attention. He told himself that once he was away, safe in some hotel, he would discipline himself again, eat, take exercise, sleep without the help of the radio. Until then he was in suspension.

He ate some bread and cheese, although a few mouthfuls were enough to check his appetite. He then went back into the sitting-room to wait for her, although it was only two o'clock. He had time in which to prepare himself, yet his mind was curiously empty of calculation. Calculation might, even now, fail him. Instead his thoughts returned to Putnam, and the strange bachelor simplicity in which they had lived their days. An atmosphere of Eden before the Fall hovered over that existence, while now the Fall beckoned, with all its dread inevitability. He marvelled that such a doubt-free existence had ever been his; even the memory of that quietude was receding by the minute. It had been replaced by this phantasmagoria which, although it was out of character, he accepted as his doom, his fate. It was enthralling, no doubt, but somehow, at this crucial juncture, he could not keep his mind on it. Instead it darted back in time, until, in a half sleeping state, he saw his past once again, saw Putnam's grin, saw his father in his racegoer's camel-hair coat, tracing a careful path towards the house, saw figures to whom he could hardly put names, grumbling elderly relatives, inert uncles, spiteful aunts, members of a quarrelsome family whom his parents had eventually discarded, preferring their own dystopia to the rival dystopias they had inherited. So it had gone on, down the generations, until it ended in him. It appeared to him, quite suddenly, that his desire never to marry or have children (for that surely was what it was) had to do with this paltry inheritance. By his own action, or lack of action, he had drawn the line under it, put an end to it. He understood now why he was alone.

He saw his mother, his poor mother, he thought with a start of surprise, forced to make do with this reduced company, with his unsteady father, with his half tearful half resentful self. How unhappy they all were! And all imprisoned, all unable to escape. His own escape might never have been made, so achingly present was he once more in that original house, whose disposition he could recollect with startling clarity.

Instinct made him try to break the spell of that half sleep, which was more like a visitation, yet when he opened his eyes he almost expected to see his old bedroom, and to smell his mother's cigarette smoke. He sat up, panic stricken. Slowly the sight of his own room reasserted itself, but the panic persisted. He felt as he had felt on the day of his final school examination, the one that was to get him into Oxford, the one that he had failed. This had surprised his headmaster, who had encouraged him. 'Were you unwell?' he had asked. 'Had anything upset you?' It was impossible that he should confess that his parents' arguing had kept him sleepless all the previous night. One did not confess such things to kindly liberal-minded mentors. He blamed no one, not even his parents, whose behaviour had become his secret. He had, he thought, just not been good enough. And maybe it was all for the best.

That had been the first of the chances missed, the paths not followed. The first, and the most crucial. By dint of failing that first and last examination his liberty had been deferred for many years. And even now it was still in question.

He padded into the bathroom and went through his usual ritual, the brushing of the teeth, the smoothing of the hair, the discreet application of a sweet-smelling lotion. He knew that all this was otiose, for she never came near him. Since that first day she had never even taken his hand, but had preferred to stand before him, on display, so that he could both admire her and measure the distance between them. No doubt she felt contempt for his grey hair, his lack of muscle. He accepted this. He knew the feeling of old. It was the feeling reserved for those outside enchantment, for those humbly precluded from the triumphs of this world. Whereas she was the scornful mocking temptress who arranges their downfall. He felt that he had foreseen this since the beginning of time.

He was outwardly composed when he opened the door at four o'clock. She was still in her bathrobe, her feet still bare. With Palmer-Harris's cheque in her pocket she had become lazy, like an animal with a full stomach.

'Good heavens!' she exclaimed, shading her eyes. 'What on earth is that?'

'It's a vase,' he said. 'I brought it from a friend's flat.' It seemed pointless to explain who Putnam was, and what had happened to him, and anyway he thought it indecent to mention Putnam's name in this context. The bathrobe, he noticed, was loosely tied, showing the cleft between her breasts, and her legs as far as the knees. He had no doubt that this was deliberate.

'I had a card from the Dunlops,' he said. 'They will be back on Tuesday.'

Her face closed. He contemplated the hardened down-cast features. Colour had flared into her cheeks, which glowed dark red.

'What will you do?' he asked.

She shrugged. 'Go somewhere else, I expect. Did you say something about tea?'

He ignored this. 'My offer of Rome still stands,' he said. 'We could take off on Monday. I'm sure it wouldn't take you long to get ready.'

She got up and started moving round the room, humming under her breath.

'Or I could move in here,' she said. 'You wouldn't mind putting me up, would you, George? Actually,' this word was drawled in her most imperious manner, 'that might be best. I could make a few calls, get a few clients together. And then in time, who knows?'

She sat down again and let the robe fall away from her legs. 'But you'd have to get rid of that vase first,' she said, with a smile which set out to be amiable but had, unknown to her, become antagonistic. Again he felt a thrill of a desire which was not a true desire, or at least not for what she was offering.

'I'm afraid that wouldn't be suitable,' he said.

'Why? It's not as if you need all this space to yourself. What do you do all day except read? Well, you only need one room for that, don't you?'

He cleared his throat. 'Actually I have a lot of business on hand,' he said. 'I have to dispose of a friend's flat. I shall be bringing all his belongings back here.'

This was not true; he had only just thought of it.

'And what's happening to his place?'

'It's sold,' he said quickly. 'I have to get the key from the agent when I want to go in.' He went into the kitchen, a knot of constriction in his chest. He faced the terrible fact that she was stronger than he could ever be.

'So I'm afraid Rome is all I can offer,' he said, putting the tray down in front of her.

'I don't need a holiday, thank you. I need a future. You surely can't have failed to get that into your head. I'll

181

come away with you, since you're so keen, but I've got to make plans. Surely you can see that?'

'I don't think I can help you with those plans. I thought that was understood.'

She regarded him without amenity, her cheeks suffused. 'My time does not come cheap, George.' She meant her company. She got up to go, tightening the belt of her bathrobe virtuously about her waist. 'Perhaps you'll think better of it tomorrow. I'll look in then, shall I? And of course if there's anything you want you'll let me know. Don't bother to see me out. I think I know my way around by now.'

He sat for a while, a cup of cold tea and a plate of untouched mince pies in front of him. He glanced around the room, seeing it with her eyes. The thought of marriage, once dismissed, occurred to him again, and was definitively abandoned. But the prospect of the lonely evening was unbearable. And his thinking, so recently imperative, seemed to have become paralysed. Yet even now, even in his disarray, he sensed a queer excitement. It was the excitement of a gambler, bent not on winning, but on suicide, when his last card is also his last chance, and all the odds are against him.

10

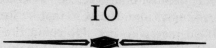

He was by now violently in love; of that there was no doubt. Or if not in love as he had previously understood it, enthralled to the point of losing his judgment, that judgment which had kept him prudently on course for many a long year. And they had seemed long, he now thought, made bearable only by a mild conscience, by accredited pleasures, by licensed indulgences. His conception of love throughout those long years – that lifetime, he reminded himself – had been courtly, *chevaleresque*: only permitted thoughts had entered his head, and he had been contented, grateful to Louise, whose expectations were as modest as his own. He had grown up with a full complement of conventional images, weddings, christenings, children, grandchildren. Where these happy families had come from he had little idea, preoccupied as he was with his own particularly inharmonious home life, and later with the escape which always seemed to him to be under threat. His fantasies then had been gently old-fashioned. Had he been promoted to the rank of husband he would have played his part faithfully, valiantly, and he had no doubt, even now, that he would have made a good father.

But if a nostalgia for that picture remained with him, he also knew that whatever happiness might have fallen to his lot would have been tinged with disappointment. And despite those primitive subconscious decisions he had made – never to marry, to bring an end to his unfortunate line – one strand of his imagination always led him to Louise. It was because Louise would have fitted in so well with the traditional idea of a wife that he had perversely put a curb on marrying her. He could imagine all too well what their lives would have been: the substantial but unpretentious house, the garden which it would be his job to tend, perhaps a weekend cottage, and his wife, in attractive yet sensible clothes, growing in authority while he sought his quietus in work. His own parents must have been like that once, before their true natures had reasserted themselves. And if Louise and he had had children he had no doubt that they would have been boys, and as unattractive as Louise's own son had been when Bland had first encountered him at the age of six. That friendly grimy boy, with his hot adult smell, had distressed Bland then, just as the memory distressed him now.

What he had missed was equally present to his mind: peace, company, reassurance, the comfort of knowing that he was acting in character. There would have been holidays when there was no need to make contact with strange women, however amiable, and to walk away from them afterwards with a feeling of disappointment. There would have been pleasant evenings, family occasions, the sort of occasions at which a bachelor always feels uncomfortable. There would even, dare he think it, have been regular meals, about which a bachelor has to make certain decisions. These days, unless he went to the club, he tended to forget about food, lacked the energy to prepare anything, and consequently ate very little.

This tendency was reinforced by his unwillingness to leave the flat for the duration of Katy's tenure, and with the thought of Katy his dilemma once again presented itself in its crudest form. Katy was the obverse of Louise, and in many ways she had brought into prominence the nature of his long affection. He was not a vain man, but when he thought of himself married to Louise he could see that he would have become self-satisfied. But why should he not have become self-satisfied? He had all the qualifications: an excellent job, a career which in those early scared days he could hardly have envisaged, the ability to provide for a family, which was no doubt why he had willed her his money. In many ways he still thought of her as his wife, the wife whom he had failed to marry. And she no doubt thought of him as one who might have been, should have been, her husband.

There was no need to shed any tears over this situation, which had lasted so long and with so little rancour on either side. By the same token it was static, non-negotiable: there was no need to develop it or indeed examine it. Nevertheless Bland had no doubt that these days he referred to the situation rather more than did Louise, for in the long run he had lost more by it than she had, and he thought his solitude rather more unbearable than hers. Indeed, he had the proof, if proof were needed, that he had blundered more disastrously than he had ever imagined, and in a way which he could never disclose, particularly to Louise, although he knew that she would love him just the same, however much he disappointed her.

Because always on the verge of succumbing to that love, and always drawing back, he had deprived himself of its undoubted blessings and its routine satisfactions. Instead he had been overcome with passion for a woman half his age, whom he hardly knew, and who was hard, cunning, venal and an opportunist to her fingers' ends. That he knew all this did not deter him. If he had once wanted to avenge himself on a life of obedience no such illusion succoured his imagination now that the hour of decisions had arrived. Perhaps he had succumbed to the charm of seeing himself in a more flattering light, as discreet and worldly, as he certainly was not, a patron rather than a lover, almost like a novelist with one of his own characters. Indissoluble from this fantasy was the image of the hotel balcony, the red sun sinking, the lightweight suit and the panama hat, perhaps a cigar, and the unhurried wait for his creation to return to him after a day given over to all those diversions which he would selflessly permit her. He had stood on just such a hotel balcony, watching just such a red sun, during his recent stay in Nice. Longing had furnished him with a companion, and brought the fantasy to life. That was how his idyll had taken shape and how it exerted power over his mind: he still, even now, saw a more ideal version of himself, in complete control, in beautiful surroundings, though these were non-specific, and somehow, mysteriously, inspiring respect. The respect was important, essential. As his own situation became more farcical he insisted to himself that once removed from present circumstances, and translated into another sphere, he would register as another character altogether, an enigma, a man of secrets, and as such make a deep impression on his entourage, the waiters, the porters, the chauffeurs, who would hasten to do his bidding. In this way he would be able, to a certain extent, to forgo the respect of his companion, who would have none, or none for him, and to accept, magnanimously, and always with that air of distinction, what little she had to offer.

He had never been so far removed from that condition as he was now. He had reached the stage of being subjugated, as he had never been subjugated before, and not merely by this mysterious woman's will, but by those impure and retrograde compulsions which he recognised as being more akin to a kind of exasperated dread than to any sort of spontaneous affection. Although physical love hardly entered into his calculations, he did not doubt that at some point he would consider her his creature, in an act of possession no less real for being divorced from contact. The idea was unseemly, and he did his best to banish it. He would continue to banish it, he thought, though it would remove one of his satisfactions. But all his satisfactions were now taboo, it seemed. He had opened Pandora's box, and Discord had broken out, revealing to him a natural hunger which he had never suspected. He almost ground his teeth when he thought of the girl, her provocation, her beady-eyed passive aggression, the limitations of a mind which, in its very idleness, wrought in him that irritated frenzy which was part of his malaise. Pandora, in the myth, had been forbidden to open the box, just as Eve had been forbidden to eat the apple. Both were allegories from the beginning of the world, with the same fatal outcome, the same dubious prohibition, the promise made and then cancelled, the endowment glimpsed and then removed. He had always shuddered at the cruelty of both stories, and in so doing had lost any simple beliefs, which had not, in any case, persisted after childhood, but having thought about the matter he preferred Pandora to Eve. Pandora let loose Discord, but at the bottom of the box discovered Hope. There was thus the relief of something saved, essential to any story, although when hope outlasted expectation the outcome was disillusion. That he was beginning to understand.

If he had any hope it was surely illusory. He knew that she would never love him. He did not blame her for this: he rather doubted whether she had ever loved anyone. And in his humble state he doubted whether he was lovable, even by Louise, since if he removed himself from the life he had always lived and embarked on this adventure Louise would cease to be near to him, to know him: he would be literally beyond her reach. The idea was chilling. He had never before been out of the range of Louise's love. But her innocence was incompatible with the life of subterfuge he would be obliged to live, the removals, the squandering of money, the lonelyheart-edness. He had once looked on it as a stimulus, a harmless hobby to be taken up in his retirement. Now he knew the grief contained in the myth, the disobedience, the sheer complexity of the world of consequences, when all had been so simple before.

He tried to trace the origins of his aberration, which he now knew to be an aberration, in all its monstrosity, but could find nothing in his life which gave any indication that he might behave in this way. Did it all date back to childhood, as the pundits, and no doubt Howard Singer himself, maintained that it did? In that case, distasteful though the task would be, he might have to search his soul for motives of revenge against those negligent forebears, whose character and appearance came so vividly to mind, now that he was almost as old – older – than they themselves. Although dead, they took up a great deal of room in his mind and memory, sometimes assuming the posture and expression – sardonic, careless, negligent, uncommitted – by which he had first known them. He saw them in every physical detail: his mother's dry brittle hair, his father's camel-hair coat. That coat, with its exaggerated shoulders, disguised the slight paunch which was the result of too many whiskies. When not worn it was slung round his shoulders. Another snapshot: his not quite handsome father's winning smile (crooked, because of badly fitting teeth) and his ruddy face smelling of violets. He could almost hear the transparent excuses, as that same father made his escape to Folkestone, or Lingfield, or Kempton Park, where he had collapsed in the very act of raising his hip flask to his lips. A fortunate death, no doubt, but not one of which an eighteen-year-old boy could necessarily feel proud.

His mother he saw as she had been in her sad latter days, in a dress with a button missing, her swollen feet in stained furry slippers, her hair wild. Years of bad luck had made her intolerant, so that she had never had a kind word to say to him, or indeed to anyone else. But there had been no one else: just himself, his father, and his mother's quarrelsome sister. It was her sister's death, rather than her husband's, that had affected her. The slight stroke she seemed to have suffered on hearing of the news had led to a marked deterioration in her behaviour, so that meals were no longer prepared, and any washing had to await the reluctant attentions of a once-weekly cleaning woman.

It was after his truncated university career and his subsequent beginnings as a clerk that she took to wandering into his room, shutting the window, and sitting there for half a day, not caring where she was, as though one place were as good as another, as no doubt it was by that stage in her life. No allowance had been made for his youth: that was surely a legitimate cause for complaint. But what good would it do him now to complain about all this? He was a grown man, he was even an old man; he had survived them. In a year or so he would have outlived them. The thought was somehow terrible.

He wondered if it were natural to be thinking so persistently of his parents, particularly as he did not miss them. He wondered if it were healthy, or desirable, to be thinking of the past just now when he should be thinking of the future. What good did it do to succumb to these ruminations at any time? If he did so would he not become as disaffected as they had been? So far he had escaped this particular affliction. He did not see this as a great achievement: the lesson had been there for any fool to learn, but age, he knew, brings unwelcome returns to earlier selves, even unknown, certainly unsuspected selves. He saw himself, an old man, sitting in his chair, a muffler round his neck. He could see this much more clearly in that the heating was still on the blink: after an initial early puff of warmth the radiators had apparently given up for the rest of the day. Maybe there was a power cut that he had not heard about; he had not been watching television, and the battery in his radio had given out. He was thus presented with a useful way in which to spend his morning: he could go to the shop in Marylebone High Street and buy a couple of batteries. The radio, of course, would have to be left behind. For now he was convinced that he must leave.

His distraction was profound. Air; he needed air, a breath of normality, however factitious. He slipped out of the building without his customary greeting to Hipwood, or to the Milsoms, the elderly couple from the ground floor who went out shopping together every day at the same time, and whom he used to see, standing behind the glass doors, surveying the weather, when he left for the office. He had always liked them: they seemed pleased with their little routines, with each other's company, although there was an air of ill health about them. Both were curiously crooked, as if they had suffered from rickets in childhood. Clearly their beginnings had not been easy, although presumably they had risen to the degree of affluence that permitted them to live in this building. Scrap metal, he had heard Hipwood, who knew everything, say; he had paid no attention. The Milsoms were shy, not daring to trust their vowels to the likes of Mrs Lydiard, but they felt comfortable with Bland, and always nodded and smiled to him. Or had done. Now they no doubt longed to ask him how he was, registering his altered appearance. At least, he supposed it was altered; he had not scrutinised it lately. In his present state of mind he could hardly give an account of himself to anyone, let alone the Milsoms, who, in their shyness, would not know how to respond, even if his remarks were calculated to put them at their ease, along the lines of 'A bit tired, you know?' Even that would bring a look of concern, a shifting of feet, a tightening of Mrs Milsom's hand on the handle of her wheeled basket. Yet he was tired, there was no denying it, and he longed to tell someone. But what he had to tell was so confusing that he had to keep all information to himself.

He walked carefully along Kendal Street, applying himself to keeping his balance, and trying to ignore the bitter cold, the dull light, as if the earth had not the energy to shift itself, as if it would be winter until the end of time. He turned up his collar and regretted his tweed hat, which he thought might be promoted to everyday wear. He no longer had the heart to wear the magnificent fur hat that Putnam had brought him back from Russia and which he had occasionally worn to the office, receiving compliments on his appearance, which had hitherto not been dramatic. He felt half dressed, as if he had forgotten some item of clothing, and for a moment wondered if he had come out in his slippers. But all seemed to be in order; it was the day that was at fault. He had to fill in the time between now and later this afternoon, when he would knock at her door, and, with an air of *désinvolture*, invite her in for a cup of tea. This would no doubt precede her answer to all his questions, most of them unstated, and her verdict on what was to be his future. He hoped that some last-minute inspiration would come to his rescue; as it was he felt dull-witted. Had he had more energy he would have gone for a walk in the park, yet at his present shuffling pace he doubted whether he would get far. He must buy some food, he thought, although he was not hungry. He did not seem to have eaten recently. Restaurants were the answer to his problem, but he had momentarily lost all memory of his surroundings, and in any event felt too shamefaced to do other than eat at home. He made a detour to Selfridges, and bought a cooked chicken and a quarter of ham. He added a bag of salad, which he knew he would eventually throw away, some pears, a wholemeal loaf, and a piece of Roquefort.

After a pause in the middle of the shop, he bought a bottle of Beaujolais. Then, much encumbered, he took a taxi home.

He surveyed his living-quarters as if he were seeing them for the first time, or the last. The sitting-room, as Putnam had once observed, looked like the waiting-room of a Harley Street psychiatrist, except that that would be warmer, with an even purring warmth designed to allay disquiet. He had never felt exactly comfortable in the flat, although he doubted whether it could now be improved, or even disturbed. It had an immemorial feel to it, as if it were the home of someone who had recently died. He tended these days to retreat to the bedroom, although that too, in the mysterious way of bedrooms, appeared sombre and uninhabited. The bed, which had been outrageously expensive, was his refuge; he had hoped, and indeed had planned, to die in it. His few drawings, mostly English, mostly from the end of the nineteenth century, hung on the walls, flanking the one decent object he had retrieved from his parents' house, a handsome gilt-framed mirror ornamented with stucco garlands. A longer cheval mirror occupied a corner: his ghostly reflection was the first thing he saw when he got out of bed in the morning.

This room was his true home, his retreat. It even crossed his mind that he might return to it some day, when his journeyings were over, and his companion no doubt lost. He would not sell the flat, he decided. It could remain as it was, ready to receive him, a broken man, at the end of his life, his money spent, or rather wasted, his hopes confounded. He lingered in the room, wondering how it would be, that last, that final state. In the half light, which was all the light that ever seemed to enter here, the grey-blue walls dissolved into kindly shadow, so that his eyes encountered no disquieting vista but rather a pregnant silence, a withholding, as if some secrets remained to be disclosed, and would not be disclosed until due time had passed. He hung his jacket in the wardrobe and put on a navy blue cardigan. Even his clothes were suddenly dear to him, infinitely pathetic, pointless, and unprotected, careful suitable garments, carefully chosen, carefully tended. They would be left behind: there would be no room for much in the one bag he intended to pack.

He turned to the window, which looked out onto gardens now bleached by the bitter weather. He was within shouting distance of Radnor Place, the scene of his first social débâcle. Since that time he had avoided confrontations of principle or belief, in the hope that his modest pretensions would allow him to pass through life unnoticed, as they had done. Until now. The supreme irony was that he had almost reached the end of his life before being visited by this powerful impulse to change it, and that the catalyst was someone of whom he equally powerfully disapproved. He could not solve this conundrum. He could only live through it and hope to survive it.

For the first time in this whole inexplicable adventure he felt a sadness at leaving, and realised that this sadness could only be mitigated by hopes of an eventual return. A sudden shower of rain struck the window, and he stepped back with a shudder. The sun, the sun! Suddenly, passionately, he longed for it, longed to cancel this pitiless nadir of the year, and of his spirits. No amount of feasting or celebration could obliterate this month, though he had done his best with it in recent years, had endured the enforced stay in the Hardwicks' Surrey house, resigned to the good cheer and the jolly routines. These kind friends looked upon his visit as forming part of a Christmas tradition, as bogus as it was instant. He had already told them that he would be away. And however strange his new surroundings, they would surely be less strange than the churchgoing and the heavy meal and the dark nights that would otherwise have awaited him. Every year he had sworn to stay at home; every year he had given in to their insistence. Now he could not even stay at home. Home was a difficult concept at the best of times, and never more so than at this moment.

He went into the kitchen and put the ham on a plate, together with a slice of the chicken. He contemplated the salad, then stowed it away, only to delay the moment at which he would discard it. He cut the bread and poured a glass of the wine, which fortunately was at the right temperature. A strange calm seemed to have succeeded his former excitement. He had almost forgotten that this afternoon was to be anything out of the ordinary. He tasted the cheese, which necessitated another glass of wine. By the time he got up to make some coffee he noticed that the bottle was three-quarters empty. No matter: he had always had a good head, and there was no danger of his losing it now, for he had already lost it. He washed up, carefully turning the fine plates which he had bought in a junk shop in Brighton; he admired once more their solid weight and their confident pattern, as if he might never see them again. He supposed that once he had disappeared the plates would be removed by Mrs Cardozo, who also admired them, along with anything else she considered to be superfluous to his requirements. He would be dispossessed, of course, but in a sense the process was already under way, and its progress was in any event ineluctable.

He had managed to avoid or to overlook the fact that his afternoon would be a long interval of waiting for the verdict to be delivered on what remained of his future. He could do nothing until Katy informed him of her decision. In a curious way the decision was no longer his: it had passed from his grasp, and with its passing he was reduced to powerlessness. A childlike feeling of sadness, together with the half-light of the room, and his tired limbs, stole over him; he felt as if he were back in the house in Reading, and as if his mother had just left his bedroom, cigarette in hand. He had always slept heavily in that room, either out of despair or out of pity for the ruined woman who wandered into it when he was not there, and left her disturbing presence to imprint the brown carpet and the Jacobean curtains. Instinctively he removed his shoes and lay down under the quilt. The wine had acted on his stretched nerves like a sedative, and was interfering with his ability to plan what he would say to Katy when she came that afternoon. He would be as reticent as he could manage: that had been his stance all along. What he feared now was a breakdown of his reserve, a rage, an outcry if she resisted him. He was on the edge. Again the deep throb of his original excitement strengthened his resolve. He felt the almost intolerable emotional tension of one who is face to face with the action of a lifetime. In that moment he left his previous life behind, and there might have been no beginning, no home, no parentage, no birthright, only the prospect of a future so uncharted that he seemed to have passed at once into an ageless adulthood, never again to know innocence, or irresponsibility, or self-esteem, but always to be on the rack of mature considerations, arrived at coldly, and without illusions.

While pondering the enormity of his situation he fell asleep. Almost at once, it seemed, he had a dream of his parents, looking young and lighthearted, but heavily made up, like Kabuki players. They appeared to be ministering to each other, but without anxiety, without rancour, the rancour which had dogged them in later years. Somehow, in this dream, he realised that he was seeing them as they had been when they were young, before he knew them, newly married, perhaps, certainly optimistic. Even in the dream he felt a pang of love and envy, and these two emotions obliterated his later distresses as though they had never been. Simply he was seeing them for the first time, as they really were, without relation to himself and his needs, and thus exonerated from his later strictures. They had been unsatisfactory as parents, that he knew. What he had never known, but knew now, was their bewilderment, their disappointment that age had not maintained the promise of youth. Now he himself, struggling with that same disappointment, knew them to be as innocent as the common ruck of mortality. Suddenly, unexpectedly, he threw in his lot with them, with their ordinary unhappiness, which was perhaps their legacy to him, and his true inheritance.

The sleep that followed this dream – for he had briefly surfaced before the tide dragged him down again – was so profound that when he awoke it was to a feeling of finality. It is all over, he thought, and knew it to be true. He was not even surprised. If the past had claimed him in one sense, the present exerted its hold in another. There would be no flight to the sun: his future lay with the bitter seasons of reality. There would be no leaving this room, which now seemed kindly, even hospitable. He saw his madness for what it was, the final upheaval of an unlived life, such as might have tormented some saint in the desert. Was not St Antony tempted by visions of lascivious women? St Antony's remedy had been to scourge himself and pray. He, Bland, would no doubt undergo similar discomfort in the light of future reflection.

He prepared the tea-tray with a feeling of gravity, arranging biscuits on a plate, as if in the hope of tempting an invalid. But when the bell rang and he opened the door it was to a Katy dressed once again in her T-shirt and jeans, her feet encased in an incongruously smart pair of black suede pumps. She wandered past him into the flat without her usual calculated greeting. Strangely, neither wanted to be the first to speak. He went into the kitchen to make the tea; that done, he placed the tray in front of her as he had done so many times before. Her inaction

made her seem listless and defeated. He was not too surprised by this: her attention span was limited. He had seen
her yawn and slump into exaggerated inanition, only to
recover her colour and her spirits if some diversion were
on offer. That, in fact, was how he had first seen her.
This, though, was different. Her hair was unwashed; her
eyes refused to meet his. There was an air of hostility
about her, different in kind from her usual anger, heavier,
more immovable.

He understood. He had been too slow for her, too old,
too prudent. Her efforts had been in vain; he had not
endowed her in whatever way she had expected; he had
not made his life over to her, together with his flat, his
worldly goods, as she had willed him to. He knew that
she cared nothing for him, that she probably felt for him
the contempt that was in keeping with her age, and with
his. Now that she was leaving – a fact of which he was
in no doubt – she did not bother to hide her dislike.

'So you're going back to America?' he said.

She nodded. She picked up *The Times*, and scanned,
with apparent interest, the temperatures on the back page.

'Back to Mr Singer?'

She tossed *The Times* to the floor. 'Well, there's nothing
for me here, is there?'

'When are you going?'

'As soon as I can borrow the money for the ticket,' she
said, careless now.

He looked at her averted face, averted not from embarrassment but from indifference.

'I can help you with that,' he said, aware of a stunning
disappointment. He hardly knew what to say, since her
responses were apparently in abeyance. 'Perhaps if I gave
you a cheque?'

'That might be best,' she replied absently.

There was a pause. 'Well, if you're sure . . . You'll let
me know when you're leaving?'

'Quite sure.'

Her expression had become severe, as if she had surprised him in some shortcoming. It was he, finally, who was embarrassed. To stem the blush he felt creeping over him he took his cheque-book from the drawer of his writing-table and made out a sizeable cheque, one which he thought might cover everything: the ticket, a hotel, a flat even, meals, new clothes. He wanted her to be safe, though he had denied her safety. But safety bored her, like his careful room, his careful solitary life. He thought it all for the best, but felt a terrible fatigue, as if he might be ill.

She examined the cheque briefly, then put it in the pocket of her jeans. No further words, it seemed, were to be exchanged. Words were in any case superfluous, since they had no need to explain themselves. She turned her back, walked towards the door, and twiddled her fingers in farewell. Already she had recovered a little of her purposiveness. When she left the silence was profound.

As one might walk carefully in a ruined building, so as not to cause further subsidence, he picked up the untouched tea-tray and took it through to the kitchen. Perhaps because of his recent dream his mother's intonations echoed in his ears. Her observations, he had to admit, were often acute, though always unfriendly. He was not yet ready for the sort of criticism which would have escaped her had a similar situation arisen in her lifetime, and he shrank from entertaining any, since criticism now was beside the point. In a way the two women were not unalike. It occurred to him to ask himself why he had seemed so young in his dream, absorbed, wondering, and he understood that he had never mastered the intricacies of adult behaviour, which would have enabled him to have dismantled this episode from the outset. His mother had been indifferent; so had Katy. Katy had indeed been vastly indifferent, and had erected her own house of cards on his life and his possessions, without ever taking the trouble to test the ground, to question him about his own likes and dislikes, his own preferences, without walking delicately around him to judge whether he was ready for her to take over, and whether she could do anything appropriate to make him more amenable. That was what had brought about his last minute reconversion, the realisation that she was profoundly indifferent to his life. If only she had asked him . . . what? Not even so much as what he wanted, as what he thought, felt, imagined! Yes, that was it: imagined. She had treated him as a prostitute treats a client, with dislike, as perhaps she treated all men who failed to maintain a significant hold over her life, like her father, like Howard Singer. He should, even at this stage, feel pity for her. Instead he felt a generalised distress that one so young could have such rudimentary sensibilities. 'Tell everyone how great you are': that ridiculous instruction had been adopted by her as others might embrace a philosophy or discover the resources of religion, and her own evangelism, learned so late in life, and grafted on to a possibly defective natural growth, had merely reinforced her blindness to the reality of otherness, to the qualities which fallible human beings rely upon to guide or support them through this life.

By comparison his own projects were only defensible insofar as they provided for both of them: some possibility of a good life might have emerged had everything gone according to plan. Otherwise he saw himself as a fool rather than a knave, a man deluded by his own folly into forgetting his age and his inclinations, his history and his dignity. He examined his conscience and found no prurient intentions. His very indifference to what her behaviour told him about herself had merely strengthened his resolve to magic her into another life, a life which he himself had somehow mislaid during what he thought of as his years of obedience. He had wanted them both to be innocent, as if they were two travellers who had met by accident, and who saw no need to burden each other with their life histories, so charmed were they to have discovered one another in a lonely and deserted place. That such innocence was too much to expect, certainly too much to demand, was now borne in on him with crushing force. Finally, it was the misapprehension that made him suffer, rather than his own inchoate imaginings. He had projected those imaginings on to someone who did not even suspect their existence, and whom he could not now blame for disappointing him. He could not condemn her for her misuse of him. In a sense his was the greater misdemeanour.

Their lives were incompatible: that was the truth of the matter. His history was a foreign country to her, one which she had no wish, no need, to visit. Compatibility is not the affair of an instant. It is preceded by knowledge, by sympathy, by understanding. It is preceded by history, the history he shared with Louise, with Putnam. He understood now why Louise was always in his thoughts, although he had done his best to ignore them, and had even succeeded. That old intuition which had always been there, that period of their lives when no explanations had been necessary, that long, that even tedious predictability: that was true friendship. He had not even felt friendship for the girl, for his brooding obsession could not be confused with true friendship. Friendship meant reliability, a telephone call which could be made, or answered, in an emergency. Friendship was what served at the end, when one was near one's last resting place. And by no stretch of the imagination could he see Katy at his bedside, although, should the need have arisen, he would be there at hers. Or would have been. Even his imagination was foundering now. The figure on the balcony, in the lightweight suit, remained merely as an image, but a potent one, as if it were the figure of an exotic stranger, one whose acquaintance he would dearly love to have made.

Though it was only just past five-thirty he went back to the bedroom and lay down again on his bed. He knew that a lonely night of reflection awaited him, and he welcomed it. He had still to overcome his enormous sorrow at not having managed to admit to his life all those elements he had somehow been at pains to exclude: licence, passion, adventure, fury, recklessness. Had he once been able to indulge such forces, to achieve a perfect liquidity of the emotions, he thought that he might have been able to face death with equanimity, knowing that nothing had been wasted. He did not in all honesty think that he had used the girl as a mere pretext for such indulgence, that it was an old man's lust disguised as philanthropy that had misled him. The proof, he thought, was that he had felt for her some of the same sadness that he felt for himself, as if they were not only unprotected but uninstructed, and if not innocent then certainly defenceless. The strange odyssey that he had planned for them had indeed something childlike about it, proof of his own childlike wishes, in which sex and sin played no part.

It seemed that extreme instinctive love of that nature was to be denied him, along with the energies that informed those wilder imaginings sanctioned by desire. He remembered in this context a conversation he had once had with Putnam. It had been shortly after the summer holidays, some two or three years earlier. He had been in Aix-en-Provence, where one of his discreet encounters had taken place. It had been perfectly agreeable, extremely appropriate to the time and the circumstances, and it left him depressed, even more depressed than usual. The utter predictability of the episode, and that included the love-making itself, filled him not with shame – that would have been easy to understand – but with longing. On his return to London he had gone on one of his long walks (Kennington, he seemed to remember: the huge incongruous churches came back to him) and had called in to Putnam's flat afterwards. It was a Sunday: they were to go back to work the following day. For Bland there was something of the apprehension of returning to school, which always afflicted him at such times.

In the rust-coloured gloom of Putnam's flat, and in the glow of his superior electric fire (synthetic orange coals, embedded in black bakelite), they had sat in silence, eating crumpets. Both were in a ruminative mood, it seemed, with little to impart in the way of information.

'You're quiet,' Putnam had finally said. 'Anything wrong?'

'Tell me something,' he had replied, out of the depths of his preoccupation. 'Why should life seem exciting only if there is the possibility of throwing it away? And not even in a good cause. Fatal passion is what I'm talking about, I suppose, and what a failure you feel if you've missed it.'

'I wouldn't give you a thank you for a fatal passion. A fatal passion can turn nasty, you know. That's why it's called fatal.'

'I seem to have missed it altogether. I seem to have almost avoided it, as if I doubted my own ability to deal with it. Maybe I was too modest.'

'Don't be so bloody vain! Only vain people proclaim their modesty.'

'Not modest, then. Unprepared.'

'You are what your destiny made you. We all are.'

'I keep feeling I've done something wrong, as if I'd been locked out of something by my own fault.'

'That's probably true. We've all done something wrong. I do something wrong every time I have a fling with a married woman. Not that there have been all that many,' he added.

'And that doesn't make you suffer?'

Putnam lit a cigarette. 'Not much,' he said finally.

'I suppose that's the difference between an affair and a love affair. I wouldn't mind suffering for the real thing. In fact I long to.'

'You're a romantic. An adolescent. Grown men don't want to suffer. It all comes from reading, you know. If we didn't have the books to go on we shouldn't put up half such a show. At least you wouldn't. I don't anyway.'

Now, lying on his bed in the dark, he thought of that conversation and how even Putnam had not understood him. Yet no doubt Putnam had been right. It made no difference. He had continued to think in terms of the seamless adventure, onto which he had so recently imposed the flight, the foreign exile, the passion transmuted into a watchful benevolence. Something had gone wrong; something was amiss. Maybe he was not up to the mark. Maybe the life he had led had been insufficient preparation. In the timeless dark it seemed to him that the passion he had always sought had become attenuated, until now it was an affair not only of longing, but of infinite regret.

I I

He did not know when she left. At some point in his
sleep he heard the chink of the keys dropping through his
letter-box. He surfaced briefly, not knowing what time it
was, but sleep reclaimed him almost at once. When he
finally awoke he saw that it was very late, nearly nine
o'clock. He had never before slept past his usual hour,
and took this as a sign that something was gravely amiss.
Yet he did not seem to be ill. Slowly he reassembled his
former self, testing reflexes and movements, not quite
daring to think. His instinct was to obliterate everything
that had happened, to expunge every sign both of her
presence and of his involvement. For the rest he would
postpone mature reflection on the significance of these
events, and of his own part in them. He would have
plenty of time in the days ahead to arrive at a judgment,
not on Katy, who now seemed to him almost innocent,
an accidental happening in his life, but on himself.

He drank a cup of tea and had his bath. Food was out
of the question. When he had dressed, as carefully as
usual, he picked up the keys, and, as he knew he had to,
unlocked the door of the Dunlops' flat. The air vibrated
with her absence, as though she had only just departed.
She had left behind her, through instinct or through carelessness, unmistakable signs of her recent occupancy. In

the sitting-room an ironing-board, with the iron up-ended on it, stood facing the television, which flickered with an old black and white film starring Fredric March. He went into the main bedroom, the equivalent of his own, where he supposed the Dunlops slept. Here a coverlet had been hastily pulled over the duvet, while a dent in the pillow showed where a head had recently lain. No attempt had been made to disguise the fact of an alien presence. A wardrobe door, half open because its contents had been disturbed, showed the orange suit pulled half-way off a hanger, one discreetly padded shoulder in the air. He knew that he would find unwashed cups and plates in the kitchen, and wet towels in the bathroom. An almost fearful inspection showed him that his suspicions were correct.

While wondering what to do about all this he had time to marvel, almost to shake his head in admiration, at her incredible insouciance. This is freedom, he thought: freedom is to take what one wants, without bothering to cover one's tracks. But that is also a definition of criminality, possibly of psychosis. He wondered why he had not seen this before. She had seemed to him phenomenal, certainly; had he not been swept off his feet he would have had time to register certain abnormalities, which she had appeared to regard as stepping-stones on the road to enlightenment. A few further moments' thought convicted and then exonerated Howard Singer, for whom he now felt a reluctant sympathy. Howard Singer's upbeat doctrine could not afford to censure the returning prodigal, although her departure, like all her departures, might have left behind some unanswered questions, and a certain amount of minor, or perhaps not so minor, damage. Howard Singer, who was obliged to think that there was no wrongdoing that could not be cured by excessive sympathy, would no doubt be obliged to greet her with enthusiasm. She had once been useful to him, although she would now need to employ all her ingenuity to convince him, all over again, of her value.

But she might even manage this. She was like the phoenix: with each fresh start she regained her strength. In the meantime the wreckage that she had left behind was difficult to ignore. He concentrated on the wreckage in the flat, postponing his own case for later consideration. He washed up the cups and plates, not daring to look in the larder or the freezer, not quite knowing where everything was kept. In the bathroom he picked up the sodden towels from the floor and rather helplessly hung them on the edge of the bath. He dismantled the ironing board and switched off the television. The rest, he decided, was beyond him. He would have to ask Mrs Cardozo to put the flat to rights, a request which would certainly be unpopular. Then, even if the flat looked odd, it would be clean. Anything that seemed out of place could be laid at Mrs Cardozo's door. Besides, she was an enterprising woman: she would find clean sheets and towels, and might be persuaded to put the dirty linen into the laundry box, which he could then smuggle downstairs for Hipwood to hand over. Hipwood would need a very generous tip this year, he reflected, as would Mrs Cardozo. But he had no further use for his money, and no future in which to make use of that money: all expenses were therefore irrelevant, and were in any case self-inflicted. He had purposely omitted to fill in the stub of the cheque he had made out to Katy, and by now he had genuinely forgotten how much he had handed over. This seemed to him the only healthy indication of the whole affair, an indication that the pitiful exchange could now be consigned to oblivion, oblivion now being his most imperative requirement.

Today was Sunday: Mrs Cardozo was due on the following day, Monday, and the Dunlops would be back on the Tuesday. He thought it sad that his plans should so immediately contain these other characters, to whom he was indifferent, while Katy seemed to have vanished into thin air. Once the trail of her presence had been tidied away there would be little to suggest that she had ever been here, despite the fact that her actual presence had been violently disruptive. Again he admired her for that mixture of idleness and calculation which had almost certainly led her to set her sights on him, simply because he was the nearest thing to hand. And she had so nearly succeeded, let down only at the very end by her own uncertain staying power rather than by any intellectual assessment of his suitability.

Even now he did not entirely regret having known her, even having been willing to suspend judgment on account of her. She was no doubt an amalgam of genuinely damaging characteristics; she was also, and probably by the same token, out of the ordinary. He did not doubt that although he saw her as a failure she was in her perverse way something of a success. He thought it entirely appropriate that her instinct had taken her back to Howard Singer, not on Singer's account, but in the hope of annexing one of the more confused of Singer's wealthy clients. He saw her set up in Bel Air, by which time she and Singer would once more be on the best of terms. Perhaps someone less susceptible than himself would occupy the position he had once coveted. At least, he hoped that the next man would be less susceptible. He himself, he thought, had been unequal, and had thus suffered unduly.

Since it was Sunday, and there was now no possibility of change, he put on his tweed hat and set out for the park. The day was fine: the clouds had lifted and disclosed a sky of icy blue, with a low yellowish sun imparting an even radiance to empty streets and frozen pavements. In the park his feet made creaking noises on the frosty grass. It was intensely cold. Because he felt tired, in spite of his long sleep, and because he had not breakfasted, he decided not to take his usual walk to South Kensington, but to sit for half an hour in the steady pitiless light and to try to form some assessment of himself that would help him in the days ahead. For there would be many in which he ran the risk of being destroyed by his own disappointment.

He sat in the small pedimented pavilion which faces the sunken garden on the Bayswater side of the park. There was no one about, although the day was so clear. He could feel the cold of the stone, unwarmed by the winter sun, through his coat, and thought that for an elderly man, a man of his age, he was perhaps being imprudent. Common sense dictated food and warmth: he had at some level decided that it was more appropriate to do without either, at least for a significant interval, which must be dedicated entirely to thought of a constructive nature. But no thoughts, let alone constructive ones, occurred to him.

He felt, as he sat undisturbed, in the light of the cruel winter sun, as if he had been shipwrecked, as if he were the only survivor of a disaster so obscure that he could never explain it, even to a friend, even to a friend who loved him. To Louise, who must never know of it. If anyone had been wronged it was Louise, to whom he had denied the offering he had been ready to make to that almost unknown girl, and for whom he now felt pity. She had had the hardness and the dynamism of youth, and he had, through no fault of his own, through the impartial agency of time, lost both. Through that same agency, and no doubt only incidentally through the agency of Katy, he had lost the opportunity to change, had lost the capacity to change. Through envisaging a future so different from his own undoubted and authentic past he had given way to the charm of an idyll, one which could hardly stand up to the light of day. That balcony, that cigar, that red sun sinking . . .

There was no rule which said that he could not still enjoy those things, but he knew that it would be useless to try. It was only the fantasy that his life might be shared, and shared by someone so alien to himself, that had enabled his imagination to open up these vistas. It had all been totally seductive, and at the same time totally unsuitable. He had been brought up against a phenomenon not previously encountered: the chance acquaintance, not even a friend, who enlivens, enables, introduces the idea of liberty, of a liberty beyond one's prudent limits. Through the completely random circumstance of meeting this girl he had nearly become another man, living an altogether more poetic life.

Of course the reality would almost certainly have been shabbier. Perhaps his best course now would be to reflect on how perfect the fantasy was, simply by virtue of being a fantasy. Put to the test he might not have salvaged the philosophical calm with which he had so complacently endowed himself, might have become tetchy, with the tetchiness of old age, and also with old age's aches and pains, the stiffness of the joints, the uncertain digestion, the dimming eyesight. In many ways it was better to stay where he had always been, making the best of a job which by most standards was not too bad, with help, however unhelpful, near at hand. That reminded him: he must prepare envelopes for Hipwood and Mrs Cardozo. He had written no Christmas cards, though he had received many. He had not yet bought a present for Louise. But Louise was a matter on which he was not yet ready to think.

As for love, the strange exasperated feeling he had had for the girl, and which was certainly a form of passion, if only an impure form – that had vanished in the light of this unnerving light. He supposed now that he would never know it, that madness of which the poets wrote. Perhaps his foreknowledge of it, his apprehension of it, his recognition of its properties, would have to be enough, although as a fantasy it had not left him much to sustain him in the life that lay ahead. A fantasy is forward looking:

one gains no pleasure from looking back on it. He would be left with his dry memories and his small routines, obliged to make his peace with what remained to him, rather than with what he had promised himself. In that way he would no doubt salvage a little outward dignity, even though his thoughts, which must be kept secret, might disclose another truth.

In his mind's eye he saw a figure in a T-shirt and jeans, the sort of figure which might pass unnoticed and unremarked in a crowd of similar figures, striding into, and being almost obliterated by, the willing confusion of an airport. He saw her hitching her holdall onto her shoulder, as they all did, and striding along the walkway into the plane. He saw the plane vibrate with banked energy, saw it take off, saw it dwindle, and then disappear. With that he got stiffly to his feet, put a hand behind him to ease his back, and made his way out into the Bayswater Road.

There was a café along here somewhere, he remembered, a cheap unpretentious Greek place, which seemed to cater for transients or for tourists too bewildered to search for anything more elaborate. In the summer there were four painted white tables on the pavement, and waiters, all talking loudly to each other, would come out from time to time to remove the thick white cups and sweep the remains of rolls and croissants on to trays. Today a Japanese couple sat impassively eating fried eggs and baked beans in the dim interior, while the coffee machine hissed and the proprietor displayed the lung capacity of a football coach. Bland sat down and ordered tea and toast. Both, when they came, were surprisingly good. He sat for ten minutes or so in the steam and noise. Then, since there was nothing else to be done, either now or in the future, he went home.

In the flat he retrieved his salad, made a dressing, and cut a couple of slices from his chicken. There was a little cheese left, and the bread was still fresh. He felt extraordinarily hungry, as if he had been fasting for days, or as if this were his first meal after a serious operation. Yet even with the food in his mouth, half masticated, he was doubled up by an excess of grief which left his face contorted and his eyes moist. He forced himself to swallow, but needed a glass of water to calm himself. The rest of the meal went uneaten. He pushed the plate aside, went from the kitchen into the sitting-room, and let himself fall heavily into a chair, appalled at what was happening to him. To engage once more in ordinary life would, he thought, take more courage than he possessed. Yet all those kind people who had sent him Christmas cards, and to whom he was so profoundly indifferent, would no doubt view his condition with concern, were they to witness it, and in the event of an illness or a breakdown, which now seemed probable, would care for him, and visit him, and shelter him if the necessity arose. He owed something of a duty to those people, and to Louise, who, he knew, would be there at his death as she had been present all his life, to whom he had not given a single thought in his current predicament, but who must never know the truth. And at that hypothetical death-bed there would be one notable absence, but it would not be that of Katy, whom he saw as eternally escaping, but of the man he might have been, and who had predeceased him, some time ago, in his sixty-sixth year.

With a supreme effort he got to his feet, irritated, despite himself, by the chilliness of the flat. He tidied the kitchen, went to his writing-table, and put a not inconsiderable sum of money, together with a suitable greeting, into an envelope for Hipwood. The realisation that it was nearly Christmas made him reflect on his social duties: he would have to buy and send cards, although it was too late now for presents. He could send flowers, perhaps. Louise presented a problem. He had never failed her before. Some excuse must be made, some reason given. He repulsed the idea of an invented illness, although he reckoned that he was so nearly ill that this might be near the truth. With his last ounce of moral strength he took a stand against the desire to let everything go, all feelings, all loyalties, all respect and care for himself. He forced himself once more to envisage buying a ticket to some distant place, but knew in the same instant that he could not stand the experience on his own, while that imaginary companion was still so present in his mind. He would have to stay where he was, and as he was, going through the motions of a normal existence until some lightening of the spirit took place, in the same mysterious, almost magical fashion that his own brief and so illusory meta-morphosis had taken place. He would have to wait for this, and in the meantime comport himself with as much dignity as possible. Nothing became a man of his age, he knew in spite of himself, so much as a certain degree of dignity.

He put on his overcoat and the soft black hat he had been in the habit of wearing to the office, seized his envel-ope, and went downstairs to the front desk. Hipwood emerged from his cubby-hole, and laid a proprietorial hand on the base of his Christmas tree.

'Compliments of the season, Mr Hipwood,' said Bland, handing over his envelope.

'Much obliged, sir,' replied Hipwood. Usually, Bland reflected, he was more forthcoming.

'And I wonder if I might ask you a favour?' Bland went on.

Ask away, said Hipwood's expression, which had not changed from a certain mournful placidity.

Bland laid a further twenty pound note on the desk. 'My heating doesn't appear to be working,' he said. 'Would you be very kind and take a look at it? I don't much like the idea of spending Christmas in a cold flat.'

'You won't be going away then, sir?'

'No. I shan't be going away.'

'Leave it with me, sir. Sometimes the thermostat needs a little adjustment.'

'If you need to go into the flat you have your keys,' said Bland. This proof of confidence, he felt, was as much as he could summon in his own defence. Besides, he knew that Hipwood was longing to get into the flat, which in his imagination was the scene of recent lechery and licentiousness. He took it upon himself, as a guardian of public morals, to keep an eye open for possible derangement. Not that he ever found it, but, as he let it be known, he had his suspicions. To these Bland had formerly been obliged to lend an ear. 'Third floor, sir,' Hipwood would say, out of the corner of his mouth. 'Have you heard anything out of the way? Only they had a visitor last night, and I have my suspicions.' The tenant, whether male or female, was always referred to as 'they'. Bland knew that Hipwood suspected all the highly respectable retired men and elderly women who occupied this building of harbouring discreditable secrets. Like many solitaries he had a disorderly imagination. Bland, who was in possession of just such a discreditable secret, saw himself performing a symbolic act in bidding Hipwood search his flat. Even now it occurred to him to wonder if any evidence of his infatuation remained. Then he reflected that all the evidence was in his head, and was likely to remain there, and bidding Hipwood a pleasant good afternoon he went out into the icy street.

His intention was to walk to the National Gallery or the National Portrait Gallery, to buy his Christmas cards, and to spend the evening virtuously addressing them, ready to be posted the following morning, or even that night, if he had the energy to go out again. He set out in a ruminative spirit, without his usual energy, but the afternoon was so fine, so calm, so depopulated, under the same cloudless sky, that he found himself increasing his pace, responding to those dear streets which had kept him company since his first arrival in London. He had spent his first feverish weeks exploring, before returning exhausted each evening to the small hotel in Earls Court where he had lived before being directed to Radnor Place, and hence to liberty. He had arrived in London with money from the sale of his parents' house in his pocket, and this had protected him from the the worst excesses of his innocence. He had learned slowly but thoroughly, setting himself to examine every neighbourhood in turn, playing with the voluptuous decision, which it would one day be his to make, of where to live, or, as he thought of it then, where to make his home. That home had proved elusive, or perhaps it was that none of his homes seemed to be the right one. Some living presence was eternally missing, yet at the same time he was prevented from introducing one. In this way Louise had escaped him, having seen his caution for what it was. And now, in the austere comfort of his present flat, undeniably expensive, undeniably his, he still felt himself to be a visitor, uncertain of his welcome, and not entirely at home.

For old time's sake he walked down George Street, down Baker Street, into Oxford Street, and then, just inside the park, to Hyde Park Corner. He had walked this way many times in the past and remembered how he had felt his heart expand with the grandeur of it all. Now it was no longer a novelty, nor did it feel so grand. Yet it was still his favourite. There were more triumphant cities, Paris, Rome, Vienna, even New York. All were more naturally festive, yet none felt like the centre of the universe as London did. Paris could be traversed on foot, or at least could have been when he was young; Rome was too cynical, Vienna too secretive. On his first visit, newly emancipated, and wide-eyed with wonder, it had seemed to him that London was one vast government building, the occupants of which went about their daily task of policing the known world. Or so it had been once. Now it was a city in decline. The dignity of the place was almost gone, yet these days he felt he understood it better. It was, like himself, secular. He gave little thought and no attention to the churches of London, which he had once conscientiously researched, but saved his acts of obeisance for the Houses of Parliament, nineteenth-century masterpiece, emblematic of the national confidence, pragmatic, sober, yet given over to Gothic pride. For a provincial like himself the sight of the building was enough to restore his spirits on a grey day.

In Trafalgar Square he became aware of crowds. For most of the day he had felt entirely alone, not seeing, or not hearing, the people who dreamily filled the Sunday streets. Forced to move more slowly now, he sought in vain a known face above the heads of the crowd, which seemed compact, murmuring. He was able to admire the light. The icy sun had now faded, but in doing so had imparted a pinkish flush to the white stone of the National Gallery. In their last hour of liberty, before the darkness sent them home, people seemed becalmed, humbled, obedient, content to drift in company along the thronged but strangely silent street. It was enough to saunter, shoulders almost touching, the warmth of strange bodies almost palpable through overcoats, one's sense of self almost in abeyance.

He bought his cards, then, suddenly tired, took a cab back to Kendal Street. After the cold and the rapidly fading light he was almost glad to get home. The flat seemed strangely welcoming. He put his hand on the radiator and withdrew it smartly: blazing hot. So Hipwood had been successful. One might even say that Hipwood had been morally successful. If this had been a morality play Hipwood would be seen as having saved the day. Moral considerations aside, however, there was no doubt that the flat was newly comfortable. He made tea and drank it gratefully, yet in the act of eating a biscuit his face contracted once more with grief. It seemed that the solitary act of eating revealed to him once again the vast areas of solitude which he now inhabited. He deduced from this that he might be wise to spend his time alone, at least until he had regained some mastery of himself, for to display such an involuntary rictus in company – the sort to which an infant is subject – would be more than he could tolerate. Work might be a palliative, but he had none. Companionship would have helped, but he had precious little of that either. His world was, temporarily, quite empty. And there was the routine of Christmas to be got through. Tomorrow he must think about food. In the meantime there were gestures of acknowledgment to be made to the outside world. He spent the evening writing and stamping a number of cards: he was astonished that he knew so many people, to whom he sent his best, even his fondest wishes. Somehow it was not possible to send a card to Louise. A loving message would have been necessary, and he did not think he could manage one, not because Louise was not lovable but because he himself was as devoid of love as if he had been eviscerated. Certainly he felt depleted, as if by surgery. And his mind was empty now, under the influence of what he recognised as extreme fatigue. He left his pile of cards, stamped and ready to be posted the following morning, and, with scarcely the strength left to remove his clothes, went to bed. At some point in the middle of the night he became just conscious enough to remember that he had failed to telephone Louise.

On the following day, Monday, he met Mrs Cardozo at the front door, and asked her, as a very great favour, if she would mind cleaning the Dunlops' flat. She was immediately indignant. 'I only work for you, George. I don't work for others.' The point at which she had decided to address him as George was now lost in the mists of antiquity. She would always be Mrs Cardozo to him, although he would have liked to call her by her name, which was Fidelia, and which he thought beautiful.

'I'll have coffee waiting for you when you've finished,' he assured her. 'And I want you to have this. Merry Christmas. Just change the sheets and towels,' he added, 'and generally tidy up. There's no need to do anything in here today,' he said, all but propelling her disapproving back across the landing. 'Open the windows,' he called after her. Then he shut his own door quickly, in order to forestall further protests.

He took the opportunity of her temporary absence to do his shopping. 'Good morning, sir,' said Hipwood pleasantly in the lobby. 'Heating all right?'

'Excellent, thank you. Good morning, Moira.'

'Good morning,' said Mrs Lydiard distantly. They were no longer friends, it seemed. He had failed to keep in touch, and he would, he knew, continue to do so. He could not bring himself to discuss Katy's departure with her, could not summon the impartial tone with which it would be imperative to mention the matter, on which she would no doubt have very decided views. He doubted whether he would exchange more than the most conventional greeting with her ever again.

The strange sun of yesterday had disappeared. The weather was grey, misty, piercingly cold. He posted his cards and made a few desultory purchases. He still could not turn his mind to everyday sustenance. Back in the flat he stood for a moment at the window, patting the scalding radiator. When Mrs Cardozo had gone he lunched on bread and cheese and a glass of wine, and then attempted to settle down with Mauriac, whose mournful steady tone he found comforting. At some point in the afternoon he darted over to the Dunlops' flat and switched on the heating.

Tuesday was even colder. He forced himself to turn his mind to everyday affairs, had lunch at the club, and bought an ample stock of provisions on his way home. He did not expect to leave the flat until after Christmas. A strange calm descended on him, and he spent the afternoon sitting in his dusky room, idle to outward appearance, not bothering to switch on the lights even when it was quite dark. In fact he was absorbed in thought, passing his life in review, and even finally managing to think of Katy with an absence of blame which was not quite, not yet, indulgence. When the doorbell rang he got up like a sleepwalker, still in the dark, to answer it. Tim Dunlop stood on the landing, holding a small box of chocolates and a Christmas card.

'Just to say thank you for everything,' he said.

'There was no need . . .'

'You've been awfully kind. The place looks much tidier than when we left.'

'I sent Mrs Cardozo over. I hope you don't mind.' He thought this truth preferable to any other.

'Mind! We're delighted!' He lingered awkwardly, anxious to get home.

'You had a good holiday?'

'Oh, splendid, thanks. And you've been all right?'

'Yes, I'm fine.'

'Going away for Christmas?'

'No. No, I shall stay here.'

'You won't be lonely?'

'Lonely? Oh, no. What I need,' he said, with a thrill of longing that almost brought tears to his eyes, like a cough, a sneeze, some irrepressible physical commotion, 'is a bit of a rest.'

'You've been overdoing it, I expect.'

'That must be it,' he said gratefully. 'Yes, once or twice I've felt myself getting a bit near the edge.'

'Yes, well, if you need anything . . .'

But he needed nothing. A rest, perhaps, one of those long sleeps that brought such illuminating dreams. And time to reflect, as a man of his age should reflect, quietly, patiently, even humorously.

'Goodnight,' he said, and shut the door onto Dunlop's retreating back. He went into the kitchen, opened the larder, and stared unseeingly at the contents. Then he went into the bedroom and turned down the bed. I have had my adventure, he thought. Now I must live my life as I have always lived it. What was it that I lacked? Courage, or the necessary folly, that *grain de folie* that the French talk about? Automatically he switched on the radio for the shipping forecast, and switched it off again when the telephone rang.

'George? Thank goodness I've got you at last. I knew you'd be worried not hearing from me, dear. But I've been out rather a lot, two nights running, in fact. We're all rather busy down here. On Sunday I went to the carol service, and the Fawcetts invited me for supper afterwards. I couldn't refuse, though I knew you'd be worried. And last night there was a little party for the older children at the hospital. You know I sometimes help out there. But that's enough about me. Now what about you, dear? Are you all right?'

'I'm fine,' he said.

'That's good.'

There was a pause. 'Have you decided to go away?' There was perhaps a tentative note in her voice.

'Louise,' he said. 'I've left it too late to make plans for this year. But I've got an idea for your present. What would you say to a cruise? In the spring?'